I0822434

THE IMPOSTER'S INHERITANCE

Glass and Steele
Book 9

C.J. ARCHER

Visit C.J. at www.cjarcher.com

❀ Created with Vellum

CHAPTER 1

LONDON, AUTUMN 1890

I'd been dreading dining with the Delanceys and their friends from the collectors' club since we received the invitation a week previously. It was not my idea of an enjoyable way to spend an evening.

Part of that apprehension could be attributed to seeing Lord Coyle again. Our meetings were never easy, but they had become even more of a trial since he'd asked me to encourage Matt's cousin, Hope, to accept his marriage proposal. Doing so would expunge the debt I owed Coyle after he gave me information to blackmail Lord Cox into marrying Hope's sister, Patience.

Information that had somehow fallen into the hands of the very man who could destroy Patience's happiness with her new husband.

Lord Cox's half-brother, and the true heir to the barony, had discovered that he had been robbed of his inheritance, and Lord Cox blamed me for telling him. The half-brother was the son of the previous baron and his first wife, a governess. The marriage had been conducted in secret, in front of strangers, so it was easy for him to set her aside in favor of a more appropriate high-born lady who also gave him a son. That second child inherited the Cox title and estate, but his parents' marriage had been bigamous, and so he was illegitimate. His older half-brother had been brought up none the wiser to his father's identity, let alone his duplicity.

I suspected Lord Coyle was to blame for informing the half-brother. I intended to find out tonight why he'd done so.

The confrontation would have to wait until after dessert, however. The marbled jelly, iced pudding, apple tart, vanilla cream and fruit selection were too delicious not to enjoy. Indeed, the food had made the evening marginally less tortuous than I'd anticipated. Being seated next to Professor Nash had also helped. I'd not been forced to endure conversation with the Delanceys, Lord Coyle, or Lady Louisa Hollingbroke. If I couldn't sit with Matt, then Professor Nash was the best dining neighbor I could have asked for. Even Oscar Barratt, sitting on my other side, wasn't someone I wanted to engage in casual conversation. I might blurt out that he was making a mistake in marrying Louisa.

The announcement of their pending nuptials had appeared in the previous day's newspaper and perhaps accounted for Oscar's invitation to dinner. Mrs. Delancey was a dedicated hostess and would have insisted he join us, along with his fiancée, as soon as she learned of the engagement.

"It's been an edifying collaboration," Professor Nash told me about his contribution to Oscar's book on magic. "I've learned some things from Barratt and, I humbly suggest, he has learned some things from me."

"I don't doubt it," I said. "Your knowledge on the history of magic is unsurpassed."

He chuckled as he scooped up a spoonful of jelly. "Thank you, you're very gracious, but we don't know if anyone else studies the topic. That's the problem with being persecuted; magicians must research and perform their art underground."

It would be ungracious to point out that he wasn't a magician. Magic had died out in his family with his grandfather, an iron magician. It was possible his family was distantly related to that of Fabian Charbonneau, my mentor and co-collaborator in furthering the study of magic, although Fabian didn't know of a connection.

"Have you ever traced your family tree?" I asked the professor.

"Only four generations back. There's no connection to the Charbonneaus, if that's what you're thinking. None that I've found, anyway."

"You read my mind."

"Speaking of Charbonneau, how are your studies coming along? Have you managed to recreate any of the remarkable spells of the past?"

I savored the last mouthful of apple tart, in part because it was so delicious but also because I wanted to think about my answer. I could only delay for so long, however. "Not yet."

"What are you working on? Something in particular?"

"We're still learning the words." I didn't tell him that Fabian and I were about to attempt to create our first spell. Matt was the only person who knew, and he wasn't thrilled with the idea. I'd assured him that it would be some time before we'd make it work—if it worked at all. We still didn't know how to pronounce many of the magical words on our list. It was going to involve a lot of trial and error.

I glanced at Matt over the bowl of exotic fruit perched on a vine-covered silver pedestal but he was in conversation with Sir Charles Whittaker and didn't notice. Mrs. Delancey appeared to be listening in, her head tilted toward them, her food forgotten.

"Have you received one, India?" Oscar asked. At my blank look, he added, "A threatening letter from some artless crackpot."

Out of the corner of my eye I saw Matt's head lift, his attention now on Oscar too.

"No," I said. "What are you being threatened with?"

"It's not specific." Oscar now had the attention of all the guests. "And it's not me who has been threatened but other magicians. My brother, for one, as well as some magicians I know who are all good craftsmen with successful businesses. That appears to be the common factor. I haven't received a letter, nor have you or other magicians of my acquaintance who don't have businesses relating to their particular magical art."

"How many of your friends have received letters?" Matt asked.

"Four." Oscar plucked up his cognac glass. "The anonymous author tells the recipient they should be ashamed for gaining their success through cheating and not through hard work like himself. He insists they cease using their magic or there will be consequences. The actual consequences aren't stated."

Mrs. Delancey placed a hand to the silver and jet cameo choker at her throat. "How does he even know who to write to? Most magicians are not open about their art."

Oscar shrugged.

"An educated guess." Lord Coyle leaned back in the chair, causing it to creak in protest at the redistribution of his considerable weight. "Once one becomes aware of the existence of magic, it's logical to assume that the most successful craftsmen and businessmen are magicians. Barratt's brother, for example."

"Who would send such letters?" Mrs. Delancey asked.

"A struggling businessman who wants to blame his lack of success on magicians," her husband said. "It's typical of that class."

I bit down on my retort.

"My dear," his wife scolded. "You forget yourself." It wasn't clear if she was reminding him they were among people from "that class" or that his own family had been in the wool trade before he turned to banking.

"And so it begins," Lord Coyle muttered with a glare for Oscar.

Oscar ignored him, as did Louisa. They seemed unconcerned that Oscar's newspaper articles about magic had propelled the topic into the public sphere. The attention had faded after he stopped writing them, but clearly anger and frustration still simmered in some quarters. His book would bring a fresh wave of interest.

And possibly a fresh wave of persecution.

Oscar didn't see it that way. He and Louisa hoped the attention would free magicians who'd lived in secret for generations. I wasn't yet sure if that would be the outcome. Hearing about these letters made me think that Matt was right all along, and bringing magic into the open would only cause trouble between magicians and the artless.

I glanced at Professor Nash. He agreed with Oscar and was writing the history chapters for his book. He pushed his glasses up his nose. The light from the crystal chandelier reflected off the lenses and made it seem as though his eyes shone.

After dessert, Mrs. Delancey rose, a signal for the ladies to adjourn to the drawing room. We headed through the door flanked by two potted palm trees and held open by a liveried footman.

The lush tropical theme had been carried into the drawing room for the occasion. Palm trees occupied all the corners, the tips of the fronds brushing the mantel and vine-covered pedestals bearing bowls of pineapples, oranges, peaches, grapes and apples. A large birdcage positioned between armchairs contained two brightly colored parrots—stuffed, of course.

A footman maneuvered between the furniture, a silver platter balanced on his fingertips. He set the tray down on a central table and poured tea into delicate china cups.

"So you are getting married, Louisa," Mrs. Delancey began. "And to a newspaperman, no less." Her disapproval was clear in her tone, there was no need for her to wrinkle her nose too.

Louisa's smile didn't reach her eyes. "Oscar is an interesting man."

"A magician, yes."

Louisa didn't offer up any of Oscar's attributes, of which he had a good number. I liked Oscar, on the whole, although he could be over-zealous in regards to magic sometimes. He was a decent man, handsome and charming. It would seem none of these things were worth mentioning by his fiancée. It was as Matt and I suspected—Louisa was marrying him for his magic.

Mrs. Delancey accepted a teacup from the footman. "Your fortune and his magical connections will make you quite the formidable couple in some circles. We don't have many magicians in the collectors club."

"Oscar isn't invited into the club," Louisa said, lifting the cup to her lips. "Coyle made that perfectly clear to me after the announcement."

"What a shame," Mrs. Delancey muttered without any conviction whatsoever.

Louisa set down her cup and rested her hands on her lap in a languid, elegant motion. She regarded me with her soft blue-gray eyes. It would have been easy to think her sweet, with such gentility seeming to run through her veins, but I knew her to be sharp and, at times, selfish.

"India, tell us about your work with Fabian," she said.

"There's nothing to tell. We're still learning."

"You must keep us informed of your progress."

"You ought to ask Mr. Charbonneau, Louisa, not India," Mrs. Delancey said. "I'm sure he'll be more forthcoming, given your long-standing friendship."

Louisa's fingers curled into fists, but her face didn't lose its smooth calmness. "Fabian and I are not that close. Acquaintances, nothing more."

They *had* been friends, but that friendship had withered when Louisa asked Fabian to marry her, and he'd refused.

I didn't feel any sympathy for her, then or now. She had asked him to marry her because he was a magician. After his rejection, she'd turned her attentions to Gabriel Seaford, the doctor magician who'd saved Matt's life, only to be thwarted when we warned him about her. Matt and I had decided to inform Oscar of Louisa's prior marital interests tonight so that he could go into the relationship with his eyes open. We couldn't withhold something so important from him.

I glanced at the door, wondering if Matt had managed to speak to Oscar alone. He'd promised he'd try, but given the cool nature of their acquaintance, I wasn't sure he'd try very hard.

We endured awkward conversation for a long twenty minutes until the gentlemen finally joined us. I knew instantly from Oscar's face that Matt had found a way to broach the subject of Louisa. The signs were so subtle that I doubted Louisa noticed, but I'd been looking and I saw the hardened jaw, the slight pursing of the lips, and the way in which he did not immediately go to his fiancée's side until she put out her hand in summons.

I wasn't the only one who noticed the change in Oscar. Lord Coyle did too, going by the way he watched them from beneath pendulous eyelids.

The rest of the evening was blessedly short. Once Louisa became aware of Oscar's moroseness, she lost her appetite for conversation, even when it centered on magic. They were the first to take their leave, and Matt took the opportunity to suggest we depart too.

Lord Coyle left with us. "What did you say to Barratt?" he asked Matt as we made our way down the front steps of the Delanceys' townhouse.

"That's none of your business," Matt said oh-so casually.

Lord Coyle grunted.

Our carriage rolled up and a Delancey footman opened the door for me. "Is there something else, Coyle?" Matt asked as he assisted me up the step into the cabin.

"I wanted to ask Mrs. Glass if she has considered my proposal any further. It has been a week since we last spoke of it." He turned his gaze to me. "I don't think I need to remind you that you owe me, Mrs. Glass, and that convincing Hope to accept my marriage proposal will absolve you of the debt."

"It's not a debt," Matt snapped. "You forced her into an impossible position."

Lord Coyle ignored Matt. "Mrs. Glass?"

"I haven't seen Hope all week," I said.

"Call on her tomorrow. I expect an answer in two weeks."

"You can't expect a young woman to make up her mind about something this important in two weeks!"

"Hope Glass isn't a silly girl. I'd wager she has already made up her mind and is just delaying."

"Why would she do that?" Matt asked.

"To make it seem as though she can't make up her mind. I may never have been married, but I do know how young women like to be the center of attention."

I rolled my eyes but he might not have seen it in the dim glow of the street light.

Lord Coyle touched the brim of his hat. "Good evening, Mrs. Glass."

"One more thing," Matt said, squaring up to Coyle. My blood ran cold. He was going to confront his lordship, even though I'd asked him not to. "We received a letter from Lord Cox stating that his half-brother found out the truth. Why did you tell him?"

"I didn't." Despite his denial, he showed no surprise at the news.

"It was unfair—cruel, even. Cox is a good man. He has children, for God's sake. They don't deserve the stigma that will be placed on them when Cox's illegitimacy becomes public."

"The half-brother hasn't made it public. Perhaps he won't pursue the matter." Lord Coyle stabbed the end of his walking stick onto the pavement.

"If you didn't inform him then who did?" I asked. "It wasn't me."

"It could have been any number of people who knew about the first marriage. Servants, a midwife, old neighbors, the vicar, the vicar's wife. A secret like that is impossible to keep forever."

"What will happen now?" I asked quietly.

"That will be up to the half-brother. You've received no more correspondence from Lord or Lady Cox?"

I shook my head.

"Then we shall wait with bated breath." He tapped his walking stick on Matt's leg. "Go home with your wife, Glass. It's late and my conveyance is waiting."

Matt climbed in and sat beside me. He closed the door and the carriage moved forward with a jerk as Sir Charles and Professor Nash came down the front steps.

"You promised you wouldn't mention Lord Cox's letter to Lord Coyle," I said.

"I never promised." Matt turned to me and lifted a lock of artfully curled hair off my shoulder. The intermittent streetlights cast his face in alternate light and shadow, and within each moment of light, he was a little bit closer, his lips a little more parted. He was going to kiss me.

I lightly smacked his shoulder. "You might not have promised in so many words, but it was still a promise."

He sat back with a sigh. "How is not promising still a promise?"

"It just is."

"Are you mad at me, India?"

"Yes. No. Perhaps." I snuggled closer to show I wasn't really mad and because it was a little chilly. He adjusted the fur collar of my stole and tucked me into his side. His warmth instantly enveloped me. "Do you believe Coyle when he said he didn't inform Cox's half-brother?" I asked.

"No. He has no compunction about lying."

"But he had no reason to tell him."

"No reason we know of."

I yawned and tucked my hand inside his jacket to feel the comforting beat of his heart. "Oscar seemed unhappy after you spoke to him. Do you think he really is in love with Louisa?"

"Hard to say. She told him about proposing to Fabian, by the way. Louisa said she'd done it out of familial duty, as their families have a long association and it was expected."

"Then why did he look so cross when he came into the drawing room?"

"Because he didn't know about Gabe Seaford."

"Ah. So now he's aware it wasn't familial obligation but a pattern that proves she's after him for his magic." I yawned. "Poor Oscar."

"They deserve each other."

"They won't have each other, now. He'll call it off, or do the honorable thing and let her end it so that she can appear to be the jilter not the jilted."

"Perhaps. Or perhaps the lure of her fortune will help him overcome his misgivings."

* * *

WILLIE BREEZED into the sitting room, took one look at me with Aunt Letitia's portable writing desk on my lap, and clicked her tongue in admonishment. "You working on a Saturday?"

"It's a miserable morning," I said, indicating the rain-splattered window. "And this isn't work. I enjoy learning about magic." It fulfilled me in a way that only tinkering with clocks and watches had in the past. Now that I no longer had ready access to broken timepieces, I found my restlessness soothed by memorizing Fabian's list of magic words and attempting to put them together to create new spells.

"Sounds like work to me." Willie slouched into a chair by the fire with a loud sigh. She sighed again when no one took any notice of her.

Matt lowered the corner of the newspaper. "Something wrong, Willie?"

"I'm bored."

"Already? You just got out of bed."

"And it's almost eleven," Aunt Letitia noted without looking up from the letter she was reading.

"I slept in because I got in late last night," Willie said.

Duke lowered the newspaper he was reading just as Matt raised his. "Were you with Brockwell?"

"Ain't none of your business who I was with."

Duke rolled his eyes and lifted the paper again.

"Fine, I'll tell you." Willie stretched her feet toward the fire. "I met a woman down by the docks—"

"The docks!" Duke cried at the same moment that Aunt Letitia said, "Spare us the vulgar details." She might accept Willie's inclination for both sexes but she didn't like discussing it.

Duke put the paper down on the table and regarded Willie with concern. "You do know those women ain't looking for love."

"Who says *I'm* looking for love?"

"The only thing you'll find there is disease."

Aunt Letitia made a sound of disgust. "*Must* we speak of these things?"

"What about the detective inspector?" I asked. "Are you two no longer a couple?"

"A couple?" Willie scoffed. "We were never that. We were just two people who like each other's company, once in a while. We still see each other some nights, but neither of us wants to make it something it ain't. We're happy."

She did seem rather happy with the arrangement. I wondered if Brockwell was too.

"Who wants to play poker?" Willie asked.

"Not me," I said, once again concentrating on the list of magic words.

"Duke?"

"I'm reading the paper," he said, picking it up.

"As am I," Matt added from behind his newspaper.

Miss Glass lifted her correspondence higher to hide her face and avoid looking at Willie altogether.

Willie crossed her arms over her chest. "I wish Cyclops was

here. He'd play a few rounds with me. Is he at Catherine's shop again?"

"He left early this morning," I told her.

"That shop'll be as clean as a drunk's empty glass by now. He's been there every day for a week."

Ever since Catherine Mason had lied to extricate him from Charity Glass's trap, Cyclops had shown his appreciation by helping Catherine and her brother Ronnie set up their watch and clock shop. The shop had opened for business a few days ago, but Cyclops insisted on being there to clean, carry things, and assist in any way he could. Willie was right; there was no need for him to be there now that the shop was in order. Tomorrow it would be closed, being Sunday. I wondered if Cyclops would invent a reason to visit anyway.

Talk of the shop reminded me of the black marble clock now sitting proudly on the mantel in the sitting room. It had been on display for many years in the shop, losing time every day, despite both my father and I working on it. While I'd managed to get every other clock and watch working, that one had always eluded me.

I'd never spoken a spell into it, however, until bringing it home a few weeks ago. The spell my grandfather had taught me didn't fix the clock straight away, but speaking the spell in conjunction with my continued daily tinkering had finally worked. The clock had not lost a single second all week. The satisfaction I felt bordered on elation.

Raised voices drifted up to us from downstairs, but we couldn't make out the words. One of the voices was Bristow's. Matt lowered his newspaper and frowned, listening.

A loud clatter rose above the voices. It sounded like the silver salver crashing onto the tiled entrance hall floor. "Stop!" Bristow shouted. "You can't go up there unannounced!"

Footsteps pounded on the stairs.

Matt, Duke and Willie shot to their feet and made for the door, but the intruder barreled through it, almost careening into them. He pulled up short, his chest heaving with the exertion of sprinting up the stairs. His gaze flew past Matt and the others and fell on me.

Aunt Letitia gasped and reached for my hand. I took it, my heart in my throat.

I recognized the man. He was a leather magician by the name of Bunn. The last time he'd come here, Bristow and Peter the footman had marched him out after I'd refused to use my magic to extend his. So why was he back, and desperate to speak to me?

CHAPTER 2

"What is the meaning of this?" Matt demanded.

Mr. Bunn finally seemed to see Matt, flanked by Duke and Willie. A formidable trio, even though Willie didn't have her gun on her. It was no wonder he swallowed heavily and glanced behind him. Bristow and Peter blocked the exit.

"I'm sorry, sir, I tried to stop him," Bristow said. A few strands of hair stood on end, and his jacket was bunched at the shoulders. For the usually impeccably turned out butler, he was positively disheveled.

"It's all right," Matt assured him. "The fault lies with this fellow." He squared up to Mr. Bunn. "I asked you a question," he growled.

Mr. Bunn's cheek twitched. He looked to be no more than twenty, but his blond curls could have made him seem younger than he was. With the bluster fading, he looked somewhat vulnerable.

"My name is Joseph Bunn. I'm a leather magician. I met Miss Steele a few months ago, here." He'd learned about horology magic and Chronos through Oscar Barratt's article and discovered the address of the magician's granddaughter through a combination of coincidences. No other magical craftsmen had sought me out since, and I had thought myself safe, forgotten. Clearly Mr. Bunn had not forgotten.

"It's Mrs. Glass now." I indicated Matt. "Mr. Glass and I are married."

Mr. Bunn removed his cap and crushed it in his hands. "Congratulations." He cleared his throat and addressed Matt. "I asked your wife to use her magic to extend mine so I could make fine leather shoes that last. She wouldn't do it then, but I thought I'd try again."

"You've wasted your time." Matt indicated the door, inviting Mr. Bunn to leave.

Mr. Bunn didn't move. "You see, I started the business and it's doing real well. Everyone likes my boots and shoes because the leather's so fine, and I sell 'em at reasonable prices while I get established." He spoke quickly, as if he realized Matt had a short fuse and he had to say everything before the spark reached the gunpowder. "But I had to borrow a lot of money to get started, and now I've got a large debt. I was hoping Mrs. Glass would take pity on a fellow magician and extend my magic to make the leather seem like new forever. Once I get a reputation for fine, *durable* boots..." His cheek twitched again with his tentative smile. "People from all over London—all over England!—will want a pair of my footwear. I ain't in a hurry, Mrs. Glass. I'm young and I can meet my repayments, for now, if things go along as they have been. People already know how good my work is, but if the magic could be extended, I'd be the best."

"Mr. Bunn, I admire your enthusiasm and entrepreneurial spirit," I said, "but my decision has not changed. I won't extend your magic."

His smile faded and his busy hands scrunched the cap tighter. "Why not?"

"Magicians already have an unfair advantage over artless craftsmen, but at least the magic doesn't last. It would be immoral of me to extend that advantage."

"How is it unfair when magic was given to me by God?"

"Don't bring God into this," Willie spat. "If He wanted you to use your magic to get ahead, He would have made your magic last forever and not fade away."

"But He gave Mrs. Glass that kind of magic."

"Let's leave religion out of this," I said. "The fact is, I won't be extending your magic. Please don't come here and ask again."

Mr. Bunn stepped toward me. "But—"

Matt grabbed his arm, and Duke grabbed the other. Willie blocked his way, hands on hips. Mr. Bunn struggled for a moment but must have realized it was pointless and stopped.

"I wasn't going to harm her," he muttered. "Just talk to her."

"What makes you think she will extend your magic now when she wouldn't last time?" Matt snapped.

"I've gone and set myself up," Mr. Bunn said. "I thought if I showed her I was making a go of it, and I could prove my business could be profitable within a few years, she'd see fit to help me."

"You've wasted your time," I said.

"And ours," Matt said. He and Duke hustled Mr. Bunn toward the door.

"I never told anyone else where to find you!" Mr. Bunn cried. "Not a single magician. I kept your secret, Mrs. Glass. Now you should help me."

"She doesn't have to do anything for you," Willie snapped.

"And if you tell a soul where to find her," Matt said, his voice like cold steel, "I will ruin your business and have your creditor call in your debt."

Mr. Bunn's eyes widened. "You! *You* sent me that letter!"

Matt's gaze narrowed. "What letter?"

"Threatening to ruin me."

"I haven't sent you a letter. I didn't know who you were until today."

"Tell us about the letter," I said, rising.

"It was from someone who threatened to ruin me, just like

Mr. Glass did. It called me a cheat for using my magic to make my business successful."

It was just as Oscar mentioned. Successful magicians all over the city were receiving letters accusing them of cheating. It was no surprise that Mr. Bunn had been one of the recipients if what he said was true and he'd built a solid business in such a short time.

"Do you have the letter still?" I asked.

"I threw it away." He looked up at Matt. "You didn't send it?"

"I have better things to do. Not to mention I'm married to a magician," Matt said. "I have no reason to send you or anyone else threatening letters. Unless you harass my wife again."

Mr. Bunn's lips twisted. "So what am I supposed to do?"

"Continue to make excellent quality shoes and boots," I said. "Just as you are now."

"That ain't enough! The quality quickly fades. How will I get ahead?"

"Through hard work," Willie said.

"That could take years!"

"There ain't no shortcuts in life."

Mr. Bunn didn't offer resistance when Matt and Duke marched him out of the sitting room. Peter followed, but Bristow remained behind.

"Can I get you anything, madam?" he asked.

"No, thank you."

"I want to apologize again for allowing that fellow to get past me."

"It's all right, Bristow. It's not your fault."

"Maybe you should get him a gun, India," Willie said as Bristow bowed out. "What do you think, Letty?"

I'd forgotten about Aunt Letitia. I turned to her when she didn't answer Willie and drew in a sharp breath. She was smiling at me with childlike innocence.

"Veronica, is Harry home?" she asked. "I'm sure I heard his voice. Go and tell him to come here." Her face darkened and her lips formed a pout. "Father has been horrid to me again, and Richard too. Our brother always takes Father's side, but Harry always takes mine, bless him."

I eyed Willie, and together we gently assisted Aunt Letitia to her feet. "Why don't I take you to him," I said.

I helped her to her room while Willie fetched Polly to sit with her while she rested. It had been some time since she'd taken a turn, and I'd begun to hope she was getting better. But the shock of Mr. Bunn's intrusion, and the subsequent confrontation, must have caused her mind to slip into the past where she thought I was her old maid, Veronica, and Matt was his father.

Matt, Duke and Willie were waiting for me when I returned to the sitting room. "How is she?" Matt asked.

"Confused but she agreed to rest." I sat with a sigh. "What a strange morning."

Matt rubbed my shoulder. "I don't think Bunn will cause any more problems."

"I should have flashed my Colt," Willie said. "That'd make sure he never came back."

"You should have told him your lover is a detective inspector with Scotland Yard," Duke said. "I reckon that would have worked better."

"She wouldn't use Brockwell like that," I said.

Willie blinked at me. "Course I would, if I thought it would work. But Matt's threat did the trick." She eyed the door through which Mr. Bunn had left. "Although the lad's got the courage and stupidity of youth, so who knows."

"I wonder if the person who wrote those letters will follow through on their threat to ruin Bunn and the other magicians," I said.

Matt sat beside me and took my hand. "It would be easy to do. If their guilds find out they're magicians, their memberships and licenses would be revoked."

If they had no license, they couldn't sell their products. It was an archaic system that worked to keep magicians out. It was why so many magicians had hidden their magic and the art had been all but forgotten by most. It was why my parents never told me about my lineage, although those in The Watchmaker's Guild had suspected magic flowed through my veins. The guilds wielded enormous power, and that made me uneasy.

***

CYCLOPS RETURNED after lunch and we spent a leisurely afternoon indoors as the rain continued to fall outside. With Willie snoring in an armchair, I retreated to the library to continue my studies. I found Matt there, reading, and we snuggled together before I got up to sit at the table with my notes.

An hour later, he closed his book and joined me. "Did Bunn's visit rattle you?" he asked.

"A little." I gave him a flat smile. "But I'm all right. I think you scared him off for good."

"I hope so." He perched on the edge of the desk and eyed me closely.

"What is it?" I prompted. "Come on, out with it."

"Am I that easy to read?"

I grinned. "Always."

He grunted. "I was wondering if you were tempted to help him."

"Not at all." I turned to face him fully. "I can't believe you had to ask me that."

"You might be able to read me, but I can't always read you, especially when it comes to your opinions on magic."

I touched his knee. "I was never tempted to help him. The only magic I will ever extend is Gabe's when you need it."

His hand closed over mine and he leaned down to kiss me. It was light and sweet and filled with promise and love. If I ever doubted I was cherished, he only needed to kiss me like that and my doubts fled.

He pulled up a chair and sat next to me. "What about the new spells you create with Fabian?"

"I can't foresee a reason to use the extension spell in our experiments."

"Have you settled on a spell to try first?"

"Making a watch fly."

"You can already do that."

"Not consciously." My watches sometimes saved my life by wrapping their chains around my attackers' necks or wrists. A clock had also once flown off the mantel and hit an assailant on the head. But I couldn't make them do it on purpose or control their flight path. "Fabian can not only make iron fly, he can also direct it. Mr. Hendry can do the same thing with paper, to a limited extent, and Oscar with his ink words. We've already tried combining Fabian's spell with my watch one but it didn't work. We're going to try to change it a little."

"What about Hendry's spell?"

"What about it?"

"Did you use the words you remember from it on your watch?"

"I don't remember any." Try as I might, I simply couldn't recall the words he'd spoken to fling papers and cards at me. I'd been too filled with panic at the time.

"I can remember two from the first time he used the spell," Matt said. "I wasn't there when he unleashed a houseful of papers on you in the entrance hall that second time, but Willie was. Have you asked her?"

"I'll rouse her now."

He took my hand before I could run off. "Not yet." He tugged me closer. "You know what she's like when you interrupt her naps."

I circled my arms around his neck and lightly nipped his lips with mine. "What shall we do to pass the time until she wakes?"

I felt him smile. "I can think of a few things."

* * *

WILLIE TURNED out to be just as bad as me at remembering Mr. Hendry's magical words. "How would I know?" she cried when we asked her after she awoke from her nap. "I was too busy trying not to get my throat sliced open."

"Death by paper cut," Duke said with a chuckle as he reached for a piece of sponge cake.

Willie slapped his hand away. "It ain't funny."

"Agreed," Matt said.

"Sorry," Duke muttered, eyeing Willie as he went in for the cake again.

"Do the words Matt remembers match any of the words from Charbonneau's flying iron spell?" Cyclops asked.

I handed him my notepad. "Only one," I said pointing to a nine-letter word. "The other is different. When I see Fabian again on Monday, we'll see if it can be slotted into his spell. If that doesn't work on my watch, we'll try a few others from this list that don't have a use or meaning attributed to them yet."

"What'll you do once you make your watch fly?" he asked, reaching for another slice of cake.

"Make something else fly."

Willie clicked her fingers, her face alight with enthusiasm. "A magic carpet, like in that *Arabian Nights* story."

"Professor Nash thinks they're not just stories," I said. "He thinks magicians from long ago used to make carpets fly all the time."

"Chronos believes so too," Matt pointed out.

"Won't you need a wool magician for that?" Duke asked.

I nodded. "Which is why one of our first spells won't be for a flying carpet. We don't know any wool magicians."

"You can always seek out Bunn and try the spell with leather," Willie said. "He could make you a flying cowhide carpet."

"Aye, but he'll want India to extend his magic in return," Duke said.

"He doesn't make leather anyway," I pointed out. "He just works with it. Specifically turning it into footwear, although I don't see why his spell wouldn't work for clothing and bookbinding too."

"So you need a tanner magician?" Duke pulled a face. "I ain't going to help you find one. Have you smelled those factories? They stink."

"Maybe tanner magicians don't need to use dog feces and whatever other muck they soak the hide in," Cyclops said. "Maybe that's the whole point of their magic."

His theory made sense. Mr. Hendry was able to make paper without additives, just by using a spell, so why not tanner magicians too? "It would make a tanner magician easy to find," I said. "The lack of smell will make the factory stand out."

"It would stand out too much," Matt said. "I don't think there are any for that reason. Someone would have noticed."

Willie poked the glowing coals in the grate with the fire iron, stirring them to life. "Pity. I'd like to ride on a flying carpet. Or cowhide."

Duke chuckled. "It's a lot further to fall off a carpet flying over the city than it is a horse."

Willie sniffed. "Ever seen me fall off a horse, Duke? You haven't because I ain't never."

"Not even when you were little?"

"Nope."

"Huh. I figured you'd landed on your head from a fall and that's why you're a bit…you know." He tapped his temple, angling his head so that Cyclops would see his wink but Willie couldn't.

She brandished the fire iron and Duke pressed back into the chair to avoid it, the smile no longer in evidence. "It's a brave man that calls me mad when I'm holding a hot poker."

"Or a stupid man," Cyclops said. When Duke protested,

Cyclops gave an apologetic shrug. "Well I wouldn't have said it to her."

"Doesn't Delancey come from a family of wool magicians?" Matt asked.

"The magic ended with his father," I said.

"There are no distant cousins?"

It might be worth checking. If Delancey lost touch with his cousins, it didn't mean Fabian and I couldn't approach them.

Bristow entered and announced a visitor. "Miss Hope Glass is in the drawing room."

Matt and I exchanged glances. This was my chance to convince her to accept Lord Coyle's proposal. But I still wasn't sure if I should, or even if I *could*. Hope wasn't someone whose opinion could be easily swayed.

"She alone?" Cyclops asked. "Or are her sisters with her?"

"She's alone," Bristow said.

Cyclops relaxed. "Think I'll stay in here awhile, just in case."

Matt and I greeted Hope in the drawing room and she responded politely if somewhat stiffly. We exchanged the obligatory pleasantries while we waited for the tea to arrive. After Bristow deposited the tray and left, closing the doors behind him, Hope finally got to the reason for her visit.

"The last time we saw one another," she began, "I warned you that I would discover what hold you have over my brother-in-law, Lord Cox."

She sipped slowly, deliberately, as if she wanted to savor every drop of tea. It was typical of her to turn tea drinking into a dramatic art. I sipped slowly too and didn't prompt her. I would not rise to her bait.

"And so I have," she said.

"Have what?" Matt asked gruffly. It would seem he wasn't going to play any games with his cousin.

"Let me start at the very beginning." Hope set down her teacup and saucer. "Patience and Lord Cox arrived in London two days ago. We dined with them at his townhouse last night. It was immediately obvious that something was amiss. Lord Cox looked drawn and anxious. He barely engaged in conversation and his nerves appeared frayed. Patience was no better, but she seemed worried about her husband rather than nervous. When I spoke to my sister alone, I asked her what was the matter. She said she didn't know, but her husband had been like this for over a week, ever since receiving a letter."

"He didn't tell Patience the contents of the letter?" I asked.

"No."

Matt and I shared everything, so it was odd to me that a husband and wife would keep secrets. Surely Lord Cox would tell Patience about his past soon. It did, after all, affect her too.

On the other hand, it might upset her deeply to learn that he had only married her because he'd been blackmailed into it by me, and he was protecting her feelings by keeping the secret.

"I knew Patience wasn't telling me everything," Hope went on. "I pressed her all night until she finally cracked and admitted she suspected you were involved, India."

"Me?"

"She saw a letter addressed to you in Lord Cox's hand, but she didn't know the content. I would have opened it before the servants sent it, but Patience was always the obedient one, despite that little incident with the rogue." She dismissed Patience's youthful indiscretion with a wave of her hand, as if it had been nothing and had not led to Lord Cox calling off their first engagement.

"Is that why you're here?" Matt asked. "To ask India why he wrote to her?"

Her eyelashes fluttered. "I know why he wrote to her. He blames India for breaking her promise to keep his secret. The secret India used to force him to marry Patience." She picked up her teacup and sipped.

Despite my shredded nerves, I did the same, keeping my features schooled.

She rested the cup on her knee and regarded me with a cool

smile. She was enjoying this. Or perhaps she was enjoying seeing her sister suffer. "When I couldn't get an answer out of Patience, I confronted Lord Cox, and he told me," she said.

"What, precisely?" Matt asked, clearly not believing she knew the secret.

"Everything."

Matt made a scoffing sound.

"He told me that his father was married to another woman before he married his mother," she said. "The first marriage was never dissolved and so the son she bore him is the legitimate heir. He told me his half-brother grew up not knowing this, but Lord Cox had learned it from his father on his deathbed. He had kept the secret to himself and thought no one else knew about it —until you used the scandalous information to blackmail him into marrying my sister."

An icy shiver rippled down my spine.

"Why would he tell you all of that?" Matt asked. He sounded calm, whereas I was wracked with guilt, horror, and utter shamefulness at my role. "I don't believe it's simply because you asked."

"I promised him I could help him," Hope said, matching his tone. "I told him I knew people who can fix all sorts of problems, even those that seem unfixable, and they specialize in problems of a personal, unmentionable, nature."

"Who?" I blurted out.

"Why, you, of course." She smiled at me then turned it on Matt.

He sat unmoving in the chair, regarding her through hooded eyes. "Why would you say something like that?"

"Because it's true. Since you are the one who informed Lord Cox's brother, India, you can uninform him, so to speak. You simply have to tell him it's not true and that you were simply being nasty out of jealousy, spite or some such notion."

"I did *not* inform him," I said hotly. "I don't know how he found out the truth, but I can assure you, it wasn't through me, Matt or any of our friends."

Her forehead creased. For the first time, she looked uncertain. I was more relieved than I cared to admit that she believed me.

"Then who did?" she asked.

"We can't fix this," Matt said. "If the information is true—and it must be or Cox wouldn't be so worried—then nothing can be done, now that the half-brother is aware of it. You need to speak to Cox and tell him we can't help him. Make sure he knows we kept his secret. Tell him to engage a good lawyer."

"No, Matt, I won't tell him a thing," she snipped off. "Because you *can* still help him. You've helped the police with all sorts of delicate matters. I believe you're even on good terms with the commissioner."

"This isn't a police matter. The commissioner can't do anything."

"He can sweep all sorts of things under the carpet."

"It's not a criminal matter."

"Then you must find another way to end this in favor of Patience and Lord Cox. After all, you owe them."

"We didn't inform the half-brother!" I said again.

"I meant it's your fault my sister married him in the first place. If not for your blackmail, he would never have proposed a second time. She wouldn't be tangled up in this mess."

I bit my tongue despite wanting to spit back a thousand retorts. It would serve no purpose to show her how angry I was. I'd *helped* Patience. She'd *wanted* to marry Lord Cox, and I suspected he loved her too. Besides, Hope had never cared about her sister's happiness. She wasn't pursuing this because she cared, she was doing it for her own selfish reasons. By being connected to an upstanding, influential peer like Lord Cox through her sister, Hope's own marriage prospects had brightened. His fall from such lofty heights could bring Hope down too.

"Did you tell any of this to Patience?" Matt asked.

"No," Hope said. "She's not aware that she shouldn't be styled Lady Cox." Her smile returned, as if she were picturing the moment she revealed the secret to her sister. "I think it's time she learned the truth." She rose. "Good day. I'll see myself out."

Even so, Matt rang for Bristow and the doors opened immediately.

Hope didn't leave, however. She stood there, frowning. "You didn't answer me earlier. If you didn't tell the half-brother, who did?"

"How would we know such a thing?" I said.

"Could it have been the person who gave you the information?" The silence that followed was so deep that I swore I heard the clock's mechanisms whir. "Where *did* you get the information, India? Someone must have given it to you. Matt doesn't have the contacts in England to find out this sort of thing, and you have never moved in the right circles."

Matt rose and indicated the open door. "Bristow will see you out."

She didn't move. The cogs of her mind turned behind her unblinking stare as she sifted through what she knew of us, who our contacts were. It didn't take long for her to settle on the answer.

"Lord Coyle," she murmured.

I offered neither confirmation nor denial, but she didn't seem to need it.

"How did he learn the secret?" she asked.

"Coyle is very well connected," was all Matt said.

Hope's gaze turned pensive.

"Speaking of Lord Coyle." I did not go on. I couldn't decide whether I should try to convince her to marry him or not. She was loathsome, but he was worse, and I wasn't sure I could bring myself to push her toward him.

"Speaking of Coyle," Matt said, picking up where I left off, "perhaps you should accept his marriage proposal. Once the situation with Cox becomes public knowledge, your other prospects will withdraw. Coyle won't care, however."

"I have no other suitable prospects," she said with a tilt of her chin. "As to Lord Coyle, I'm capable of making up my own mind without my dear cousin telling me what to do."

"I'm merely advising."

"I get quite enough *advice* from my parents, thank you. If I do accept Coyle's offer, it will not be because you or anyone else wishes it." She strode out, her skirts swishing around her ankles.

"It wasn't a refusal," Matt said, sitting again. "But we need her to accept him within two weeks."

I rubbed my forehead, unable to focus on the prospect of their marriage. I was too consumed with wild ideas for helping Lord Cox keep his title. "Is she right, Matt? Is there something we can do to make the half-brother give up his claim?"

He settled beside me on the sofa with a deep sigh. "We could try reasoning with him, and tell him Cox is a good man who doesn't deserve to suffer for his father's sins. We can point out how it will affect Cox's four children."

I could tell from his deflated tone that he didn't think it would work. It would be a very generous, selfless man to give up the prospect of wealth and privilege for someone he didn't know.

"Cox should offer to give his half-brother an allowance in return for giving up all rights to the title," Matt said. "That's what I'd do if I were in his shoes."

I suspected Matt would give up the title to the rightful heir, no matter the consequences to himself, but he was a different man to Lord Cox.

"Hope will tell Patience, and she'll hate me for the part I played in her engagement," I said with a groan.

Matt put his arm around my shoulders and kissed my forehead. "She loves him. She should thank you."

I gave him an arched look. "That's not how she'll see it."

"You don't know that. Besides, it's Cox she should be angry

with. He knew he wasn't the legitimate heir and yet he proposed to her anyway. The first time, I mean. He had no right to do that when it could all come tumbling down at any moment. "

"But that's the thing," I said. "He never expected his half-brother to find out."

"Still…" He kissed the top of my head again.

I pulled away and clasped his hand in both of mine. "I want Lord Cox to know that it wasn't me who informed the half-brother. I hate him thinking I've betrayed him."

He nodded. "We'll visit tomorrow."

CHAPTER 3

We drove to Lord Cox's townhouse immediately after Sunday morning's church service in the hopes we would catch them before they left to make calls. Being recently arrived in London, I expected them to be busy seeing friends. It would be important to keep up appearances, in case word had got out.

I was worried we wouldn't be received, but the butler showed us into the drawing room after checking that his master and mistress were home. We were greeted with stony faces. Lord and Lady Cox sat at opposite sides of the drawing room, not at all how a newlywed couple should be in one another's company.

Patience knew. It was a relief to know that they'd had the awkward conversation. I didn't want to be the one to inform her.

"I'm glad you're here," Lord Cox said without so much as a "good morning." "It saves me a visit." He waved at the sofa and we sat.

"We'll have tea now," Patience said to the butler.

"No tea." Lord Cox dismissed the butler with a lift of his finger. "They won't be staying long."

I swallowed heavily.

Patience's glance flicked to mine then away, as if she couldn't bear to look at me. She seemed worn out. Her eyes were puffy and her nose red. Her husband looked just as exhausted, and there was none of the soft, amiability in his face that I'd seen before.

I swallowed again. "It wasn't me," I said quietly. "I didn't tell your half-brother. I don't even know his name."

"I don't believe you," he said without looking at me.

"My wife isn't a liar," Matt growled. "She didn't inform him. Nor did I. If I were still a betting man, I'd put money on Coyle."

Lord Cox's gaze finally snapped to mine. "Coyle?"

"He's the one who told me about your…predicament," I said. "He wanted me to owe him a favor, so he gave me the information to use. I'm sorry, Patience. I really am, but…it worked out for the best, didn't it?"

She looked away, her face pale, her lower lip quivering.

"How did he discover it?" Lord Cox asked.

"I don't know," I said.

The muscles in Lord Cox's jaw worked as he stared straight ahead. "Why would he want *you* to owe him a favor, Mrs. Glass?"

"That's none of your affair," Matt said.

"She owes me answers."

"She owes you nothing. She didn't tell anyone your secret."

"She blackmailed me!"

"Into something you wanted anyway."

Lord Cox's lips thinned and he stared straight ahead again. He did not refute it, at least.

"He wants me to owe him a favor because I'm a magician," I said, "and he has an interest in magic objects."

Lord Cox snorted. "That's absurd."

I'd given him an explanation; I wouldn't beg him to believe it.

"Have you spoken to your brother yet?" Matt asked.

"Half-brother." Lord Cox crossed his arms, and I thought he was going to remain silent, but after a long, awkward moment, he blew out a breath. He closed his eyes and rubbed his forehead. "I've written to him, offering him an allowance if he signed an agreement stating he wouldn't pursue the matter further. He refused."

"Offer him more."

"It was a sizeable amount! More than generous. More than I can afford," he added in a mutter.

Patience winced. She looked to be in pain as she watched her husband's demeanor change from defiant to defeated. I wished she would go to him, comfort him, but she remained seated.

"Ask to meet with him," Matt said. "If you can explain the impact it will have on your family face to face, he might give up the claim."

"That's why I'm in London, to see him. He traveled here to meet with a lawyer, according to the letter. He wants to meet me too, but not to get to know his brother better," he bit off. "He wants to look the man who cheated him out of his inheritance in the eye. That's how he worded it."

That was either the rash reaction of a deeply hurt man or the thoughtless reaction of a cruel one. I sincerely hoped the brother was the former, because the latter was going to be impossible to reason with. "I'm sure once he meets you both and sees that he would be hurting good people, he'll change his mind," I said.

"I doubt it. He asked me to bring the family coronet to the meeting and hand it over as a symbol of good faith."

"Coronet?"

"A priceless heirloom, given to my ancestor by Charles II after the restoration of the monarchy. My family fought for the Royalists in the civil war. It's kept under lock and key on the estate and only worn on special occasions."

"Did you bring it with you?" Matt asked.

Lord Cox nodded.

"You're not going to give it to him," I said, aghast.

"Why not? It's his."

"Legally, yes, but…" I didn't finish. He was right, and the brother had the law on his side. If I hadn't known the protagonists in the story personally, I would have been on the brother's side too, hoping he would take what was rightfully and morally his.

My relationship to Patience had colored my judgment and sent my own moral compass pointing in the wrong direction. I bit my lip, folded my hands in my lap, and remained quiet.

"After I hand over the coronet, he'll want the rest," Lord Cox said heavily. "If I don't walk away from...from everything, he'll take me to court."

Patience dabbed at her eyes but tears still spilled down her cheeks. Her husband cast an anxious glance at her from beneath lowered lashes but she wasn't looking his way and wouldn't have noticed.

"When are you meeting him?" Matt asked.

"Tonight," Lord Cox said.

"On a Sunday night? No lawyer will agree to that."

"It'll just be us."

"Let me come with you," Matt said. "I have enough legal knowledge to know if he's bluffing."

"Fine. We're meeting here." Lord Cox rubbed his forehead again. "If it weren't for my family...I don't know if I'd bother fighting."

"Why?" Patience blurted out. "You'll lose everything, Byron. The home you grew up in, your lands and tenants, your livelihood! Not to mention your reputation will be in tatters, and your friends will abandon you."

I was about to retort that true friends would rally around him, but I kept my mouth shut. Perhaps Lord Cox didn't have true friends who looked beyond his title. He certainly didn't leap to their defense. Indeed, he remained quiet. I'd never thought of him as middle-aged, with his smooth face and full head of blond hair, but in that moment, he looked every bit his forty-odd years.

Patience retreated into silence too, as if her outburst had never happened. Husband and wife didn't make eye contact.

I signaled to Matt that I wanted to speak to Patience alone. At least, I tried to signal to him. When he simply frowned at me when I jerked my head at the door, I winked. He still didn't understand, however, so I had to resort to a more obvious method.

"My lord, my husband has an interest in historical objects from the English civil war period," I said. "May he look at your coronet?"

Lord Cox blinked at Matt. "I would never have guessed you to be an enthusiast of English history. I'll fetch it."

Matt smiled and watched him leave.

"What about the civil war fascinates you?" Patience asked.

"Just the whole thing, really," Matt said. "The Royalists and the…"

"Roundheads," I filled in.

"Fascinating stuff."

I cleared my throat but Matt still didn't understand my hint and remained seated, a rather blank look on his face. It would be up to me to draw Patience away instead. She wouldn't speak openly if Matt were listening in.

"What a lovely clock," I said, moving to the mantel where a tortoise shell and gilt ormolu clock stood proudly in the center between two ornate gilt candlesticks. "Tell me all about it, Patience."

"I don't know anything about it," she said.

I held out my hand to her. "Then let me tell you what I know. It's in the style of Louis XIV but is a modern reproduction."

"You can tell that just from looking at it?" she said, joining me.

I took her hand and urged her to face the mantel with me, our backs to Matt. "I wanted to tell you something," I whispered. "Something between just us women."

She withdrew her hand. "If this is your way of apologizing for your meddling then…then I don't know if I'm ready to forgive you, India. I'm sorry. Perhaps one day."

"I'm not sorry that I helped him make up his mind to marry

you," I said quietly. When she went to walk off, I grabbed her elbow and held tightly. "Listen to me, Patience. I want you to know that I'm not sorry because Matt's right. Lord Cox did really want to marry you. I knew it then, and I know it now. If there was no admiration on his part, no affection, I wouldn't have gone ahead with the blackmail."

"Affection? For me?" she scoffed. "You had to *push* him towards me, India."

"It was just a little nudge."

"It was blackmail. You threatened to expose a dreadful secret that could ruin him. It took *that* for him to propose."

"He proposed once before."

"Precisely. *Before*. Before he found out about my past indiscretion. I disgust him so much that once he found out, he had to be coerced into proposing again. He loathes what I did, and he loathes it even more that he had to marry me."

I took her hands in mine and didn't let go when she tried to pull away. "I don't see that. All I see is a man who didn't know how to set aside his pride and act on his feelings. I gave him a way to do it."

"Is that what you tell yourself to lessen the guilt?"

I deserved the verbal slap, but I wasn't giving in yet. Something Matt said occurred to me. "I don't believe he's dwelling on your past, Patience. Matt told me Lord Cox was happy at the wedding."

She looked away. "Things were fine, for a time."

"Until he received the letter from his half-brother?"

"Yes. But if he trusted me, loved me, he would have spoken to me about it. He would have shared the burden." Her chin shuddered and her eyes pooled with tears.

"Not if he's angry with himself. Angry and ashamed."

She blinked back her tears. "Why would he be angry with himself? It's not his fault."

"Because he married you despite knowing his father's terrible secret. This coldness is because he feels ashamed that he married you under false pretenses. Perhaps he feels *he's* no longer worthy of *you*. You are a baron's daughter and he's…well, he's the illegitimate son of a bigamist."

"D—do you really think so, India?"

"Yes." I squeezed her hands. "Speak to him. Reassure him that you love him anyway, and always will, no matter what happens. You will love him unconditionally, won't you?"

"Of course."

Lord Cox entered carrying a golden crown on a red velvet cushion. It was in remarkably good condition for its age, with hardly a scratch on it. The gold shone brightly around the garnet and tourmaline gemstones, as if it had been recently polished.

"It's lovely," I said. "What do you think, Matt?"

"A very fine piece," Matt said dutifully.

Lord Cox presented it to Matt. "You may pick it up, if you like."

Matt did so, turning it around and making a show of studying it. "How old is it?"

"About two hundred and twenty years."

"It has survived well. There's not a dent on it."

"It's kept in a locked box."

Matt handed the coronet to me. Luckily he kept hold of it because I immediately let go as faint magical warmth spread up my arm.

"Something wrong, Mrs. Glass?" Lord Cox asked.

"No." I took it from Matt and I brushed my thumb over the smooth golden surface, one of the garnets, then back to the gold again. The magic was definitely in the gold, not the jewel, but it was quite mild.

I placed the coronet on the cushion. "Thank you for showing us. Matt, shall we go?"

Lord Cox promised to let Matt know when he was meeting his half-brother and we departed.

"It was magical, wasn't it?" he asked as we headed down the front steps.

"How did you know?"

"The condition was far too good for something so old, even if it is kept in a box. Your reaction when you touched it was also a giveaway."

"I wonder what Lord Cox would think if he knew."

"Going by his reaction when you told him you were a magician, he wouldn't believe you."

"Lord Coyle would pay a tidy sum for something like that," I said. "Gold magic is incredibly rare." So we'd been informed by Mr. McArdle, a gold magician we'd met when we were searching for the mapmaker's apprentice. According to McArdle, gold magicians once knew a spell to make gold multiply, but the spell had been lost in ancient times. "If that coronet is only two hundred years old, then Mr. McArdle was wrong."

"The coronet could have been fashioned from an older artifact. The magic in it could be ancient."

"True. The residual heat did feel faint." I accepted his assistance up the step into the carriage. "Even so, best not to mention it to Lord Coyle. There's no telling what he'd do to get his hands on it."

* * *

WE ARRIVED home to find Willie, Aunt Letitia and Duke trying to cheer Cyclops up. Even Mrs. Potter seemed to have contributed to the effort in the only way she knew how, but the shortbread, slices of Madeira cake and sponge on Cyclops's plate hadn't been touched.

"What is it?" I asked, pausing in the doorway, hat pin and hat in hand.

"He's too good for Catherine," Aunt Letitia said huffily.

"It ain't her fault," Cyclops muttered.

"Let me rephrase. He's too good for the Masons. Horrid family. How could you be friends with them, India?"

"Did something happen at church?" Matt asked.

Cyclops had attended the Masons' local church instead of joining us at Grosvenor Chapel for the Sunday service that morning. "I shouldn't have gone," he said. "Everyone stared."

"You should have come with us," Aunt Letitia said.

"If he avoids them then they'll never get used to him." Duke picked up the plate and offered it to Cyclops. "Have one of Mrs. Potter's shortbread. They always make you feel better."

Cyclops accepted the plate but didn't eat.

Willie reached over and took the slice of sponge. "Duke's right. You got to go again. You ain't a quitter, Cyclops. Anyway, you got a right to go to any church you like. I say you go back there next Sunday and the Sunday after and the one after that."

"I don't want to go where I ain't wanted."

"You shouldn't care what people think." Willie took an enormous bite and a waterfall of crumbs cascaded onto her chest. "I don't."

Duke rolled his eyes.

Matt clapped Cyclops on the shoulder. "Willie's right, in a strange way."

Willie tossed Duke a smug look.

"This is about you and Catherine, not her family. Hear me out," he said when Cyclops protested. "If her family love her, and I believe they do…"

"They do," I chimed in.

"Then they'll accept you for her sake, if they see she loves you and you love her. Give it time. Be persistent but don't rush them. They'll come to see you for the good man you are. Everyone does."

Cyclops gave a deep sigh and a nod of thanks for Matt.

Willie went to take one of the shortbread, but Cyclops moved the plate out of her reach. "Mrs. Potter gave these to me," he said. "Get your own."

Willie pouted as she watched Cyclops eat one biscuit and pick up another. "You'll get fat."

He ate the second biscuit and smiled at her, his mouth full.

She *humphed*. "Mrs. Potter never bakes me shortbread when I got romantic troubles."

"See what we mean," Duke said to Cyclops. "Everyone likes you. Mrs. Potter doesn't try to feed everyone just because they're sad. Case in point." He indicated a morose Willie.

She poked her tongue out at him.

Bristow cleared his throat to get our attention. I hadn't heard him enter. "Are you at home for Oscar Barratt, sir?"

Matt looked to me and I nodded. "Is he alone or with Lady Louisa?" I asked.

"Alone." He bowed out and returned a few moments later with Oscar.

"Ah, cake," Oscar said. "Excellent timing."

I asked Bristow to bring in refreshments for everyone. Willie sat up straighter and rubbed her hands together.

"What can we do for you, Barratt?" Matt asked.

I scowled at him. He might not like Oscar, but he should at least exchange pleasantries with our guest before getting to the point.

"I believe congratulations are in order," Aunt Letitia said, smoothly. Perhaps she didn't like Matt's abruptness either and being a more experienced hostess than me, knew precisely what to say to rescue the situation.

"No, Letty," Willie hissed. "He found out Louisa cast her net wide only days before she proposed to him. Remember?"

"I remember," Aunt Letitia whispered back. "But it's his place to say so, not yours."

Willie shrugged. "So are you calling off the wedding?" she asked.

Oscar cleared his throat and flattened his tie. "I see your friends and family all know about my life, Glass."

"They like to stay informed," Matt said.

"We don't gossip," Aunt Letitia assured him. "Even Willemina's very discreet, despite evidence to the contrary. Go on, what was it you wanted to tell us?"

Bristow returned with a tray of shortbread and bowed out. I made sure Oscar got two biscuits by way of apology for the interlopers.

"I felt as though I owed you an explanation after the other night," he said to Matt. "You see, Louisa and I are still engaged."

"Really?" I blurted out.

"However, in light of her past liaisons, I am no longer under the illusion that she's marrying me out of love."

"Oh, what a shame." Aunt Letitia clicked her tongue. "I do so enjoy a happy story, and I'm afraid this one will end in tears."

I eyed her carefully, wondering if she'd had one of her turns. Her eyes had that dreamlike quality they sometimes got when her mind slipped into the past.

Oscar finished his first biscuit while we all waited for him to go on. He swallowed, cleared his throat, and reached for the second.

"Why are you going through with the marriage if you know she doesn't love you?" Duke finally prompted. "Do you love her?"

Oscar considered the question. "I thought I did, for a while. But…I don't know. I don't think so. I was crushed that night of the Delanceys' dinner party when Glass told me she tried to court Dr. Seaford, but I think it was simply my manly pride that was hurt. When I thought about it, I realized I didn't mind that I'd never been the object of her affection. What I did mind was that she'd hoodwinked me. I told her so this morning."

"And?" I asked.

"And she apologized and promised to be honest with me from now on. She said she still wanted to get married if I did."

"And you do?"

"Why not? What have I got to lose?"

I frowned. "But…you're willing to marry a woman you don't love and who doesn't love you, because she has a fortune?"

He shrugged. "You make it sound strange, India. People have been marrying for reasons other than love since the institute was invented. At least neither of us is under any illusions. We both know this is a marriage of convenience. Besides, I like her and she likes me. We'll get along fine."

I stared at him. He smiled back.

"Don't worry about India," Willie said. "She thinks everyone should have what she and Matt have. People like you and me—sensible, logical people—know love ain't for everyone." She stretched out her legs and crossed them at the ankles. "And that's all right by me."

"I think it's commendable that you've both come to an agreement and are going into the marriage with honesty," Aunt Letitia said. "Too often the young lady is unaware and is disappointed when she learns her husband is only after her fortune. Lady Louisa *is* aware that you're marrying her for reasons other than love, isn't she?"

"She is now."

"Are you sure this is what you want?" I asked. "Marriage is for life."

He smiled. "I'm well aware of that. This is what I want, India. My work is too important to me to give it up."

"Work?" Matt echoed. "Are you referring to the book?"

"Yes, and any future books I wish to write. With Louisa's money, I can pay the printers well to minimize the risk of them pulling out of our agreement like the last one did. I can even afford to leave my job at the *Gazette* and throw myself into research, although I enjoy journalism, so I haven't decided whether to stay or not yet." He gave me a flat smile. "I'm flattered that you're trying to talk me out of this, India."

"Don't read something into her reaction that's not there," Matt growled. "India and I know what Louisa is like. I don't think you're fully aware of how manipulative she can be."

"She did lie to you about Gabe," I said to Oscar.

"It wasn't a lie," he pointed out. "She just failed to mention him. Besides, she didn't propose to him, just to Charbonneau."

"But she would have if we hadn't warned him and he hadn't put some distance between them."

"She wants to marry a magician. After Charbonneau, Seaford was the next logical choice. It made sense she'd pursue him. I don't mind. I know my magic is neither rare nor particularly powerful."

I sighed and appealed to Matt. He, however, simply thrust out his hand toward Oscar.

"Then congratulations," he said. "I hope you'll be happy together. Or at least not want to kill each other in five years."

Oscar chuckled and shook his hand. "Marriages of convenience can work, Glass. And who's to say we won't fall in love eventually anyway?"

Aunt Letitia clapped her hands. "That's the spirit. It will be a romantic ending after all."

* * *

I MANAGED to convince Matt that I ought to come along to the meeting with Lord Cox's half-brother as a support for Patience. Considering she and her husband weren't on good terms, I suggested she might need me.

He saw right through my ruse, however. "If you want to meet him, just say so," he said as we drove to Lord Cox's townhouse in the early evening. "No need to hide behind Patience."

"I am not hiding behind anyone. Wipe that smirk off your face, Matt."

His eyes gleamed in the darkness. "You wipe it off. With your mouth."

"Americans," I muttered in imitation of Aunt Letitia. Then I kissed him.

A few minutes later, we were received into the drawing room where we met our host and hostess. Both looked nervous, glancing at the door at every sound. Conversation quickly stalled, and I searched for something to say to break the tension while we waited.

"Will you be redecorating?" I asked Patience. The drawing room had a woman's touch in the pale pink and mint green color scheme and spindly-legged furniture, but it was a good ten years out of date. The previous Lady Cox must have put her stamp on it when she first married and Lord Cox hadn't changed a thing since.

"I don't know," Patience said, staring down at her lap.

We fell into silence again, and it was almost a relief when Ned Longmire arrived. He entered the drawing room with a confident step and a defiant manner about him, as if he were daring Lord Cox to challenge him then and there. He wore a new suit, though not an expensive one, with shoes polished to a high sheen that looked as if they'd hardly been worn. His necktie was a deep blue, tied with a simple knot. A silver watch chain hung from the buttonhole of his dove gray waistcoat. The outfit was all wrong for eveningwear, something I wouldn't have known before I moved in with Matt.

I wasn't sure if Mr. Longmire noticed the difference between his clothing and the dinner jackets, white shirts and white bow ties worn by Matt and Lord Cox. He seemed far too interested in his half-brother's face, perhaps seeking out any resemblances. I saw very few. They were both fair in coloring with light blue eyes, but that was where the similarities ended. Lord Cox's face was slender, his top front teeth protruding somewhat, and he had a full head of hair whereas Mr. Longmire's receded into a peak. Mr. Longmire was also more physically imposing than his half-brother with a broader, taller build.

"Good evening," Lord Cox said stiffly. "May I introduce my wife, Lady Cox."

Patience put out her hand, and Mr. Longmire paused before shaking it. Going by her frown, she'd expected him to bow over it. Or perhaps she was annoyed by his mere presence. He was, after all, attempting to destroy her new life.

"This is my wife's cousin, Mr. Matthew Glass and his wife, Mrs. India Glass."

Mr. Longmire wagged a finger at me. "I know you," he said in a strong Yorkshire accent.

"Oh?" I said. "Perhaps you bought a watch or clock from my father's shop when I worked there. Steele's on St. Martin's Lane."

The finger wagging continued. Beside me, Matt shifted his stance. I hoped he wasn't considering snapping the finger off.

"You used to be India Steele?" Mr. Longmire said.

"That's right. Was it a watch or a clock?"

His top lip lifted in a sneer. "I wouldn't buy nowt from you."

"Oh?" I said, a sick feeling settling in my stomach. I suspected I knew where this was heading.

"You and your kind are ruining us," he went on.

"That's enough," Matt snapped.

"My guild contacts here in London told me to watch out for you." Mr. Longmire looked me up and down, far more thoroughly than he'd inspected his brother, and with more disdain too. "They said you're the spiritual leader of the magicians."

I took a step back beneath the force of his ire. "I—I don't know what you mean. I no longer have a shop."

"You don't need a shop to rally your kind. They all look up to you, so I hear. They say you're powerful." He stabbed his finger in my direction. "You lot are ruining us, and you don't bloody care!"

Matt grabbed him by the lapels and shook him, hard. "I said, that's enough."

Mr. Longmire tried to push Matt off but failed. "All right, all right. You win. I'll save my accusations until after this meeting."

"You won't speak to my wife again unless she wishes it. Is that clear?"

"I say, steady on," Lord Cox said, keeping his distance. "Let's all take a deep breath and calm down. All this talk of magic is somewhat speculative anyway."

"It's real," Mr. Longmire told him. "Mrs. Glass might not have a shop anymore, but her father did, and her grandfather, and they were successful too."

"Only moderately," I said.

"They were successful because they cheated. All magicians are cheats. We hard-working, honest businessmen can't compete when the other players don't follow the rules."

I frowned. His words sounded very familiar.

Matt shook him again. "If you don't close your mouth—"

"Matt." I laid a hand on his arm. "Let him go. You're crushing the suit he bought especially for tonight's meeting."

Matt released him, but not before giving him a shove.

"Mr. Longmire," I said, "have you been writing threatening letters to magicians in London?"

Mr. Longmire smoothed over the creases in his jacket. "What of it?"

"You can't go around threatening people like that!"

"People?" he spat. "You magicians shouldn't even call yourselves that. You're not natural, you're definitely immoral, and you're just plain cheaters."

Oh dear. He really shouldn't have said that.

Matt grabbed Mr. Longmire by the shoulder, jerked him around to face him, and punched him in the nose.

CHAPTER 4

"Mr. Longmire!" Lord Cox cried. "Are you all right?"

"Matthew," Patience scolded, sounding very much like Aunt Letitia. "Was that necessary?"

"Yes," Matt said.

"His nose is bleeding," I pointed out. "It'll get on the carpet."

Matt handed me his handkerchief and I gave it to Mr. Longmire. He snatched it off me, not in the least grateful.

"You bloody arse," he spat at Matt as he dabbed at his nose.

"There's no need for that language in front of the ladies," Lord Cox said.

Patience rang for the butler. "We'll go in for dinner now," she instructed. "I think we could all do with a glass of Madeira."

I didn't think adding wine to the hostility would make things better, but on the other hand, I might need it to get through the evening.

"I'm not staying for dinner," Mr. Longmire said.

"Oh." Lord Cox's shoulders slumped. "I thought we were going to talk about this like decent, civilized folk and nut out a solution."

"He ain't civilized." Mr. Longmire nodded at Matt. "And she

—" He cut himself off before he could say something that would earn him another punch on the nose. "Anyway, there is only one solution." He pulled out a document from his inside jacket pocket. "Sign this. I had my lawyer draw it up."

Lord Cox looked over the pages, his face growing paler with each passing moment. "I—I need time."

"For what?"

"To think about things. This is all very sudden."

"It is for me, aye, but is it for you? My source says you already knew about our father's bigamy."

Lord Cox winced and made a show of reading the papers again.

"He needs his lawyer to look over it," Matt said.

"I can tell you what it says." Mr. Longmire sniffed and dabbed at his nose again. "It states that you will hand over all land and chattels that belong to the barony, as well as the title itself. You give up any claim to styling yourself Lord Cox, and your heir gives up all rights of inheriting."

Patience gave a little sob into her hand.

Lord Cox winced again. "I would still like my lawyer to look over it. As you can imagine, this isn't a simple matter."

"It is to me," Mr. Longmire said.

"How can you be so cavalier?" I snapped. "You are changing their lives and the lives of Lord Cox's children. Can you not see how upsetting this is?"

"I have no sympathy for any of you. Your class have looked down on mine for generations, *my lord*. You are about to get a taste of your own medicine."

"My husband is nothing but generous and kind to his tenants and everyone in the village," Patience said with more backbone than I'd seen her exhibit before. "What you're doing to him is despicable, cruel." She pressed a hand to her stomach and drew in a fortifying breath. "Please, be reasonable, Mr. Longmire, and accept my husband's offer of an allowance. That way everyone gets something out of this sordid mess. A mess that was not of my husband's making any more than it was of yours."

Mr. Longmire looked as though he were considering her suggestion, but in the end, he shook his head. "I want what's mine. I have no sympathy for him. He had a life of privilege, while I grew up poor."

"Our father gave your mother an allowance," Lord Cox growled. "You were hardly destitute."

"An allowance! Do you think that made up for the way my mother was treated? Her family shunned her. She was jeered at by people in the village because they didn't believe her when she said she was married. They spat at her and called her disgusting names. I had to fight off bullies every day. When we moved, she was able to make a fresh start only by telling everyone she was a widow. But she never married again, and now I know why. She was a decent woman who would never break her vows." His eyes glistened for a brief moment before he bared his teeth. "She didn't deserve that life. And neither did I."

Lord Cox rubbed his forehead. "I'm sorry. I really am. You're right and you and your mother should have been treated better. If it helps, he wasn't a nice man, our father. He was very cold and distant. He ruled the household with an iron fist."

"*If it helps*," Mr. Longmire sneered. "*You* did nothing after he died. *You* kept the secret, hoping this day would never come. Now that I see what company you keep." He thrust his chin in my direction. "I'm not surprised you're a cheat too."

"For goodness' sake," I muttered.

Matt squared up to Mr. Longmire, who merely glared back at him. "Go ahead. Hit me again, Mr. Glass, and I will have you up on charges of assault."

Matt's brittle chuckle held no humor.

Mr. Longmire swallowed and backed away.

"It's time you left," Lord Cox said sitting heavily in an armchair. "I will look over these papers."

"Not without the coronet," Mr. Longmire said. "I told you I

wanted it as a show of goodwill." He put out his palm. "Hand it over."

Weighty silence settled around us, smothering and dense. I found it hard to breathe, to think. Patience went to her husband and touched his shoulder. He covered her hand with his own. It was the first sign of affection I'd seen between them and it seemed to rally him.

"I can't," he said. "I promised I would, but there's a lot to think about. My children, my wife…"

"Hand it over," Mr. Longmire growled.

"Let me go through these papers with my lawyer and then—"

"No! I want the damned coronet! It's *mine*. I deserve it." He stepped toward Lord Cox, his jaw and fists clenched.

Matt grabbed him by the arm and spun him around. He was going to hit him again.

"You don't want it," I said quickly.

Nobody paid me any mind.

"You don't want it," I said to Mr. Longmire. "It's magical and you hate magic."

Everyone stared at me. A warning flashed in Matt's eyes, but not censure. There was no point in holding back now. Everyone in that room knew what I was.

"What are you talking about?" Mr. Longmire snarled.

"When we were here earlier today, Lord Cox showed us the coronet. I touched it and felt magical heat."

Mr. Longmire scoffed. "You're making that up. Magic doesn't have any heat. I've felt a magical object before, Mrs. Glass, and it wasn't hot."

"Only magicians can feel it in things that have had a spell cast on them during the manufacturing process. It's a different kind of warmth than that created by the sun or fire. I can't explain it, but I do know when I feel it. And when I touched the coronet this morning, I felt its magic warmth."

"Is that why you immediately let it go?" Patience asked.

I nodded. "Do you really want it if you hate magicians and

magic so much, Mr. Longmire? Wouldn't it be considered *cheating* if you were to possess such a thing? I wonder what your friends in business would think if they knew you coveted a magical crown."

The muscles in his face twitched and twisted as he fought to control his anger. He swallowed whatever retort was on his lips, however, and simply threw Matt's bloodstained handkerchief on the floor. Either he really didn't want anything to do with magic or Matt's threatening stance worried him.

Lord Cox tugged on the bell pull. "Good evening, Mr. Longmire," he said evenly.

Mr. Longmire put a finger down his collar and stretched out his neck. "I'll be back for the contract."

"Show Mr. Longmire out," Lord Cox instructed the butler.

Matt put up a staying hand. "Just a moment. Who told you about your father?"

"I received an anonymous letter along with copies of all the documentary evidence to prove the claim," Mr. Longmire said.

"Are you sure the documents weren't fabricated?"

"Pardon?"

"With the right equipment and an excellent forger on the payroll, fake copies of birth certificates and parish records are easy to come by. I assume you checked everything before marching to London with your threats."

Mr. Longmire looked a little less sure of himself. With a rallying sniff and another stretch of his neck, he said, "Of course I did. Besides, it must be true. Cox hasn't tried to deny it."

"That's not the point. The point is, lawyers want proof."

Mr. Longmire turned to Lord Cox. "You can keep the coronet for now. I'll collect it when I get the rest of what's rightfully mine."

We waited for him to go before we took our seats again. I felt somewhat shaken after the confrontation and clasped my hands together on my lap to steady them. Matt must have sensed it because he placed his hand over mine and caressed my knuckles with his thumb.

"Well," Lord Cox said with forced cheerfulness, "shall we go in to dinner?"

I didn't feel like eating. Nor did Patience. She pushed her food around her plate and hardly touched her dessert, even though I'd decided by the time the banana cream was served that there was no point sacrificing delicious food for Mr. Longmire.

The men had briefly discussed legalities and the contract, but it wasn't clear by the end of the night whether Lord Cox was going to sign or not.

"Do you still think it was Lord Coyle who informed him?" Patience asked me as tea was served in the drawing room after dinner.

"I do. He ought to be ashamed of himself for causing this trouble."

"I just want to know why," she said on a sigh.

As did I, and whether it had anything to do with magic. Perhaps Lord Coyle thought Longmire's hatred of magicians tied in with his own plans to keep magic secretive. By issuing threats to successful magicians, Longmire might be frightening some into remaining hidden. That would suit Coyle nicely. But why inform Longmire about his father? That was a separate matter entirely.

"What line of business is Mr. Longmire in?" I asked.

"Rope," Patience said. "He's part owner in a small factory."

"Part owner?" Matt echoed. "I thought he said he and his mother were poor. That's quite a rise."

"They weren't poor," Lord Cox said. "My father's allowance was generous. Longmire was educated well too, mostly by his mother. My father told me she was intelligent, witty and beautiful. I sensed he was in love with her, even years later."

"He abandoned her and their child," Matt pointed out. "That's not love."

Lord Cox eyed the legal papers as if he would set fire to them with his glare if he could. "He won't give up until he has what's rightfully his."

Patience pressed her fingers to her lips, her eyes filling with tears as she gazed at her husband.

"What should I do?" Lord Cox asked Matt in a thin voice.

"I can't answer that for you."

"You can't give up the barony for that man," I blurted out. "He's horrid."

Matt squeezed my hand. "But he has the legal and moral right to take it."

* * *

WITH HIS ALLOWANCE reinstated after his recent incarceration, Fabian Charbonneau could afford to move out of my grandfather's small house and into a residence near Berkeley Square. It was there that we met to learn the language of magic and attempt to create new spells.

For the first time since starting this endeavor with Fabian, Matt had decided to join me, claiming he had little else to do that day. He sat with us for a while, listening in as Fabian and I assembled words in what we hoped was the right order, but moved to sit by the fire with the newspaper after twenty minutes.

"It's not right," I said, shaking my head at the watch Fabian had placed in my hand. "There are too many words in this spell."

"How do you know?" Fabian asked.

He was immaculately turned out, as usual, with a rich burgundy waistcoat adding some color to his otherwise somber suit of dark gray. The waistcoat looked bare without the gold chain of his watch decorating it. The Patek Philippe chronometer timepiece had a lovely solid feel to it and had grown warm from my attempts to speak our experimental flying spell into it. But it hadn't moved.

"I don't know how," I said. "I just do. This spell is wrong."

Fabian studied the words again. "It has the common words from my iron spell and the paper flying spell mixed with your watch fixing spell. What else can we add to it?"

I shook my head. "It's not what we need to add. All the words are here but they're not in the right order."

"How do you know?" he asked again.

"I just do," I said, repeating myself. "Sorry, Fabian, I know you want definitive answers but I can't give them."

"It is all right, India. Your magic is strong, and I suspect you use this." He tapped his chest. "Rather than this." He tapped his forehead.

"Intuition," Matt said from behind his newspaper. "She uses her innate sense of magic."

Fabian smiled. "Intuition, yes. You are a marvel, India. I have not met another magician like you. Now, play with the words. Move them around or change the way you say them. Use your intuition, not your brain."

I rearranged the order of the words but none worked and my intuition told me they were wrong anyway. I rearranged them again and again, but still something was off. I knew it wasn't the pronunciations. Despite Fabian's accent, I was quite sure we had that part right.

Too many words. There had to be. "Say your iron spell again," I said.

He repeated it and the broken nail he used for practicing lifted off the desk. The spell seemed longer than the one Mr. Hendry had spoken to make paper fly. If only I could hear that one again to be sure.

I crossed out one of the words in Fabian's spell and, for what seemed like the hundredth time, inserted the watch words in place of the iron ones. Then I spoke the new combination.

The watch flew off my palm, skimmed Matt's newspaper, and smashed into the fireplace.

I covered my squeal of surprise with my hand and stared at

the pieces on the hearth. "I broke your watch. I'm so sorry, Fabian."

He grinned. "I will get another."

"But it was a Patek Philippe."

"A *flying* Patek Philippe"

Matt retrieved the pieces and poured them onto Fabian's cupped hands. "Were you trying to decapitate me?"

"Sorry," I said. "I think I need practice."

"Perhaps I should move to another room."

"That would be wise. Just until I can control it." I turned to Fabian. "How do you control where the iron goes?"

He tapped his temple. "I think where I want it to go."

"Interesting." It would seem the magician's unspoken thoughts contributed significantly to making the spell work. "Let's try it again," I said, as Matt left with the newspaper tucked under his arm. "I'll think about where I want it to go."

"And the speed," Fabian said, chuckling. "Slower, this time."

"Oh, but we don't have another watch. We can't use mine. I've worked on it too many times and it might respond too well. We need an unadulterated timepiece."

He opened the desk drawer and pulled out a plain open-faced watch. "I have another."

"Why didn't we use this one first and save your good one?" I eyed the pieces he'd placed on the desk. I could put the innards back, but I couldn't fix the dented case and smashed glass.

Fabian placed the second watch in my palm. "Try it again, but concentrate on speed and direction. Fly it onto the sofa."

I steadied my breathing, slowing it down, and stared hard at the sofa, then at the watch then at the sofa again. I imagined the watch rising gently from my palm and floating toward a soft landing on the cushion.

I repeated the words in the modified spell, carefully and deliberately. The watch rose and drifted to just above the sofa where it hovered before gently lowering.

Fabian clapped. "You did it! Well done, India."

I retrieved the watch, grinning. "That wasn't hard at all."

We tried it twice more and both times, I steered the watch and controlled its flight. I couldn't stop my smile. It felt marvelous to have achieved something so remarkable. Mere months ago, I would never have suspected I could make a watch fly. The applications of what we'd learned today stretched before me like a hall runner.

Speaking of carpets… "We should try it with a small rug next time," I said. "Or perhaps a piece of leather. But we'll need the right kind of magician."

"I do not know any magicians in London," Fabian said.

"And I don't know many who won't ask for a favor in return."

"What favor?"

"To extend their magic and make it last." I told him about Mr. Bunn, the leather magician.

He grimaced. "Did Glass scare him away?"

"For now." I sighed. "He might return."

"So who will we ask?"

"Mr. Delancey is from wool magic stock. He says it died out with his father, but perhaps he has distant cousins who still possess magic. We could ask him and since he has already received such a magnificent gift of your key, he won't ask for something else." I hoped not, anyway. The Delanceys might just be greedy enough to ask for another magical item to add to their collection.

"We must try," he said.

Matt appeared in the doorway, a look of mystification on his face.

"I did it," I told him. "I controlled the watch's flight."

"On her first attempt," Fabian added, his eyes alight.

"Wonderful," Matt said, absently.

"What is it?" I asked.

He held out the newspaper. "Your butler just handed me this," he said to Fabian. "It's a midday issue, printed this morning." He pointed to an article at the top of the page. "Read that, India."

It was the gossip page. "'Lord ____ to disinherit after secret older brother found,'" the headline read. "My God," I murmured. "This is terrible."

The first paragraph of the brief article said the reclusive lord, who was not named, was reeling from the news that he should never have inherited his father's title and estate. His older brother was suing for everything and the matter was in the hands of lawyers.

"Do you think Lord Coyle told the columnist?" I asked Matt.

"Coyle?" Fabian all but spat out the name. After the earl attempted to blackmail him by paying off the debt that saw him released from prison, Fabian had no liking for Coyle. His family paid back the debt, but Coyle had insisted Fabian still owed him. We suspected Coyle had manipulated the moneylender into calling in the debt in the first place, which only made his demand harder to swallow.

"He denied it," Matt told Fabian. "But he is probably behind this." He explained Lord Cox's predicament without naming names then turned to me. "India, read the rest. You haven't got to the most interesting part yet."

I read the second paragraph and gasped. The article stated the older brother asked that a symbolic gift be made of the family heirloom, a priceless coronet. He had "nobly" refused it when he discovered it had been made with magical gold.

"Magic?" Fabian repeated. "Gold magic does not exist anymore."

"I touched the coronet," I told him. "I felt magic heat and it could only have come from the gold."

"Remarkable," he murmured.

"So it's true? Gold magic has died out?"

"Over a thousand years ago, yes."

"We met a gold magician once," I told him. "He could feel

gold magic, but he didn't know any spells. He claimed they'd been lost and the magic line was now impotent."

Fabian indicated the newspaper. "You say Coyle is the source for this?"

Matt shook his head. "While I do think Coyle informed Longmire that he is the rightful heir, I don't think he orchestrated this." He slapped the newspaper with the back of his hand. "It's not in his best interests. Not if he wants to keep magic a secret."

"It's very public," I agreed.

I read the article again. The wording was interesting. He or she did not speculate on the existence of magic, or scoff at it. It was stated as factual. "My first thought is Oscar Barratt," I said. "But this is mean spirited, and he's not cruel."

"I think it was Longmire himself," Matt said. "The half-brother," he added for Fabian's benefit.

I read the article once more and this time I could almost hear Mr. Longmire's voice in the words. It had to be him. "Why mention the magic coronet at all though?"

"To taint the unnamed lord," Matt said. "To Longmire, magic is unnatural and despicable. By associating the illegitimate lord with magic, no matter how loosely, he thinks he's painting a picture of him as unworthy—unholy, almost."

"But that's absurd. It's his family coronet too."

"He 'nobly' refused it." Matt pointed to the line. "He wants to be seen not only as the rightful heir, when names are finally revealed, but he wants the general public to think of him as the better man who refused a valuable object because of its unnatural origins."

Fabian muttered something in French that I suspected wasn't a nice word about Mr. Longmire or his assumption.

"Do you think he's right?" I asked weakly. "That the public thinks magic is something to be reviled and avoided?"

"Most of the public are still skeptical, despite Barratt's early articles," Matt assured me. "Many don't realize magic is real."

"But they would agree with Mr. Longmire if they knew it existed," I said heavily.

"We don't know that yet."

Perhaps not, but once Oscar Barratt's book came out, we would find out for certain.

CHAPTER 5

We dined that evening with Catherine and Ronnie Mason. The invitation had been extended by Cyclops, with an assurance that I would agree to it.

"I hope you don't mind," he'd said to me that afternoon. "Ronnie wanted to show you a letter he received so I told him to come for dinner. I had to invite Catherine too, of course."

"Of course," I said slyly.

Ronnie showed us the letter as soon as they arrived. Even though it wasn't signed, we knew it was from Mr. Longmire. This one was a little different to the others, however.

"It's accusing me of selling timepieces that you've put your magic in," Ronnie explained as I read. "But I'm not. The Guild knows I'm not. I had to show them the storage facility full of clocks and watches they made us remove from the shop before we re-opened."

"Ignore this," I said, handing it back. "It's written by an angry man with a chip on his shoulder by the name of Longmire."

"That's what Nate told us," Catherine said. Her lips curved into a mysterious smile that turned her pretty face into an interesting one. "But he wouldn't say more than that."

"It ain't my business," Cyclops said.

The dinner gong sounded and we filed into the dining room. Aunt Letitia had elected not to join us, citing a headache, but Duke and Willie were pleased to eat a hearty meal after spending the cool autumn day fixing the schoolroom roof at the Sisters of the Sacred Heart convent.

"Will you tell us who this Longmire fellow is, India?" Catherine asked.

"And why did he send me an angry letter?" Ronnie added.

"He's part owner in a rope making factory in Yorkshire," I said. "He believes magicians are cheating, giving them an advantage in business."

"Are there magician rope makers taking his business?" Ronnie asked as Peter placed a bowl of mock turtle soup in front of him.

"I don't know. He's riled on behalf of the artless in every field of manufacturing."

"Tell them the rest," Willie said, tucking her napkin into her collar.

"Matt and I met Mr. Longmire last night. Our meeting didn't go well."

"Matt gave him a bloody nose," Willie said proudly.

Catherine gasped and Cyclops gave Willie a warning glare.

"Mr. Longmire deserved it," I said. "He's a horrible man. I suspect he sent you the letter after our encounter because he knew it would get back to me. He dislikes me because I'm a magician."

"Tell them how he's Lord Cox's older brother," Willie said. "And how he should have inherited Cox's barony, only he didn't on account of his father was a bigamist."

Catherine gasped again.

Cyclops sighed.

Ronnie lowered his soup spoon with a clank on the edge of the bowl. "Is Lord Cox the one everyone's talking about?"

I glanced at Matt but he was looking at Ronnie. "Everyone's talking about the newspaper article?" he asked.

Ronnie nodded. "Gossip spread up and down the street as soon as the newspaper came out. No one knew who this mysterious illegitimate lord was, although plenty made guesses."

"It's quite a scandal," Catherine added.

"Don't repeat his name to anyone," Matt warned. "Not until it's made public."

"We won't," Catherine assured him. "Isn't he your cousin's husband?"

Matt picked up his spoon. "Patience. They married recently."

"How awful for her. For both of them. So is it true? He really is illegitimate and this Longmire fellow is the real heir?"

"It seems so."

"It's unclear if Lord Cox should give everything to him yet," I said. "He's seeking legal advice."

"He should give it up," Ronnie said. "It's not his. Everything should have gone to this Longmire fellow."

"He's a turd," Willie cut in. "So India and Matt say."

"I guessed that from the threatening letter he sent us," Catherine said.

"It seems to me he thinks he's entitled to everything without working hard for it," Duke chimed in. "A successful business, the barony."

"That's hardly fair," Ronnie said. "If he's the rightful heir, he should have it."

"Aye," Cyclops agreed. "And it can't be easy to compete against a magician in the same kind of business. Especially a magician who ain't afraid to use his magic."

"Good point," Ronnie said before tucking into his soup. "I'm glad we don't have any watch magicians with shops or we'd struggle to sell a single piece."

"Ronnie," his sister hissed with a glance at me.

"India's different. Her father didn't practice his magic. He used hard work, experience, and know-how, just like I plan to."

"*I* used my magic," I told him.

"That's different. You didn't know you were using your magic. You can't be blamed for that."

I thought his logic a little skewed, but we dropped the matter, thankfully. The subject of Mr. Longmire didn't come up again through the next four courses or afterward, as we played cards.

Willie joined us in the drawing room only briefly. "I have an appointment with a nurse to keep," she said, smiling.

"A nurse?" Duke asked. "Not the same one who broke your heart."

"A different one. And my heart weren't broken. It was bruised and it's fine now."

Duke huffed as he stretched out his legs. Like Willie, he elected not to play poker with us. "You sure about that? And anyway, does Brockwell know about this nurse?"

"It ain't his business."

I lowered my cards. "Of course it's his business. You and he are together."

"Except when we ain't."

I frowned. "I'm confused."

"So am I," Ronnie added.

"I'll explain later," Catherine whispered from where she stood behind a seated Cyclops. She'd claimed she didn't know how to play poker so would watch and learn. She'd stood at Cyclops's shoulder the entire time.

"Look, India," Willie said huffily. "Jasper and I have an understanding. He can see other women if he wants, and so can I. Or men. Whatever takes my fancy."

Ronnie eyed her as if he'd never truly noticed her before. His curious little smile gave away his thoughts before he returned to studying his cards.

I pointed my hand of cards at Willie. "Brockwell *says* that, but does he really mean it?"

"Why would he say it if he didn't mean it?

"Because he's trying to appease you. He wants to keep you happy and he thinks he needs to let you be free to do that."

She thrust her hands on her hips. "I do want to be free and he does know that, but that don't mean he hates the idea of it. He ain't the jealous sort, and he ain't got no truck for your sentimental nonsense, India. He likes our arrangement just fine."

"India's right," Duke said.

"What do you know about it? I know Jasper better than all of you, and he ain't pining for me or just going along with it to please me. He's got his work and that's all he really cares about. If I don't see other people then I'll pester him when he's busy trying to solve murders, and that ain't a sight no one wants to see."

"London thanks you for your sacrifice," Matt piped up. He pushed a pile of matchsticks into the middle. "Who's still in?"

"That's an audacious bet," I said.

"I'm out," Ronnie said, throwing his cards down.

I also threw in my cards.

Cyclops stroked his chin and studied his hand. Behind him, Catherine watched, biting her lip.

"Go on," Matt said. "You can afford it."

"Give me a minute," Cyclops said.

"Or just fold like I know you're going to.

Cyclops glared at him through his one eye then tossed down his cards with a click of his tongue.

"You knew you'd won that, didn't you?" I said to Matt.

He smiled as he raked in his winnings.

"How?" Ronnie asked.

"You were all distracted," Matt said. "If you'd paid attention to the game and not Willie's conversation, you'd have realized I also had nothing." He showed us his hand. He didn't even have a pair.

"I wasn't listening to her," Cyclops said, crossing his arms.

"And yet you were the most distracted. I knew you had a poor hand, although I suspect it was still better than mine."

"A pair of queens. How did you know?"

Matt's gaze lifted to Catherine, although she didn't notice. Cyclops gave a good-natured grunt.

"India, I saw your cards when you pointed them at Willie," Matt told me.

"Did I?"

"And me?" Ronnie asked, picking up his port glass. "How did you know you could beat me?"

"Er…"

"Because you're just easy to read," Willie said. "Duke you should give him some help."

Duke finished off his port and stood. "Not tonight. I'm going to a real game. Cyclops?"

"Not me," Cyclops said.

Willie clapped Duke on the shoulder. "Come on, we'll leave together. Woodall can drop me off then you, then he can wait and—"

"Don't ask Woodall," Matt said. "It's getting late, and I won't have the staff waiting up for you. Take a hansom."

Willie grumbled as she left with Duke.

We didn't play much longer before Ronnie and Catherine left too. Cyclops walked her to the door, her hand on his arm, their voices low as they talked.

After they left, I sidled up to him. "You two seem happy. Does this mean you're going to speak to her parents soon?"

"No."

"But you looked so content together."

"We are, and I ain't risking that by going to her parents and declaring myself."

"But you must!"

"It's too soon. We're going to take it slow. I'll go to their church again this Sunday, and the next Sunday, and the one after that. You all gave me the idea, and I think it's a good one. I'll let them get used to me there. In the meantime, I'll keep seeing her at the shop."

"Catherine could invite you to her parents' house for tea. That might help things along."

He shook his head. "We prefer our way. We've got patience."

"Unlike some," Matt said innocently.

I took his arm. "I have patience. I'll show you just how patient I can be by delaying bedtime. I'm going to read."

"In bed?" he said, hopeful.

"The drawing room."

Matt waited until we were alone in the drawing room, then he shut the door. "You win. You have more patience than I do."

"I'm still going to delay bedtime." I circled him, tapping my chin and appraising him as I did so. He looked very handsome in his dinner suit, his dark eyes blazing so fiercely with desire that I thought I might melt. "But I'm not going to read."

***

"WISH I'D GONE WITH DUKE," Willie said as she poured a second cup of coffee at the sideboard. To our surprise, she'd joined us for breakfast. Usually after a late night she slept in, but it turned out her night wasn't that late after all.

"It were slim pickings at the poker table," Duke told her. "I didn't stay long."

"You should've gone somewhere else," she said.

"I was tired."

Willie sighed as she sat. "We're getting old. You don't like late nights no more, Cyclops wants to settle down, and I'm getting mighty fussy about my lovers."

"What was wrong with the nurse?" I asked.

"Bad teeth."

"Crooked? Missing?"

"She complained of a toothache the entire time and her breath was as foul as a pigsty on a hot day. I told her she should see a dentist but she refused. She's scared of the pain."

"Dentists ain't so bad," Cyclops said. "Not if they use cocaine or laughing gas."

"Anyway, she turned out to be as dull as a puddle on account of all the whining."

"Go and see Brockwell instead," I said.

"Maybe I will, maybe I won't."

Bristow entered, carrying a letter for Matt.

"It's from Cox," Matt said, opening it. He shook his head as he read. "They were burgled last night and the coronet was stolen."

"Is everyone all right?" I asked.

"It doesn't say." He passed the letter to me. "He wants us there when the police call, since we have experience with these matters."

"We have experience with murder, not theft."

"You're over qualified," Duke said with a chuckle.

I read the note and passed it back to Matt. According to Lord Cox, he thought we'd do a better job than the police in recovering the coronet since there was a possibility it was stolen because it was magical in nature. He might be right about that.

* * *

MATT and I arrived at Lord Cox's townhouse shortly after the police. A young detective inspector by the name of Walker was in the process of interviewing the servants, one by one. He was in the library with a maid at that very moment.

"He won't let me listen in," Lord Cox said, pacing the drawing room. "They're my staff, this is my house, and it's my coronet. I should be entitled to hear what they say."

"They won't say anything, because there's nothing to say," Patience said gently. She turned to me, sitting beside her on the sofa. "My husband questioned them as soon as we discovered the theft and no one heard or saw anything until this morning."

"How was the theft discovered?" I asked.

"The maid went into the study this morning to light the fire and saw the coronet's storage box was open. She notified the housekeeper and it was she who woke us." She touched the lace of her high collar. "To think, someone broke in here while we slept. It's terribly unsettling."

"Thank goodness the children didn't travel to London with us," Lord Cox murmured.

"It must have happened after midnight," Patience said thoughtfully. "We dined with my family last night, at their house, and arrived back at about eleven-thirty. Byron went into the study briefly but didn't notice anything amiss."

"Did you find the point of entry into the house?" Matt asked.

"One of the footmen says the service door has been forced," Lord Cox said. "The police have inspected it but haven't reported to me yet. Detective Inspector Walker is playing his cards close to his chest."

I got the distinct impression Lord Cox didn't like being kept in the dark. For a man in his position, giving orders came more naturally than receiving them.

"He should be finished soon," Patience assured him. She spoke with remarkable composure, her voice soothing, while her husband continued to pace. The only sign that this incident troubled her was the way she knotted her fingers together in her lap and the way her gaze followed Lord Cox from one side of the room to the other.

"Patience suggested I ask for your assistance, Glass, but I'm not sure it's necessary," Lord Cox said. "Even though I stated in my message that the theft could be because the coronet contains magic, I don't believe the suspect is someone interested in it for its magical qualities. I suspect the culprit is someone more obvious."

"Longmire," Matt said.

Lord Cox threw up his hands. "Who else could it be? Nothing else appears to be stolen. An ordinary thief would have taken the silver, but this thief went straight for the box."

"But Longmire didn't seem to want it once he learned about the magic," I pointed out.

"Perhaps that's what he wanted us to think so we wouldn't suspect him. Or perhaps he changed his mind and decided he wanted it after all."

"Then why not get it through legal channels?" Matt asked.

"That would take too long."

Lord Cox continued his pacing again, his hands clasped behind him, his strides purposeful.

Patience appealed to me, her eyes full of concern.

"We should still consider the possibility it was stolen because of the gold magic," I said. "The coronet's magic properties were mentioned in that article."

Patience winced.

Lord Cox stopped dead. "That blasted column!"

"Nobody knows it was about you," Matt assured him. "Nobody could even begin to guess."

"If your theory about the theft is correct, then somebody guessed." Lord Cox sat and buried his head in his hands. "This is a nightmare."

Patience perched on the chair arm and rested a hand on the back of his neck. "It's been very trying for my husband," she told us. "He has done nothing wrong, and yet he's being punished by Longmire. I wish he would just leave us alone."

I shared a glance with Matt. We had to do something, but finding the coronet wouldn't be easy, and it would be even more difficult to be discreet. But we had to try. I didn't want to add to Lord Cox's burdens.

The detective inspector and a constable entered and Lord Cox introduced us. "Mr. and Mrs. Glass have some experience with detecting," he said. "They're going to help us find the coronet."

"That's our job," Walker said. "We'll find it for you." He was mid-thirties, young for a detective inspector, with a small frame that seemed smaller as he stood in front of the burly constable.

"I feel better having Mr. and Mrs. Glass look too," Lord Cox said. "They're experts."

"Glass, eh?" The detective eyed Matt up and down. "I've heard of you."

"We assist Scotland Yard from time to time," Matt said. "Detective Inspector Brockwell can vouch for us."

"I'm sure he can, but I have little to do with him." Walker spoke quickly, as if dashing off the sentence with as much haste as possible so he could get on with the next item on his list. He was Brockwell's opposite in that respect.

"What have you learned so far?" Matt asked.

"Nothing of use."

"Nevertheless, perhaps you can tell me what the servants told you."

"It's police business, sir. Of course, you may interview them yourself." He stepped aside.

"I will," Matt said amiably.

That amiability saw the detective's disdainful smile slip. He didn't know how to react to it.

"India?" Matt extended his hand to me. "Shall we begin?"

We left together with Patience in our wake.

"Shouldn't you find out what he learned?" she whispered. "It could expedite your investigation."

"I'd rather form my own opinions," Matt said.

"Could you inform the maid who discovered the theft that we'd like to speak with her," I said. "We'll start there."

* * *

"The box was wide open," said the young maid, pointing to the cherry wood box on the desk. The lid was still open and the velvet cushion beside it. "That cushion was on the floor. That's what I noticed first. I picked it up." She bit her lip. "I know I shouldn't have, but I wasn't thinking. I didn't know there was a burglary then, see."

"It's all right, Mary," Patience said. "Please, just answer Mr. and Mrs. Glass's questions."

Mary swallowed audibly. "Well, there ain't much more to tell. I put the cushion on the desk and that's when I noticed the box was open. I knew that's where his lordship kept something real precious, but I didn't know what."

"Really?" I asked, skeptical.

"As God is my witness," Mary said, eyes huge. "You got to believe me. I didn't know what was in it until that policeman told me a crown was stolen."

"At what point did you alert the housekeeper?" Matt asked.

She nibbled on her lip and dipped her head.

"Mary," Patience said. "Mr. Glass asked you a question."

"I—I didn't tell her straight away. I didn't know it was important, at first. I just thought Lord Cox opened the box. It wasn't until later, when I heard the downstairs door had been broken, that I mentioned it to the housekeeper. She came in here, took one look, and informed Lady Cox." She clasped her hands together, as if in prayer. "I'm sorry, my lady. I should have said something straight away, but I didn't know it was important."

"It's all right." Patience glanced at Matt and he shook his head. "You may go, Mary."

"She's very nervous," I said after the maid left.

"A guilty conscience, perhaps?" Patience asked.

"Perhaps," was all Matt said as he inspected the box. He pointed to the lock. "No sign it was forced, but I suspect it would have been an easier lock to pick than the downstairs door."

"Shall we look at it now?" I asked.

Patience rose. "I'll have the butler show you."

She left us in the capable hands of the elderly butler, with instructions to answer all our questions, no matter how uncomfortable they made him. The butler showed us the door, its broken lock, and the cabinet where he kept the silver.

"I immediately counted it, upon seeing the door, and it's all there," he said. "As word got out to the other servants about the break in, Mary remembered the box."

He introduced us to the footman who'd discovered the door. "I've remembered something that may be important," the tall youth said. "I heard a noise during the night. I should have got up and made sure everything was secure, but...but I didn't hear it again and I thought I dreamt it. I only just thought of it now as the detective questioned me."

"Do you know what time it was?" I asked.

"Ten to two. The moon was full and the curtains in my room are thin. I could just make out the hands on my watch. I keep it beside my bed."

Matt thanked him and inspected the lock next, using a magnifying glass he'd brought with him.

"There are scratch marks in the lock itself," he said, handing me the magnifying glass.

The wood had splintered where a sharp tool had forced open the lock. That would account for the sounds that had woken the footman. I looked through the magnifying glass and saw the scratch marks in the metal. Someone tried to pick the lock and failed, resorting to more desperate measures. Still, the intruder hadn't made much noise, considering the damage they'd inflicted on the door. They knew what they were doing.

We stopped by the kitchen on our way back along the service corridor. Mary was there, both hands wrapped around a cup, and another maid rubbed her shoulder. The portly cook was in the middle of lecturing her, but she stopped when she saw us and returned to the stove.

Mary quickly stood to attention. She'd been crying.

"Is something wrong, Mary?" I asked gently.

"No, madam."

"Is there something else you need to tell us?"

She shook her head, tears pooling in her eyes. "I did nothing, I swear!"

"A word, if you will, sir," the butler said from behind us. I hadn't heard his footsteps.

We walked away from the kitchen, out of earshot. "Is there something more?" Matt asked.

The butler glanced past us toward the kitchen. "I'd like to assure you, the staff are not guilty. Most have worked here for years and have a great deal of respect for Lord Cox. Only the maid, Mary, is new, but she came highly recommended by a friend of the housekeeper. Her references were excellent."

"Thank you. You can tell them none are under suspicion."

The butler's thick white brows rose. "Sir? That policeman, Walker, suspects the staff."

"Is that what he said?" I asked.

"Not in so many words, madam. He alluded to it, however, both in his interview with Mary and with the footman."

"You can assure them that I don't suspect them," Matt said. "And I'll tell Walker as much. It's clear the door was forced open. If the thief received assistance from inside the house, there'd be no need for force."

The butler looked relieved. "I'll tell the staff, sir. Thank you, sir."

Matt and I headed up the stairs and were met in the drawing room by Lord Cox and Patience. There was no sign of the police.

"Well?" Lord Cox asked. "What did you learn?"

"Nothing to rule Longmire in or out," Matt said.

"It's him." Cox rubbed his temples. "It must be."

"I think it's more likely the coronet was stolen for its value as a magical object," Matt said. "A magical golden coronet is very valuable, particularly in certain circles. Mention of it in that article will have made quite a few collectors take notice."

Coyle knew that article was about Lord Cox and he would love to add a magical golden object to his collection. Something so rare must be worth a fortune. He was ruthless enough to send someone to burgle for him, too.

"Walker thinks it's an open and shut case," Lord Cox said bitterly. "He's a fool."

"Let me guess," Matt said. "He thinks the servants are involved."

"According to him, in nine thefts out of ten, the staff are either stealing directly or leave a door open on purpose for the thief to get inside. He wouldn't listen when I pointed out that force was used."

"He scoffed when we told him we trust our staff," Patience added.

"I'm going to ask for someone else to be assigned to the case."

"Leave it with me," Matt said.

Lord Cox looked relieved for the first time since our arrival. "Thank you, Glass. I appreciate your help."

We made to leave, but instead of ringing for the footman, Patience walked us to the front door. "Please, don't tell my family about the theft," she said, glancing back at the drawing room where we'd left her husband. "It's awful enough that they know about Mr. Longmire's claim. I can't endure any more cruel jibes."

"Jibes?" I prompted.

"My mother says Byron should pay us compensation for his false representation, and my father says he should have realized something was amiss because Byron never acted like a nobleman. He called him soft."

"How awful. And your sisters?"

"I've hardly seen Charity since my return to London, and the only time I did, she didn't speak to me. She just hummed. And Hope seems sympathetic, but..." She shook her head.

"Go on."

"I saw the smile she tried to hide. That's the thing about Hope. She can be lovely to your face, but secretly, she's plotting your downfall. I half expect her to use the information to her advantage, one day."

I squeezed her hand. "Rest assured, we won't tell them a thing."

"Why did you tell them about Longmire in the first place?" Matt asked.

"I don't know," Patience said on a sigh. "Hope caught me at a vulnerable moment and I blurted it all out. At that point, I thought you two were to blame for informing him, and I felt I had no one else to turn to. I thought I'd have their support." Poor Patience. She looked utterly defeated.

* * *

MATT and I didn't immediately go to Scotland Yard, but instead went to the address Longmire had given Lord Cox. It was a modest boarding house for "gentlemen of good character," according to the sign in the window, located in a quiet street.

"He isn't in," said the landlady crisply. "He rises early, takes breakfast in his room, then goes out for the rest of the day. Would you like to leave a message with his man?"

"Thank you," Matt said.

"What is Mr. Longmire like?" I asked as she led us up the stairs.

"Courteous," she said over her shoulder. "Quiet. Keeps to himself."

"Was he here last night?" Matt asked.

"Of course," she snipped. "I run a respectable household. No gentleman should be out past eleven, but if he does lose a sense of time then he absolutely *must* be in by midnight. Only undesirables roam the streets at that hour and I can assure you, all my lodgers are decent, rule-abiding men with impeccable references."

She knocked on a door on the second floor. It was opened by a small man with neat hair, dressed in a dark suit with a stiff shirt collar and perfectly tied tie. He looked as well turned out as

Bristow. Or he would have been if not for the frayed cuffs of his jacket and trouser legs.

The landlady made the introductions then left us with Mr. Longmire's servant, Mr. Harker. Mr. Harker showed us into the small sitting room and closed the far door to hide the bedchamber. Before he did so, I spotted another door leading to an even smaller bedchamber where Mr. Harker must sleep.

The valet eyed the armchair and the wooden chair positioned at the small table, perhaps wondering if he should offer them to us. A newspaper had been laid out on the table upon which stood a pair of shoes and polish. The accommodations were so small that he had to work in Mr. Longmire's sitting room whenever his employer was out.

"How long have you been Mr. Longmire's valet?" Matt asked.

"Only a matter of days, sir. I was hired here in London."

"Did he say why he didn't bring his regular valet?"

"No," Mr. Harker said, not meeting Matt's gaze.

Matt waited. Mr. Harker cleared his throat.

"What do you make of him?" Matt asked.

"He's pleasant enough, not too demanding." Mr. Harker tugged on his cuff.

"But?" Matt prompted.

The valet looked pained. "I don't like to speak ill of the man who pays my wages, sir."

Matt placed some coins on the table. "Now I pay your wages too."

The valet eyed the coins hungrily before scooping them up. "I don't think Mr. Longmire has a regular valet, sir. He doesn't seem to know what to do with me and has left me up to my own devices."

"Then why hire you?" I asked.

"A great deal of my employment comes from young country gentlemen who couldn't bring their own valets to the city. They stay in accommodations similar to this and hire a temporary servant to see them through. But almost all have access to a valet in their country home and know what is expected of a servant such as myself. Mr. Longmire seems to only want me for the sake of appearances."

"Was Mr. Longmire home all night last night?" Matt asked.

Mr. Harker hesitated. Matt placed some more money on the table and Mr. Harker squirreled it away. "He went out briefly between the hours of one and two."

"Did he give a reason?"

"No, sir."

"Do you have any inkling where he went?" I asked.

"No, madam, but I will say that it's not the first time he has gone out that late."

Matt frowned. "The landlady says she doesn't want her lodgers coming and going at all hours."

Mr. Harker glanced at the door and leaned closer to us. "I suspect she doesn't know. Mr. Longmire is very quiet."

"When do you expect him back today?" Matt asked.

"Late in the afternoon. He returns to change for dinner then dines out at one of the chop houses. He doesn't appear to belong to a club," he added with a hint of derision.

Matt and I left and asked Woodall to drive us to Scotland Yard. "Longmire isn't all that well off," Matt said. "He doesn't have a valet or he would have brought him to London. He doesn't belong to a club and he dines at chop houses."

"His rope factory must be struggling," I said. "No wonder he blames magicians for his financial difficulties."

"Magicians might not be the cause of his problems. It could be incompetence, lack of capital, or a number of other reasons. We don't know enough about him to make that judgment."

"I'm not sure it matters what the reason is. In his mind, magicians are to blame."

Matt's lips flattened in displeasure but he didn't contradict me.

* * *

DETECTIVE INSPECTOR BROCKWELL looked pleased to see us, or as pleased as I'd ever seen the pedantic, plodding policeman. The only other times he'd shown more enthusiasm was when he happened to arrive at mealtime and we invited him to dine with us.

"This is an unexpected surprise," he said. "But a welcome one." He clasped his hands over his stomach and leaned back, his craggy features lifting ever so slightly in a smile. "Are you here about Miss Johnson?"

"No," Matt said. "About Lord Cox's theft."

Brockwell's face fell. "Of course."

"We can discuss Willie if you like," I said.

"After the other business," Matt added. "Brockwell, on behalf of Lord Cox, we've come to request that you take over the investigation into the burglary at his home."

"I can't." Brockwell sat forward and moved his clasped hands to the desk. "Walker has been assigned to it. I believe you two were there this morning when he interviewed the servants. Would you care to tell me why?"

"The coronet is magical," I said.

"So I read in a nasty little article."

"Lord Cox tasked us with retrieving the coronet and bringing the thief to justice," Matt said. "He doesn't think Walker is up to it, and I tend to agree. Walker assumes the servants are involved."

"Servants usually are involved, in one way or another."

"We're quite sure they're innocent of this crime. Either the half-brother did it or it was someone who read that article and realized the lord mentioned in it was Cox."

"Someone who wanted the magical coronet for themselves," I added. "We think it's Lord Coyle, as he knew Lord Cox was the unnamed baron and he's a collector of magic objects."

Brockwell rubbed his sideburns on his left side then switched to the right. "If Coyle is involved, there's very little I can do. He'll have the investigation suppressed."

"That's outrageous!" I cried. "He can't do that."

"Men like him can do anything they want and get away with it. Regarding the half-brother, I'm sure Walker will question him."

"He didn't go straight to Longmire's lodgings," Matt said. "We did."

"And what did you learn?"

"I can't tell you that." Matt leaned forward. "Unless you handle the investigation."

Brockwell put up his hands. "I can't simply waltz in and take over. That's not how things are done here."

"Then we won't bother you any further." Matt rose and buttoned up his jacket. "Good day, Inspector."

"Before you go." He cleared his throat. "How is Miss Johnson?"

"Fine," Matt said.

"Good, good." Brockwell stood and smiled stiffly. "Give her my regards."

"You should stop by," I said. "I'm sure she'd be pleased to see you."

"No, no, I wouldn't want to get in her way. She made her position very clear to me."

"Oh? And what position is that?"

"That she'd like to see other men. She's not interested in commitment. That's fine by me. I don't have the time for a wife." He adjusted his tie. "But if you could perhaps mention to her that such an arrangement suits me and that I would still like to, er… continue, I would be most grateful."

"We will," Matt assured him.

Once we were back in the carriage, I turned to him. "Did you notice how he said Willie wants to see other *men*?"

"I did. I suspect he doesn't know about her women."

"She should have told him."

Indeed, this pause in their relationship didn't add up. Willie had made it seem as though Brockwell wanted it too, but I was no longer sure.

She wasn't at home and didn't return before Matt and I went out again to confront Mr. Longmire later that day. We arrived at his lodgings only to be told by the landlady that he hadn't returned yet.

We were considering whether to leave and come back when a figure stumbled on the pavement just outside the front gate. When he righted himself, I gasped. It was Mr. Longmire, and he was in a bad way. His mouth and nose were covered in blood and his left eye was swelling up.

"What happened?" Matt asked, going to his aid.

Mr. Longmire spat blood onto the pavement. "I was set upon in an alley."

"By thugs?" the landlady asked, her face paling. "But this is a good neighborhood!"

"Not thugs. Magicians."

CHAPTER 6

"You have to notify the police," I said as Matt and Mr. Harker helped Mr. Longmire into the armchair in the sitting room.

Mr. Longmire winced and clutched his side as he settled. "The police are hopeless."

The landlady bustled in carrying a cloth and basin of water. She dipped the cloth into the water and went to dab at Mr. Longmire's nose.

He snatched the cloth from her. "Get going," he growled.

"But—"

"Out! You too," he said to Matt and me as she left. "I don't need your help."

"We're not here to help," Matt said. "We've got questions."

"I'm not answering them. Harker, get rid of them."

Mr. Harker sized up Matt. "I don't think I can, sir."

"This won't take long," I said, pulling up the other chair. "Allow me."

He ignored my outstretched hand and continued to wipe the blood off his face.

"You're not doing a very good job." I indicated he should give me the cloth. "I'll be gentle."

He hesitated before passing the cloth to me.

"Let's start with the assault," I said as I carefully cleaned his face. "Can you identify your attackers?"

"Two men. Strangers."

"Would you recognize them again?"

"Maybe." He hissed as the cloth touched the bruise forming above his top lip.

"Thieves are everywhere in this city," Mr. Harker said. "Even in respectable neighborhoods like this one. It's very troubling."

"What did they steal?" Matt asked.

Mr. Longmire shifted until I ordered him to sit still. "Nothing," he finally said. "They gave me a warning. They told me to go home and to stop stirring up trouble in London."

"Trouble?" Mr. Harker echoed. "What sort of trouble?"

Mr. Longmire removed his tie and handed it to the valet. "Clean this. And close the door."

Mr. Harker took the bloodstained tie and retreated to the bedchamber, a troubled look on his brow.

"Magicians know you wrote the threatening letters," Matt said to Longmire. "And they're angry."

As if he just remembered that I was a magician, Mr. Longmire snatched the cloth off me and waved me away. "I don't know how they found out I wrote them." He glared at me. "Unless you informed your friends."

"It wasn't me," I said. "And I certainly don't know anyone who goes around beating people up."

Mr. Longmire's gaze lifted to Matt. "Don't you?" he bit off.

"Matt doesn't skulk in alleys," I shot back.

"Go away, both of you. I'm busy."

"One more question," Matt said. "Did you steal the Cox family coronet last night?"

Mr. Longmire's hand stilled. "It's been stolen?"

"Yes."

He sniffed. "Must have been the servants."

"It wasn't."

Mr. Longmire shrugged. "I don't know who stole it, Glass, but it wasn't me."

"Where were you between the hours of one and two last night?"

"Here."

"No, you weren't."

Mr. Longmire glared at the bedchamber door. "I went for a walk. I didn't go anywhere near Cox's place. Look elsewhere for the thief, Glass. It wasn't me."

"Did you inform the newspaper gossip columnists about your brother's illegitimacy and mention the coronet?"

"Half-brother." Mr. Longmire gave a rueful smile as he dabbed at his lip. "If you don't mind, I'd like you both to leave. Good day."

"We'll leave," Matt said. "But I urge you to report the attack to the police. We would look into it for you, but we haven't got the time. Our focus is finding the Cox family coronet."

"He's still a horrid man," I said, as Matt assisted me up the carriage step. "But what happened to him is awful. Just awful."

"The question is, who told the magicians that Mr. Longmire sent those letters to them?"

"Coyle?" I said, shrugging. "No, not him. He doesn't know Longmire is to blame."

"Nor does he have a reason for attacking Longmire. Longmire's threats serve to keep magicians hidden, and Coyle is happy with that."

I wasn't really listening to him. There was a large hole in this theory that I couldn't see any way to fill. "We are the only ones who knew Mr. Longmire sent the letters. Us and Lord Cox, but I doubt he would send thugs to beat someone up."

"Someone else must know or has worked it out," Matt said, sitting beside me.

"Oscar knows of four magicians who received letters. We should ask him who they were and start there."

Matt said nothing. It would seem he was quite serious about

not helping find Longmire's attackers. I, however, thought justice ought to be meted out. Even Mr. Longmire didn't deserve to be attacked so viciously.

"Do you believe him when he says he didn't take the coronet?" I asked, changing the topic.

"Actually, I do. He didn't even try to deny he told the newspaper gossips, yet he denied the theft."

"Theft is a different matter entirely to spreading gossip. It's a criminal act."

"Not if it's his coronet," he said. "That's another point in his favor—why steal it when he's most likely going to obtain it through legal means eventually?"

I sighed. "So we're back to having no suspects."

"Not at all. We have quite a number of suspects who'd want a magical golden object. An entire club's worth, in fact."

* * *

I HAD ALMOST FORGOTTEN about our tickets to the opera until Aunt Letitia reminded me upon our return home. She pleaded a headache and said she was staying in, leaving us a ticket to spare.

Cyclops merely raised an eyebrow in response when I suggested he use it. Duke refused too, and Willie barked a laugh.

"I hate the opera, unless it's a comedy," she declared. "Theater's more my thing." She clicked her fingers. "Let's go see a show tonight," she said to Duke and Cyclops. "Something funny. I could do with a good laugh."

"You won't get tickets this late to anything decent," I said.

"That's fine by me. I prefer indecent shows anyway."

"Why not take Brockwell with you?"

"He's probably busy with a case."

"Actually, he's not. We were just there and he asked us to give you his regards."

"Consider them given." She reached for her teacup and

frowned into it. "I'm sick of tea." With a glance in Aunt Letitia's direction to check that her eyes were still closed, she removed a flask from her pocket and added a few drops of clear liquid into the tea.

"Why are you ignoring him?" Matt asked.

"I ain't," Willie said. "Anyway, he knows where to find me."

"He thinks you're seeing other men."

"He told me that was fine by him. He ain't interested in courting or getting a wife. Why you getting all preachy, Matt? India's prudery is rubbing off on you." She looked at the tea then drank from the flask instead.

"The point I'm making is that you didn't tell him you're seeing other women."

"Men, women, it's all the same to me. He knows I'm seeing others, not just him. Like I said, he's fine about it. He told me so."

Cyclops put down the magazine he was reading. "Just because a man says he's fine with that arrangement doesn't mean he is. He might be just saying that to keep you happy."

"Which in Brockwell's case, we believe is true," I said.

"You should tell him about the women," Duke told her.

"Why?" Willie spat. "So he can judge me? Ignore me? Treat me like I've got a disease?"

"Because it's who you are."

"I've told men before and it always ends the same way. They either want to get married and have me all to themselves or they're revolted. I like Jasper. I don't want him looking at me like I disgust him. Right now, he and I are in a good place, just giving each other some space and having some time apart, so it'll be good when we're together again. I don't want to ruin that." She pointed the flask at each of us in turn. "Got it?"

Matt put up his hands. "I tried," he muttered.

"Brockwell will still like you if he knows you also like being with women," Cyclops assured her. "He sees all sorts in his line of work, and he'd understand."

"And if he don't," Duke said, "then good riddance."

Cyclops shot him a glare. "That ain't no help."

Willie pocketed her flask, drank her adulterated tea, and rose. "I'm going to find a show. Something bawdy that Jasper wouldn't like. Cyclops, Duke, you coming?"

Cyclops shook his head. "I'll keep Miss Glass company and maybe write a letter."

"I'll come," Duke said. "Bawdy is my kind of theater. I'll leave the opera to you toffs."

Matt rolled his eyes. Willie left, chuckling, and I followed her out.

"Willie," I whispered, catching up to her.

"Why you whispering?" she asked.

"Because I have a question to ask you, and I don't want anyone overhearing." I glanced around to make sure we hadn't been followed and there were no servants within earshot.

"This sounds like it'll be good," she said, amused. "Go on. You want to know what it's like being with a woman?"

"No! In there, you made it sound like you, er, know a lot of men. How many men have you actually…you know?"

"Known?" she asked. "As in carnally?"

I felt my face heat and knew it must have gone quite red from Willie's chuckle. She leaned in to whisper. "A lady never tells, India."

I cocked my head to the side and gave her an arched look. "A lady?"

She grinned. "I never tell neither." She walked off toward the staircase, a sway in her step rather than her usual swagger.

* * *

OPERA WASN'T REALLY my cup of tea either. I preferred to watch the audience members rather than the stage, and spent the first fifteen minutes staring through my opera glasses at our neighbors in their private boxes. We'd hired ours for the evening, and it looked rather empty with just the two of us occupying it.

"We should have invited someone to join us," I said.

"We did," Matt said. "They didn't want to come."

"Someone other than Willie, Cyclops and Duke."

"We don't know anyone other than them. Except for my relatives, and I don't want to spend any more time with them in a confined space than I have to. Besides, they're already here."

I swiveled around. "Where?"

He nodded at a private box on the other side of the theater where Lord and Lady Rycroft sat behind Hope and Lord Coyle.

"That's quite a statement having Coyle there, beside Hope," I said.

"It's probably his box. Everyone's been staring."

I turned the opera glasses onto the stage so as not to be one of those oglers but couldn't help sneaking another peek. "Coyle looks rather pleased with himself."

"Hope doesn't look entirely displeased, surprisingly."

He was right. Hope seemed to be doing her duty by chatting to Lord Coyle, smiling at the things he said, and generally looking pretty in her soft pink dress cut low enough to show off the creamy skin of her décolletage and the exquisite pendant nestled in the hollow of her throat.

"Is that an emerald?" I said.

"Hard to tell from here."

"Don't be glib. If that's an emerald, then she's sending a signal that this evening with Coyle is important. Otherwise her mother would be wearing it."

Matt smirked. "You have settled into the ways of the aristocracy quickly. I wouldn't have thought of that."

"It's not an aristocratic thing, it's a female thing. If a woman is trying to impress a man and wants to send a signal, she always tries to look her best."

His lips curved at the edges. "Is that what you did with me? Wear your best dresses in my presence?"

"Matt, I came to live with you wearing my only dress, and it was rather a plain one. *You* bought me nice dresses."

"It might have been plain but it was a snug fit." His heated gaze dipped to my bosom.

"Eyes on the stage. People are watching."

"Let them watch." He sat up straight nevertheless, that secretive smile still on his lips.

"Shall we visit them before or after the interval?" I asked, once again watching the Rycroft clan through my opera glasses.

"I prefer the third option of not visiting them at all."

"We have to visit. It would be rude not to. Don't worry, I won't question Lord Coyle tonight. We'll save the interrogation for when he's alone. Oh look. Patience and Lord Cox have just arrived."

Patience took a seat beside her sister at the front of the box while her husband sat behind her. After a brief conversation with the other family members, they concentrated on the performance. The exchange between Lord Coyle and Lord Cox appeared cordial, as if there was no ill feeling between them.

"I wonder how Cox feels about sharing the same air as Coyle," I said.

"Coyle denies informing Longmire about his father," Matt said. "Perhaps Cox believes him."

"Or perhaps he's far too polite to bring it up in a public arena. Even so, I would find it difficult to be pleasant to him if I were in Cox's position." I turned to Matt. "I just had a thought. Perhaps Coyle has asked them into his box as a way of showing support just in case people start guessing that Cox is the lord gossiped about in the papers."

"It's possible," Matt said. "Particularly if he's trying to impress Hope. By throwing his considerable weight behind Hope's brother-in-law, he's sending a signal not only to the family but to anyone who dares spread gossip."

"That would explain why Cox is here tonight, in Coyle's private box, when he ought to loathe him right now. He's willing to accept any help Coyle offers."

Unlike her sister, Patience seemed to enjoy the opera. Hope's gaze, like mine, scanned the audience. At one point we happened to look at one another at the same time. I nodded a greeting and she nodded back before saying something to her mother behind her.

Lady Rycroft's frosty gaze settled on us. I quickly looked away.

Not ten minutes later, a footman entered carrying a note that he handed to Matt. He waited for a reply.

"It's from Coyle," Matt said. "He's asking if he can visit us. What do you think, India?"

"I think it's an excellent idea."

Matt gave the footman our reply and he bowed out. "You're going to question him, aren't you?" he said. "I knew you couldn't wait."

"Are you saying I'm impatient? That's twice this week. And anyway, it's not impatience, it's simply expedience. Why visit him tomorrow when we can question him tonight?"

Lord Coyle did not come alone, however. He brought Hope. She looked even prettier up close with a string of pearls woven through her hair. The blush pink silk dress with rosettes and pearls sewn into panels down the front, sides and back, was of the finest quality and showed off her tiny waist.

Her beauty and youthfulness was in stark contrast to the heavy-set, white-haired Lord Coyle.

"If I'd known you liked the opera, I'd have invited you to my box tonight too, Glass," he said.

"I don't think there'd be room for us," Matt said, inviting them to sit.

Lord Coyle presented Hope to the chair beside me then sat on her other side. "Enjoying the production, Mrs. Glass?" he asked.

"Very much so," I said. "And you, Hope?"

"I adore the opera." She smiled beatifically. Lord Coyle looked pleased.

It was the strangest exchange I'd had in quite some time. I

wasn't sure who was forcing this politeness more, us or them. I tried to gauge Hope's state of mind, and if she was truly enjoying Lord Coyle's company, or if she'd been coerced into this evening by her parents. I knew her capable of putting on a good act, and I found it impossible to read her thoughts.

"You and Cox seem to be on good terms, considering you're the one who told Mr. Longmire about him," Matt said after the soprano finished her solo. "Did he tell you that you're on our list of suspects for the theft of his coronet?"

So much for not bringing up the situation until tomorrow. And Matt called *me* impatient.

Beside me, Hope drew in a sharp breath but continued to stare straight ahead at the stage. As did I.

"Cox is a thorough gentleman," Lord Coyle said. The unspoken implication was that Matt was not.

"Good of you to invite him to your box tonight," Matt went on. "Guilty conscience, Coyle?"

Lord Coyle chuckled. "Careful, Glass. This isn't America. If you want to succeed here, you'll play the game. Follow Cox's lead. You can learn a lot from him."

"I won't stand idly by while you destroy him. He's a good man."

"Destroy him? I'm rescuing him. His association with me is the only thing that will save him from utter ruin."

"Don't pretend with me, Coyle. I know you told Longmire, and you probably stole the coronet too, for your collection." The words sounded as if they'd been ground between Matt's teeth. It was rare for him to get so angry these days, and I hadn't expected it, considering he'd been amiable up until now. Sometimes he could still surprise me.

"It wasn't me," Coyle said, his own voice sharper than usual. "There's an entire club of people who would desire a piece like that coronet."

"Give me one good reason why I shouldn't suspect you."

"Why would I risk being discovered for burglary when I can

legitimately purchase the coronet off Longmire when he inherits?"

"What makes you think he would sell it to you?" I asked. "It's a family heirloom. It's priceless."

"Everything has a price, Mrs. Glass." He patted Hope's hand. "And you're assuming Longmire cares for his father's family. Besides, I suspect he'll be selling off everything he can as quickly as possible after he inherits."

"Why?" Matt asked. "Is the estate entailed?"

Lord Coyle chuckled. "It certainly is, and I'd wager he doesn't know it yet."

An entailed estate meant the current holder of a title and the accompanying estate couldn't sell it. That way each heir through the generations inherited the land intact. With the Cox estate entailed, Longmire would effectively be a custodian after he inherited, not an owner. He couldn't sell a single acre.

"Isn't it a wealthy estate?" I asked. "I know it's large and has many tenants. Surely the income will be more than enough to keep him satisfied."

"It draws a good income from the tenants, but Cox's father borrowed heavily." Lord Coyle winced as the soprano hit a particularly piercing note. "Cox is a good manager and has no difficulty meeting the repayments, but my sources tell me Longmire hasn't got the same business head as his half-brother."

"What about his rope factory?" I asked.

"Struggling."

An idea came to me and I shifted in my chair to face him. "Perhaps someone ought to tell Mr. Longmire that he would be taking on an enormous debt. He might decide it's not worth pursuing legal action after all."

Lord Coyle simply smiled. "Shall we return to your parents, my dear?" He picked up Hope's hand and kissed it. I could almost hear the ladies in the other private boxes twittering with excitement as they watched through their opera glasses.

Lord Coyle rocked out of the chair and heaved himself to his feet before assisting Hope. They exchanged smiles.

Matt stood too. "I want a list of names of those from the club most likely to steal the coronet," Matt said. "Or I will put Scotland Yard onto you."

"No need for the threat, Glass. I was going to send a list in the morning anyway." He bowed over my hand. "I would like to say how much I enjoyed our conversation at Delancey's dinner, Mrs. Glass. When was it? Ah yes, four evenings ago."

As soon as they'd left, I turned to Matt. "Did you hear that?"

"I did."

"He reminded me that I only have ten days to convince Hope to marry him if I want the slate wiped clean."

"I know."

I blew out a breath. "Do you think he assumes I had something to do with Hope accompanying him tonight?"

"I hope so. It would be nice for something to go in our favor in regards to Coyle for once."

Matt focused on the stage again, but I suspected he hardly saw the performance. Despite his amiable features, his eyes were hard.

I took his hand. "Did you notice how he denied the theft but not your accusation that he was the one who informed Longmire about his father?"

"I noticed."

I sighed and tried to concentrate on the performance, but in truth, I wasn't enjoying it. Lord Coyle had ruined my evening. "I wish we'd joined Willie," I said. "A bawdy show sounds infinitely better than enduring Lord Coyle and Hope's display."

"It's not too late." Matt's sly grin was just the tonic I needed to lift my spirits. He stood and extended his hand to me. "Shall we, Mrs. Glass?"

"I'd like nothing more."

* * *

THE FOLLOWING morning brought a flurry of letters to number sixteen Park Street, and only one of those was from Lord Coyle. The rest were about him, and addressed to Aunt Letitia.

"Goodness," she said, reading the first one in front of the fire in the sitting room. "Could it be that she accepted him?"

"Are you talking about Hope?" I asked.

She waved the letter at me. "Why didn't you tell me, India? Why let me hear it from other people?"

"I'm not sure there's anything between them," I said. "It wasn't clear last night."

"Not according to this letter from my friend Lady Dresham. She wants to know if there's an understanding between Hope and Coyle."

"Let me see." Willie leaned on the back of the sofa and read over Aunt Letitia's shoulder. When she got to the end, she gave a *whoot* as if she'd successfully herded cattle into a yard. "Lady Dresham reckons they must be engaged because of the way they behaved at the opera. What'd they do, India? Kiss in front of everyone? Did he touch her in an unmentionable place?"

Aunt Letitia made a sound of disgust in her throat. "Honestly, Willie."

"It wasn't like that," I told them. "They sat beside each other in his private box, then came to our box together, briefly. When they left, he kissed her hand and sort of looked into her eyes. She smiled back at him."

"That's it?" Willie scoffed. "Your friend needs glasses, Letty. You tell her that from me."

"She saw them through her opera glasses," Aunt Letitia said, as if that made all the difference. "And she's quite right to assume there's an understanding between them. A lady and gentleman sit together in a private box when they wish to make a statement about their relationship. The hand kissing is not significant on its own, but if they did exchange knowing looks, then that's another matter."

Willie threw herself into a chair and crossed her legs. "Seems like a lot of fuss over nothing to me."

"You have to remember that Lord Coyle has not been linked to a woman in a very long time. Not even in passing. There have been very few ladies he has given his full attention to over the years. It's no wonder everyone thinks Hope is special."

"She is special to him," I said. "But whether she is reciprocating, I'm not sure. She's very hard to read."

"What tone did she use when she spoke with him?" Aunt Letitia asked. "Charming and playful? Curt? Biting?"

"She hardly spoke at all when they were in our box."

"That *is* unlike her."

A second message came from another acquaintance of Aunt Letitia's in the post, along with two more. The post also brought Lord Coyle's list of collectors' club members he thought would burglarize a peer's home to steal a magic gold object.

Matt received it in his study and came downstairs to show me. At the top of the list was a name I recognized.

CHAPTER 7

"Sir Charles Whittaker," I said, pointing to the first name on Coyle's list. "That is intriguing. We haven't seen his collection of magical objects, despite being in his house. He must keep it hidden, like Coyle."

"I suspect that's why Delancey isn't on the list," Matt said. "They're wealthy enough that they can get into a bidding war over the coronet, like Coyle, and they like to display their items in their house, not keep them locked away. It would be impossible to display a stolen piece let alone brag about owning it."

"There are three other names," I said, eyeing the list. "I don't recognize any. Shall we start by questioning Sir Charles? I will write to Fabian and tell him I won't be able to work until later."

Matt tapped the letter with his finger and appeared lost in thought.

"Matt?" I prompted. "Shall we speak to Sir Charles?"

"Of course." He addressed Bristow, still hovering nearby after delivering the post. "Have the carriage brought round. We'll go immediately."

* * *

WE EXPECTED Sir Charles to be at his place of business. We planned to ask his housekeeper where his office was located, but it turned out that he was at home. As our carriage drove up, the front door opened and Sir Charles himself peeked through the gap. Spotting our conveyance, he quickly closed it again.

"That was odd behavior," I said.

"Most definitely." Matt opened the window and ordered Woodall to drive on and park around the corner.

We alighted as soon as the carriage came to a stop and hurried back to the street on which Sir Charles lived in a row house as neat and well-maintained as the gentleman himself. We'd hardly got very far when Matt put an arm out to stop me.

"The door's opening again," he said. "Let's not frighten him back into his warren this time."

Instead of Sir Charles emerging from the house, a woman stepped out. Her big black hat obscured her face as she walked in the opposite direction to us. The front door closed but Sir Charles himself was nowhere in sight. He'd remained inside.

"Well, well," Matt said. "It's Mrs. Delancey."

"How do you know? Her back is to us."

"She has a distinctive gait, all swaying hips yet a rigid spine."

I eyed him. "Should I be worried that you're observing how other women walk?"

He grinned. "Come on. Let's speak to her."

I caught his arm and held him back. "Are you sure that's a good idea? If they're having a liaison, do we really want to get involved?"

"Are they having a liaison of a sexual nature or is something else going on? I'd wager it's something else, and if so, I'd like to know what."

I hesitated. It wasn't the first time they'd been seen together without Mr. Delancey. I'd spotted Sir Charles leaving her house once when her husband wasn't home. But there couldn't have been anything untoward in that visit. Not with the servants there. Here, however, where Sir Charles lived alone, was another matter.

"I'm not so sure," was all I said.

Matt took my hand. "Come on, before she disappears."

We strode quickly to catch up to the retreating figure. "Mrs. Delancey," I called out when we were only a few feet behind.

Her pace quickened.

"Mrs. Delancey, we'd like a word," Matt said. "Or we can visit you tonight when your husband is at home and ask what you were doing at Whittaker's house."

She stopped and turned. "Goodness!" she said, cheeks flushed. "I wasn't expecting to bump into anyone I knew. How delightful." From her strained smile, I'd say our meeting was anything but.

"Were you visiting Sir Charles Whittaker just now?" Matt asked. "How…irregular."

Her face froze, and in that seemingly endless moment, I could see her mind weighing up all the things she could say. Unfortunately for her, she chose the wrong option.

"No."

"We saw you leave," Matt said.

Mrs. Delancey looked as though she would refute the claim again, but then she grasped my hand. "Do not tell my husband. He wouldn't understand."

"Of course not," I assured her then wondered if I'd been too quick with my response. Did I want to be complicit in their affair?

"It's not what you think," she went on. "Please, India, you must believe me. It's nothing of *that* nature."

"Then why keep the meeting from your husband?" Matt asked.

"As I said, he wouldn't understand."

"We will." Matt used his most reassuring voice. "Tell us why you were seeing Whittaker."

She adjusted her hat, angling it further over her face. "We simply had tea together."

"You must have talked about things."

"Of course."

"What sort of things?"

"This and that. Oh." Her face lit up as a thought occurred to her. "That article in the newspaper. The gossip about a certain lord's illegitimacy and his magical coronet. We speculated about it, that's all."

"Did you come to a conclusion as to who it might be?" I asked.

"No, alas. My husband would dearly like to make an offer for the coronet."

"Make an offer to whom, Mrs. Delancey? The lord in question? The older brother? Or the thief? The coronet was stolen."

"Was it? I suppose it doesn't matter who has it as long as we can learn the name of the thief. We don't care who we deal with, although I rather suspect a thief might part with it more readily." A small frown connected her brows. "Unless they know a magical golden object would be priceless and they stole it for their own collection. Then no amount of money will suffice."

"Do you know of anyone who would steal it?" Matt asked. "Anyone from the collector's club, for example?"

Her eyes widened. "Mr. Glass! How could you infer such a thing? The members are the best of London society. Lords, ladies, bankers, industrialists. We're not *thieves*." She spat out the word as if it contained poison. "We broker deals with one another and magicians to *acquire* our items."

Considering she'd just told us she'd be willing to buy the coronet from the thief, she clearly didn't consider buying stolen goods to be wrong.

"Speaking of members," Matt went on, "have you seen Whittaker's magic collection?"

She went to respond, stopped herself, and finally said, "He keeps it to himself. He's a very private man."

"So he has never shown a single magical object to any of the members?"

"I didn't say that. I said *I* have not seen any part of his collection. I can't speak for other members. Now, if you don't mind, I must go." She checked the small watch attached to a chain pinned to her military style jacket.

"Just one more thing," I said. "Do you know if your husband has any cousins?"

She looked longingly in the direction she'd been heading. "He doesn't," she said, somewhat absently.

"Not even distant ones? Aunts? Uncles?"

"There is a distant cousin, I believe."

"On his mother's or father's side?"

She frowned, her attention suddenly on me. "Why?"

I waved off her question.

"Do you want to know if there are any wool magicians left in his family?"

"I was merely curious," I said.

"There isn't, alas." She sighed. "Imagine if I could have something magical made. A lovely coat, for example, in finely spun wool. Anyway, such a garment is not to be." She offered us a tight smile and a little wave and was on her way.

"Do you believe she and Whittaker chatted about the gossip column?" I asked when she was out of earshot.

"It's likely it was one topic of conversation, but not the real reason for her call," Matt said. "This was a deliberate visit. A lady doesn't call on a gentleman in his house, alone, unless she has very good reason. Gossip isn't a good enough reason. It's also too early for social calls."

My breath hitched. "So they *are* having an affair?"

"Goodness me, India, how your mind does leap to the most scandalous conclusion."

I nudged him with my elbow. "Come on. Let's speak to Sir Charles and get his version of events."

We crossed the road and knocked. Sir Charles answered the

door with a delighted smile and warmly invited us inside. "What a pleasant surprise. Were you in the area?"

"We drove past just a few moments ago," Matt said, stepping into the hallway. "You saw us."

"No," Sir Charles said lightly. "I saw a conveyance. I didn't know it was yours."

"Then why did you duck back inside when you saw it?"

"I forgot something. Then I looked at the clock and realized I didn't have to leave just yet anyway."

"So it wasn't because the coast wasn't clear for Mrs. Delancey to leave at that moment."

Sir Charles cocked his head to the side. "Pardon?"

"We just spoke to her and she admitted she was here."

Sir Charles blinked slowly. "What did she admit to precisely?"

"She said you were exchanging gossip," I told him. "Specifically about the matter of the stolen magical coronet and the lord who is losing his title to his brother."

"Ah. Yes. That's true." He smoothed the graying hair at his temple with his fingertips. "A most curious business. Do you know the lord in question, Glass?"

"No," Matt said. "The thing is, we don't believe Mrs. Delancey was here just to gossip with you. So why was she here?"

Sir Charles's throat worked with his swallow, but his face remained unchanged. Indeed, it was rather too smooth, too schooled, considering Matt had just accused him of lying.

"May I speak to you alone, Glass?" Sir Charles said.

"Whatever you tell me I will tell my wife later."

"Even so. I cannot bring myself to confess in front of Mrs. Glass."

"I'll wait through here." I indicated the adjoining room.

It was a cozy sitting room that captured the morning sunshine, making it a perfect room for taking breakfast. There was no evidence of breakfast having recently been consumed there, however. It was tidy, clean, and rather cool. A fire had not been lit.

A moment later, Matt and Sir Charles joined me. "Now, what can I do for you?" Sir Charles asked, as if a conversation had not just transpired between he and Matt.

"May we see your collection?" I asked.

"My what?"

"Your collection of magical objects. May we see it?"

He put up his hands. "No, no. It's private. I am sorry, Mrs. Glass, but I don't show anyone and I won't change that, even for you."

"Then how do we know you even have a collection of magical objects?"

He chuckled. "Why would I pretend to have a collection if I don't?"

"To get into the collector's club."

"But why would I want to belong to a club of collectors if I am not one too? Mrs. Glass, this suspicion is unfounded." He sounded amused, as if he were speaking to a silly woman who'd asked a silly question. "Ask Coyle. He has seen my artifacts."

Coyle must have seen them or he would never allow Whittaker into the club. He certainly wouldn't have put him on his list of suspects if he didn't believe he was a collector.

"Are you unwilling to show us because you have items in it that you should not have?" Matt asked. "Stolen items?"

Sir Charles gasped. "Certainly not!"

"The magical coronet was stolen. The one mentioned in the newspaper gossip column."

His eyes briefly flared before smoldering. "I didn't take it. I don't even know the fellow mentioned in the article. Why would you think I do?"

"We're asking the same question to every member in the club," Matt said. "We asked Mrs. Delancey just now."

Sir Charles glanced toward the window. "No one is going to simply confess to the theft, Glass. You're naive if you think that."

Matt smiled. "Thank you for the advice."

We took our leave and returned to the carriage. "Do you believe him?" I asked as we walked.

"About the theft? Hard to say. As to Mrs. Delancey's visit, I think they're both lying. She didn't come here just to gossip. However I doubt they're having an affair, despite him telling me they are."

"Is that what he told you in private? That's an awful thing to say, especially if it's untrue. A gentleman should never tell another about his affair."

"He wanted to throw us off the scent of the truth. So if they're not having an affair, what *are* they doing?"

"Whatever it is, she doesn't want her husband to find out." I paused as we reached our carriage. "To me, that implies she *is* having an affair."

"But why Whittaker? I know I'm not a woman, but he doesn't seem all that appealing to me. He's not rich, handsome, or witty."

"He is quite dashing." I stepped up into the cabin. "But more to the point, he is a bachelor and not her husband."

Matt joined me, frowning. "What are you implying?" he asked.

"He's not her husband so that makes him exciting. An illicit affair is exciting, for some women," I added when his frown deepened. "Some women who are bored, for example."

He gave Woodall instructions then closed the door. He was still frowning. "How will I know if you grow bored with me?"

"Me? Grow bored with you?" I laughed. "You must be joking. Matt, how could I ever become bored with a man with a carefree attitude and a dangerous past; a former alcoholic and gambler that likes to solve mysteries, has friends in the police force in two countries, and relatives ranging from lords to criminals? And I haven't even mentioned your magical watch. Matt, I'm more in danger of being overwhelmed by you than bored."

He looked pleased with my assessment. "Good. But let me

know if that's not enough for you anymore, and I'll consider adding another vice to the list."

* * *

SIR CHARLES WAS RIGHT; we wouldn't get anywhere if we asked the suspects if they'd stolen the coronet. We needed to find out where they'd been on the night of the theft and look for the coronet in their magic collection. Both tasks required the help of Willie, Duke and Cyclops.

We were close to Mr. Longmire's lodgings, however, and decided to call on him before heading home. He was not pleased to see us, which was hardly surprising.

"What do you want?" he grumbled when Matt pushed past Mr. Harker.

"A word," Matt said.

Mr. Longmire rose, wincing. His face had swollen even more with dark bruises forming around his eyes. By the way he held himself, I'd say his ribs hurt too. "Catch the fellows who did this to me yet?"

"We're not looking for suspects," Matt said. "If you want them caught, inform the police."

Mr. Longmire eased himself back into the chair with a grunt. "So why are you here?"

"We learned something last night that we thought you should know," I said. "The Cox estate is entailed. You can't sell off any of it."

"Is this your attempt to get me to drop the lawsuit?" He made a scoffing sound. "The land is rich, the tenants are good. The income from the farms are all I need."

"It's also heavily mortgaged," Matt added.

Mr. Longmire rubbed a hand over his jaw, only to touch a bruise and stop with a hiss of pain. "You lie."

"Cox is careful with money, but most of the income goes to paying back the loan. He's not wealthy."

As if Mr. Longmire suddenly remembered Mr. Harker was there and ought not to listen to the conversation, he dismissed him. "I want something for supper. Something sweet." After Mr. Harker left, he regarded us coolly, as if he didn't believe us. But the simple act of banishing his servant would imply otherwise. "Cox never said a word. If what you say is true, he would have told me himself to dissuade me from claiming my birthright."

"He's too proud to mention the debts," Matt said. "We just wanted you to know."

"So I'll drop the lawsuit? Ha! You're mistaken, Glass. It's not about the money." He stood again and limped to the door. "It's about what's rightfully mine. Good day."

"That went well," I said to Matt as we headed down the stairs.

"What makes you say that?" He doffed his hat for the landlady as we passed her in the hall. "He says he won't give up the claim."

"Nobody got punched or called nasty names."

The landlady gave a small squeak of horror. I smiled at her and thanked her for opening the door. "One never knows with Mr. Longmire," I went on. "Anyway, we've given him something to think about. He might change his mind in time."

* * *

THERE WERE three more suspects on Lord Coyle's list, the perfect number for our small band of associates. Matt had gathered them in the library and gave brief instructions.

"They are all wealthy," he said. "All have servants and servants can usually be bought." He passed a pouch of coins to each of them. "If they can't be bought, you'll have to think of something else."

"No guns," Duke said with a pointed glare at Willie.

"I won't use my Colt," she protested. "I don't shoot innocent people."

"Willie, you can visit the house of Mrs. Rotherhide," Matt went on. "According to Coyle's list she's a wealthy widow." He handed her a slip of paper with an address on it. "Duke, you can go to the household of Mr. and Mrs. Landers. She inherited a vast sum from her father and married a financier who already had a vast sum at his disposal. She's twelve years younger than him." He passed a piece of paper to Duke and another to Cyclops. "Cyclops, please speak to the servants at Lord Farnworth's residence. Apparently he's an unmarried bachelor in his late twenties who inherited an estate that he seldom visits. He prefers London and likes to collect rare things. Not just magical objects, but rare books, ancient artifacts and exotic beauties."

"Beauties?" the rest of us asked as one.

"That's what it says on Coyle's list." He showed it to me. It did indeed say "exotic beauties."

"Do you think he means women?" Duke asked.

"Course he does." Willie held out the piece of paper with the address of the widow to Cyclops. "Swap with me. I'll go to the lord's house and you check on the widow."

"Why?" Cylcops asked.

"Because you got Catherine. You don't need exotic beauties in your life. I do."

"What about me?" Duke whined.

"I got in first." Willie shook the paper at Cyclops.

"I gave Cyclops the Farnsworth household for a reason," Matt told her. "If 'exotic' means what I think it means, Cyclops might have a better chance of befriending one or more of the beauties."

Willie scrunched up the paper in her fist and stamped it on her hip. "I can befriend an exotic woman just as well as he can. He's too gentlemanly to betray Catherine to do what might be necessary, but I ain't got the same problem on account of me and Jasper having an understanding."

"What about me?" Duke said again. "I ain't got no one to betray, and I like exotic women too. I like *all* women."

"Besides," Willie went on. "Cyclops ain't exotic. He's just tall and looks mean." She indicated his eye patch and the angry scar disappearing behind it.

Cyclops crossed his arms. "That's insulting."

"I could have said you were fat, but I restrained myself."

"I ain't swapping with you. Or you," he said when Duke opened his mouth.

"I'll tell Catherine," Willie warned.

"Go ahead."

Willie flattened the piece of paper and sighed. "Why do I have to get the dried up old widow?"

Duke rolled his eyes. "Swap with me then. I don't care."

They exchanged papers and filed out, discussing how they'd make their first approaches, what disguises they'd use or stories they'd make up. They were more animated than I'd seen them in some time. Investigative work invigorated them.

"What about us?" I asked Matt. "What should we do while we wait?"

"I'm going to speak to my uncle," he said. "He might have some knowledge about these suspects."

"Is that wise? He'll want to know why and you promised Lord Cox you wouldn't tell them about the theft."

He thought about it a moment then smiled. "Very well. I'll ask my uncle to invite me to his club instead. Then I'll ask around there. Discreetly, of course."

"Do you think he'll want you at his club? He doesn't like you and a gentleman's club is his sanctuary, so they say."

"I am his heir, and if he wants me to fit in, he'll want me seen at his club. I might even ask him to nominate me for membership."

"Why not ask Lord Cox instead? He'll be more than happy to take you as his guest."

"If I fail with my uncle, I'll ask him." He kissed my cheek. "What about you? What are you going to do this afternoon?"

I had an idea but I doubted he'd like it. I was considering

how to make it sound like a good idea when Aunt Letitia entered the library.

"India, let's go for a drive," she said. "I've been cooped up inside too long."

"An excellent idea," Matt said, striding past us. "Enjoy your afternoon."

Aunt Letitia gave me an expectant look. "We ought to change before we go out."

"What's wrong with this?" I asked, looking down at the deep green day dress with the rose colored silk waistband and collar. The new outfit came with a matching hat and jacket with peaked shoulders, and I thought I looked very well in it.

"Nothing's wrong with it. It's quite suitable for morning calls with Matthew. But afternoon calls with me require something…different."

"Different?"

"Different to what you wore this morning. Do hurry along, India, we haven't got all day."

"Very well, I'll change. But our first call is to someone I need to see. Then we can go wherever you like."

CHAPTER 8

The offices of *The Weekly Gazette* were located on Lower Mire Lane, just off Fleet Street where the more prestigious daily newspapers had offices. Aunt Letitia poked her head out of the carriage door after I stepped down, took one look at the discarded newspapers piling up in the dirty, smelly gutters, and insisted on waiting in the carriage.

The front desk was unmanned, but I'd visited Oscar's place of work enough times that I knew where to find his office. I was a familiar figure so no one stopped me as I marched past their desks, strewn with papers and artwork, typewriters and inkstands. I even greeted some of the staff by name. The hum of the printing press in the basement below provided a rhythmic, almost soothing, backdrop as they worked.

"India!" Oscar cried as I entered his office. "What a pleasant surprise. Do sit down." He looked past me. "Are you alone?"

"Matt's aunt is in the carriage, so I must be quick." I sat on the chair opposite his desk. "I have a favor to ask."

He smiled. "Does Glass know you're here?"

"Why?"

"Because he wouldn't like that you're asking me for a favor. He doesn't like me."

"He doesn't *dislike* you, Oscar. He merely worries about the book you're writing and what impact it will have on me."

"It goes deeper than that, India, and you know it." He put his pen in the holder and leaned in. The smirk warned me of what was to come. "He doesn't like me because he worried you and I were more suited than you and him." He clasped his hands. "But that's all in the past now. You're happily married, and I'm happily engaged."

"So you are happy?"

"Of course." His smile was genuine. "Marriage to Louisa will not be dull."

"I believe you're right on that score." I returned his smile. "Now, to my favor. Can you tell me if any magicians who received one of those nasty anonymous letters are thuggish in nature?"

"That's an odd question. Why do you want to know?"

This was the part where my plan fell down. I didn't want to give Mr. Longmire's name to Oscar, but I had to tell him a certain amount of the story to satisfy him enough to help me. I wasn't sure he would, but I had to try. Unlike Matt, I couldn't ignore Mr. Longmire's situation. Someone knew who had sent the threatening letters to magicians and had then meted out their own punishment, and I wanted to find out who.

"Matt and I discovered who sent the letters. He was subsequently set upon near his home, most likely by someone he sent the letters to."

Oscar leaned forward a few more inches. "Who is it?"

"I won't tell you."

"Why not?"

"Because you can't be trusted with the information."

"I say, that's a bit harsh. I wouldn't beat him up, just talk to him, reason with him, show him we're not bad people."

"We've tried reasoning with him, and it didn't change his mind. I doubt you can make matters better, Oscar, but I'm quite sure you could make them worse."

He drummed his thumb on the desktop as he regarded me through narrowed eyes. "If you won't tell me who it is, I won't give you the names of magicians I think are capable of assault."

"I suspected you'd say that. How about I tell you something else?"

"It will have to be interesting," he said carefully.

"It is. You see, Fabian and I created a new spell together."

His thumb stopped drumming. "You did? That is interesting. Go on then, tell me. What does the spell do?"

"You must promise not to tell anyone or put it in your book."

"I'll have to tell Louisa. We don't keep secrets from one another."

I considered that then nodded. "We made a watch fly."

"Oh. Is that all? I don't mean to dampen your enthusiasm, but your magic is strong. Your watch has always responded to you."

"Not always," I said snippily. "Not the new one. Even my old one could not be controlled. Anyway, it was Fabian's watch that flew using a new spell we created."

"That is interesting. Well done, India. Give my congratulations to Charbonneau. Now, a deal is a deal. I can tell you that none of the magicians I know who received threatening letters would hurt anyone. They're good men."

"But you made me tell you my information!"

He laughed softly. "I didn't trick you. I said none of the ones who received the letters are thuggish, but I know of two others who are. Perhaps they did it on behalf of the entire magical community. But the problem is, how did they find out the anonymous author's name?"

"That is a mystery, I admit. I'll be sure to ask them."

He dipped his pen in the inkwell. "James Teller is a brick magician, and Donald Grellow is a carpentry magician." He wrote down the addresses of both men's workshops on a piece of paper and passed it to me.

"Thank you," I said, waving the paper to dry the ink.

"What are you going to do with the information?" he asked.

"I'm not yet sure. Matt isn't interested in bringing anyone to justice for it. He thinks the fellow deserved it."

"For once, he and I agree." He indicated the piece of paper. "I can go with you to interrogate them."

"It's quite all right. I'll take Matt."

"But you just said he's not interested."

"Not in bringing them to justice, but he'll accompany me to speak to these men once I tell him I'll go alone if he doesn't."

He chuckled. "You sound like Louisa. She always manages to get her way too. Sometimes I don't even realize until after I've agreed."

There was a knock on the door and a young man opened it. "There's someone looking for you, Mrs. Glass. She seems confused."

I shot to my feet and rushed out. I spotted Aunt Letitia immediately, sitting on a chair behind one of the desks, studying a caricature of the prime minister. Thank goodness she hadn't wandered off. If she'd found her way into the basement where the printing press operated… I shuddered. It didn't bear thinking about.

"Come with me. I'll take you home." I held out my hand, but she ignored it.

"In a moment. I'd like to look at these pictures. You're very talented," she said to the man hovering nearby. He beamed. He must be the artist. "Who is it?"

The artist's smile faded. "The prime minister," he said, rather stupidly.

"Oh no." She put down the sketch. "I take it back. You haven't got him right at all. Lord Palmerston doesn't have a beard."

The artist looked to me, his brows raised.

I sighed. "The current prime minister is Lord Salisbury," I told her as I assisted her to her feet. "Come along. There are no more calls for you to make today."

* * *

I INFORMED Matt of his aunt's state as soon as he returned home. "She's resting," I said. "Polly is with her."

He frowned as he sat on the sofa beside me. "What were you doing at the *Gazette*?"

"Asking Oscar if he knew who was most likely to have set upon the author of those letters, if they learned the author's name."

"I see."

"You're cross with me for asking him."

"I'm not happy about it. Why didn't you tell me?"

"Because you'd forbid it, we'd argue, and I'll do anything to avoid an argument with you."

His gaze narrowed. "How can you be sure we won't argue now?"

"I'm not." I sidled closer and wrapped my arms around him. "But it's easier to ask for forgiveness than permission."

His gaze narrowed further. "I like to think I'm a modern man, India. I don't forbid my wife anything, nor do I expect her to ask permission for something she deems unnecessary."

"So you don't mind. Oh good, I was worried." I let go and picked up my sewing. "There were only two magicians Oscar suspected were capable of beating someone up, although neither were recipients of the letters. I took the liberty of making a copy of their addresses for you earlier. It's on your desk. When shall we call on them?"

He didn't respond.

"Matt?" I asked, looking up.

He stared back. "What just happened?"

I smiled and kissed him lightly on the lips. "You agreed to call on the two men with me. When shall we go?"

"I, er…" He shook himself. "After we recover the coronet. One investigation at a time."

"Very well. How did your visit to Lord Rycroft's club go?"

"Quite well, although it took some convincing for my uncle to go along with the idea. In the end, it was Hope who convinced him to do it." Something in his tone implied there was more.

"Did she ask for something in return?" I prompted.

He shook his head. "Nothing like that. I took the opportunity to ask her if she had given any more thought to Coyle's proposal."

I set my sewing down on my lap. "Ah. I see. Now I know why you wanted to go there in the first place. You wanted a chance to convince her to marry him. Matt, I'm still not sure how I feel about pushing her in that direction."

"Well I'm sure I want her to agree and in the timeframe Coyle set, too. Call me selfish, but I don't see a problem. We all benefit if she accepts."

"But it's Lord Coyle!"

"I think the things we dislike about him are exactly what appeals to her."

"What do you mean?"

"When I brought the subject up, she said she's still considering his proposal. She didn't immediately say she would refuse him or that she thought him horrible. She actually had a gleam in her eye as she asked me how much I thought he was worth."

I pulled a face. "Why doesn't it surprise me that she wants to know his value?"

"When I was alone with my uncle in the carriage, I asked him if he thought they'd marry. The mention of it also brought a gleam to his eye." Matt smirked. "But he doesn't know her mind. Apparently Hope is keeping her cards close to her chest."

"You didn't tell either of them she must make up her mind soon, I hope. That's precisely the sort of thing that would irritate her. She could very well turn around and delay her decision out of spite."

He smiled slyly. "Give me some credit."

"So what did you learn about our suspects at Lord Rycroft's club?"

"Not much. Lord Farnsworth keeps a Nubian princess as a mistress in a separate apartment."

I wasn't sure what to make of that so waited for him to go on.

"The only thing I learned about the others is that no one at the club really knows them. Mr. Landers, the rich financier, belongs to a different club frequented by men of trade. A snide upturn of the lip tended to accompany that statement. My uncle's club is full of peers, not self-made men."

"And what about the widow, Mrs. Rotherhide?"

"Nothing," he said. "Hopefully Duke has found a way to gather more information."

* * *

WE WERE JUST SITTING down to dinner when Cyclops entered the dining room. Bristow set another place and Peter poured him a glass of wine. Cyclops rubbed his hands together and surveyed the platters with a hungry eye.

"How did you get on at Lord Farnsworth's residence?" Matt asked, passing him a plate of potatoes.

"You were right. Exotic women means dark women. All the maids are from India or Africa." Cyclops forked a potato and grinned at us. "Also, the lord needs a new coachman. I'm starting tomorrow."

"Good work. Any word on a collection of magical objects?"

"I didn't get the opportunity to ask, but I've seen where the butler keeps the keys. I should be able to borrow them."

"The artifacts could be kept at the mistress's apartment," I said.

"Mistress?"

"Who's got a mistress?" Willie asked as she sauntered in.

Bristow set her a place then discreetly left and closed the double doors.

"Lord Farnsworth keeps a Nubian princess at his beck and call," I told Willie and Cyclops. "She has her own rooms, paid by

Farnsworth, somewhere in the city. It might be a good place to hide a stolen coronet."

"I'll find out where the apartment is," Cyclops said, helping himself to slices of beef.

"Who does this Farnsworth think he is?" Willie cried. "He ain't no king."

"He's a rich lord," Matt said with a shrug.

"You're a rich lord, and you don't go around holding women against their will."

"She's his mistress, not a prisoner. Besides, I'm not a lord yet."

"If she's held against her will, we'll see that she's freed," I assured Willie. "Tell us what you learned about Mr. and Mrs. Landers."

She piled oysters onto her plate then reached for the herring. "They're either arguing or giving each other the silent treatment, according to the maid I talked to. She's a silly woman."

"The maid?"

"Mrs. Landers. The maid reckons her mistress's only interests are shopping, gossiping and scolding Mr. Landers. It's the shopping that interested me most. The maid reckons Mrs. Landers buys lots of hats, dresses, ribbons and the like, but also knick knacks. Some of the knick knacks end up on display—artwork, vases, decorative boxes. But the maid reckons a lot is never put out for others to see." Willie set down her knife and fork and regarded each of us in turn for dramatic effect.

"Go on," I said. "Where does the maid think those knick knacks are?"

"In a locked cabinet in the drawing room."

"The ideal place to show off to guests after dinner," Matt said. "They don't have to leave the room and the servants can't see what's inside."

"Only the butler has seen in the cabinet," Willie went on. "The maid reckons he won't reveal what's in it. He's real loyal to Mrs. Landers."

"Not Mr. Landers?"

She shook her head. "He was her family's first footman and got the butlering job when she married Mr. Landers and they moved into the Knightsbridge townhouse."

"How'd you find out all this?" Cyclops asked. "Flirting?"

"I paid the maid. She didn't need much convincing to betray her employers. She was real keen to tell me all the gossip she could think of. She ain't happy with her employment. She reckons being in service to the Landers is the worst job she's ever had. The butler's mean, the housekeeper's meaner, and Mr. Landers expects perfection. If there's even a smudge of ash on the hearth, he raises the roof with his temper."

"They sound like a charming couple," I said wryly.

"There's more," Willie said, her face glowing in the gaslight. She was certainly enjoying being the center of attention. "I asked the maid if she remembered if her master and mistress were home on the night of the theft. She reckons they were out, but she doesn't remember where or when they arrived home." She calmly cut through her beef, a small smile on her lips that grated on my nerves. "The maid thinks the butler went out after the servants went to bed. He was tired the next day, yawning all the time, and not noticing when things were out of place. The maid says that's not like him. Then she saw him sleeping in his office late in the afternoon. That's unheard of."

"It was him," Cyclops declared. "It must be. He stole the coronet for his mistress."

"Well done, Willie," Matt said. "All we have to do now is see inside that cabinet. It's likely the coronet is in there."

"Don't you dare suggest breaking in during the night, Matt," I said. "There are too many servants."

"Willie's maid could let me in," he said.

I opened my mouth to protest, but Willie got in first. "Not you, me. I'll go. She'll let me in, I reckon, for a price."

"That'll only put her in jeopardy," I told them. "The Landers will notice the coronet missing and will immediately suspect the servants if there's no sign of a break in."

"A very good point," Matt said.

"We shouldn't dismiss our other suspects yet anyway. Not even Whittaker. And we haven't heard from Duke."

Willie glanced at the door, but it didn't open.

"I'll continue to investigate Lord Farnsworth," Cyclops said. "I'll find out where the mistress lives."

"Catherine won't like it," Willie said in a sing-song voice.

"This ain't nothing to do with Catherine. Besides, she and I are…not together."

"Yet."

He stabbed a slice of beef and shot her a withering glare.

"I can definitely break into Whittaker's place," Matt said. "He only has a live-in housekeeper. Whittaker goes to work during the day, so all I have to do is wait for her to leave and pick the lock."

"What if the neighbors see?" I asked.

"I'll enter through the back door."

"Good plan," Willie said with a nod.

"And what about me?" I asked. "What shall I do while you're all finding ways into our suspects' houses?"

"Stay home and worry," Willie said. "You're real good at that."

A better idea began to form, but I needed to think about it more before I mentioned it.

Bristow entered and handed a note to Matt before retreating and closing the door.

"It's from Duke," Matt said, reading. "He says not to expect him tonight."

"At all?" Cyclops asked.

"Give me that." Willie snatched the note from Matt. "Huh. It ain't specific. I reckon it means don't expect him for dinner." She put the note down and pulled the plate of sliced beef closer. "More for us, eh, Cyclops?"

Cyclops and Matt exchanged glances. They both smiled.

* * *

DUKE FINALLY CAME HOME during breakfast the following morning. He greeted us with a smile and went straight for the sideboard. "I'm starving," he declared.

"Where've you been?" Willie asked. "Find a good poker game?"

"I was at Petronella's. That's Mrs. Rotherhide."

"The dried up old widow? Christ, Duke, I thought you had standards."

He chuckled as he poured coffee from the pot. "She ain't old or dry. She's early-thirties and a lot of fun." He leaned back against the sideboard and smiled into his cup.

Cyclops clapped him on the shoulder as he passed.

"You're lucky Letty ain't here," Willie said. "She'd be shocked. Look at India. She's as red as a radish."

"I am not," I declared. "Very little shocks me these days. Living with you has cured me of prudery."

Willie snorted.

Duke blushed but his smile didn't waver. He piled up his plate and sat beside me then tucked into his breakfast with relish.

Willie watched on. "You're just going to sit there and eat like you didn't just do something foolish?"

"Foolish?" Duke asked.

She threw her hands in the air. "She's a suspect. She could be a thief." She suddenly clicked her fingers and pointed at Duke. "*That's* why you did it. To get close to her and find out if she's got a magic collection and was out the night of the theft. Good work, Duke. I didn't think you had it in you to be deceptive like that. Not where women are concerned."

"I didn't spend the night with her to get information. She told me everything I needed to know before we...became better acquainted."

Willie sat back and stared at him. "Huh."

Duke grinned around a mouthful of sausage. Once he'd swallowed, he drank his coffee and cut up his bacon, all while Willie watched on with her arms crossed and a scowl on her face. My sympathy was with her as my frustration mounted with every passing second.

"She does have a collection, it turns out," he finally said. "I pretended I was a traveling American interested in magic and I'd been given her name by an acquaintance who claimed she had some interesting things in her collection. I hinted that I'd like to see it, but she didn't take the hint. I also found out she was at home at the time of the theft, although she'd been out earlier."

"That doesn't mean she didn't hire someone to steal the coronet," Cyclops said.

"True. But I'm a good judge of character and I don't think she's a thief."

Willie rolled her eyes. "Course you'd say that."

"Why?" Duke asked.

"Because you ain't thinking. Not with your brain, anyway. She could be pulling the wool over your eyes."

Duke sighed and returned to his food. "Why would she do that? Petronella doesn't know I was looking for the coronet. We did talk about it. She wondered who the lord was who owned it and she reckons there'd be lots of collectors interested in it after reading that article."

"Including herself?" I asked.

He shook his head. "She says her late husband was the collector and she rarely looks at the things now. She didn't seem interested in the objects she already owns, let alone acquiring something new. I think we can take her off the list."

Matt, Cyclops and I agreed.

Willie struck the top off her boiled egg with a slash of her knife. "I reckon she needs further investigation."

"Fair enough." Duke winked at her. "I'll do it."

Willie rolled her eyes.

Cyclops finished his breakfast and left to take on his duties as Lord Farnsworth's coachman. The butler had told him there was no need to hurry as his lordship never rose before noon. He departed with a sack full of his belongings to make his temporary home above Farnsworth's stables.

A short while later, Matt departed too with the intention of breaking into Sir Charles Whittaker's residence. He wore a dark suit and hat and packed his lock picking tools.

"What about us?" Willie asked. "What are we going to do?"

"I'm going to pay Mrs. Delancey a visit," I said. "You can stay home with Aunt Letitia. She had a turn yesterday so don't overexert her."

She crossed her arms and kicked the leg of a chair. "I want to investigate."

I turned away but my conscience wouldn't let me walk away. I sighed. "You can call on Mrs. Delancey with me, if you like."

"I'll get my hat."

"Leave your gun at home," I called after her as she raced up the stairs.

* * *

I'D DECIDED the best way to meet the Landers was to be officially introduced by a mutual acquaintance. Although I disliked asking Mrs. Delancey for a favor, I couldn't see any other way. She was delighted to receive me but looked upon Willie with an air of horrified curiosity.

"Mr. Glass's cousin, you say," she whispered to me as Willie sauntered around the drawing room, inspecting the objects, some of which I knew to be magical. "How…delightful. Oh, do put that down, Miss Johnson," she called out when Willie picked up the iron key Fabian had used to free himself from prison. "The cabinet maker is making a glass case for it, but it won't arrive for another week."

Willie tossed the key and caught it.

Mrs. Delancey reached her fingers into the air, as if she would catch it, despite being too far away. "If you could give it to me…"

Willie handed the key to Mrs. Delancey. Mrs. Delancey folded it in her fist and buried her fist in her skirts.

"You've got some nice things," Willie said, waving a hand at a tabletop crowded with statuettes of an Egyptian nature, a stuffed bird, a vase of flowers, three picture frames, a book and fan. "How many of these contain magic?"

"Quite a number," Mrs. Delancey said weakly. "Perhaps if you'd like to take a seat, Miss Johnson. Tea will soon arrive."

"I'll look around until it does."

"Mr. Glass's cousin, you say," Mrs. Delancey muttered again. "They're not at all alike."

I laughed. "Thank goodness."

Tea arrived and Willie finally sat, much to Mrs. Delancey's relief. "What a pleasant surprise this is, India. Our encounters seem to come out of the blue lately." She handed me a teacup. "Did you speak to Sir Charles about the stolen coronet? Not that he would know anything about it, of course. He's not a thief any more than I am." She laughed a tinkling laugh and sipped.

"We spoke to him."

"You ought to look closer to home for the theft," Mrs. Delancey said.

Willie dropped her teacup onto the saucer with a loud clatter. "You accusing *us* of stealing the coronet?"

"No!" Mrs. Delancey cried. "Not at all. I meant someone close to the coronet's owner. The brother, for example. He might think it's rightfully his."

"Why would he steal something he'll probably inherit soon?"

Mrs. Delancey sat forward, every part of her alert, like a bloodhound on the scent of a fox. "So the claim *is* legitimate?"

"I didn't say that," Willie muttered into her teacup.

I tried glaring at her, but she wasn't looking my way.

Mrs. Delancey pressed her hand to her chest. "This is thrilling. Mr. Delancey will laugh and laugh when I tell him. We have no love for the upper classes. They look down their noses at people like us, even though we're richer than most of them. They'll do business with my husband when they have to, but they'll never invite us to dinner. They think we're no better than tradesmen simply because Mr. Delancey works. Lord Coyle and Louisa are our only friends among the nobility, and sometimes I think they look down on us too. Tell me, India, who is it?"

"I can't say," I said.

Mrs. Delancey appealed to Willie. "I'll give you a hundred pounds, Miss Johnson, if you tell me."

"No," Willie said.

"Two hundred."

Willie reached for a slice of sponge cake. "I don't need money. Why do you want to know, anyway?"

"To offer to buy the coronet off him—or his brother—when it's returned, of course. I have every faith in India's abilities to find the thief and retrieve the coronet."

"You'll just have to wait for his name to come out in the papers," Willie said.

"But then everyone with an interest in magic will descend on his doorstep and offer to buy the coronet."

"Lucky him."

Mrs. Delancey sighed. "It's going to cost a small fortune. A magical golden coronet will enhance anyone's collection a thousand-fold. Imagine the value in five years' time!"

"Who among your collector friends could afford to get into a bidding war over it?" I asked.

"Aside from us? Lord Coyle. Louisa—but she doesn't collect objects. Her interests lie in the spells and theories, like Professor Nash."

"What about Lord Farnsworth?"

She shook her head. "Most of his wealth is tied up in his estate. He hasn't got a lot to splash around."

Willie nodded thoughtfully. "It's prob'ly expensive to keep a Nubian princess."

"Is that some kind of statue?"

"Yes," I said quickly. "And Mr. and Mrs. Landers? Could they afford to buy the coronet? I hear they're well off."

Mrs. Delancey sipped her tea, her gaze lowered.

"*Are* they well off?" I prompted.

"I shouldn't gossip."

"This ain't gossip," Willie assured her. "It's a nice chat among friends. We don't spread gossip, do we, India?"

"Definitely not," I said. "Anything you tell us will remain a secret."

Mrs. Delancey put her cup down. "The Landers are in our close circle. Not only are they members of the collectors club, but Mr. Landers and my husband are both in the financial business. We see them quite a lot socially. They've never lacked for anything. She always had the finest clothes and jewels and he has the latest conveyances and the finest horses. Until about a year ago, that is. That's when they began selling off London properties like a dog shakes off water. My husband noticed the properties coming on the market at regular intervals and sometimes selling for less than what they were worth to ensure a quick sale."

"Do you know why they began experiencing financial difficulty?" I asked.

"Gambling debts, most likely, but we don't know for certain."

So neither the Landers nor Lord Farnsworth could afford to buy the coronet legitimately. That must be why they were on Lord Coyle's list in the first place.

"Would you introduce me to Mrs. Landers?" I asked.

"I'd be delighted. Oh, I know! They're hosting a soiree tomorrow night. I'm sure she'd be delighted to meet you again."

"Again?"

"Don't you remember? You met here once before, along with several other female members of our little collector's group. She was the one wearing a diamond tiara. A little much for a simple gathering, but that's Dorothea for you. Why do you want to meet the Landers?"

"I feel a little sorry for them," I said. "They've lost so much and I thought I could put some of my magic into one of their watches. It might make them feel a little better about their plight."

I could feel Willie's stare boring into me, no doubt wondering at my weak excuse. Thankfully Mrs. Delancey didn't suspect anything.

"How charitable of you," she said. "You have a good heart, India. I'm sure they'll be delighted." She put a hand on my knee and her smile turned to a frown. "Be sure not to let them know that you know about their plight."

"I won't."

She patted my knee and sat back. "I've been thinking about the coronet ever since you told me it was stolen. Mr. Delancey and I spoke about it last night. He thinks that whoever stole it had the right idea."

I almost choked on my tea as I sipped. "Pardon?"

"A bidding war, as you put it, India, is unlikely to happen. An item as valuable as the coronet that also has sentimental value would never come up for sale. The only way to get one's hands on it would be to steal it. Pity," she muttered into her teacup.

Later, as Willie and I were in the carriage, she said, "I got the feeling she's disappointed she didn't think of stealing it herself."

"So did I. Yesterday she was horrified when we suggested she might have stolen it. She's a hypocrite."

"That's what money does to some people, India. It makes 'em do and say strange things. Like that widow, Mrs. Rotherhide." She turned to me, all earnest frown and serious eyes. "If she's rich and young and fun, why does she need Duke? She can have any man."

"Duke's kind and sweet. He's handsome, too, and strong."

She grunted.

"She might also like that he's American and working class. Some women of her standing find that interesting, desirable."

She screwed up her nose. "See what I mean?" She drew little

circles at her temple. "I don't think it's a good idea for Duke to get involved with her."

"Because she might be mad?"

"Because she's a suspect."

"I thought we agreed she wasn't. Duke saw her magical collection and the coronet wasn't there."

"She could be hiding it elsewhere," Willie said.

I let the silence settle for a few seconds to give my next words more impact. "I think you're jealous."

"Of Duke? I haven't even met the woman, how can I be jealous of him?"

I laughed. "I meant jealous of *her*. I think you hold a small candle for Duke."

"*You're* mad. Me and Duke go back a long way. If I wanted him, I could have had him."

"I suppose."

"Your problem is you're a romantic. You want everything tied up in neat bows, especially relationships. You and Matt, Cyclops and Catherine, me and Duke, or me and Jasper. But relationships aren't neat. They're messy. You just got to learn to embrace the mess, India. Like me."

Sometimes Willie was the oddest creature. And sometimes she made more sense than anyone.

CHAPTER 9

A note arrived in the early afternoon from Cyclops. It contained the address of Lord Farnsworth's mistress, a Miss Angelique L'Amour.

"That ain't her real name," Willie said. "I bet she has a fake accent, too. All the whores do."

"She's a courtesan, not a whore," I said.

Aunt Letitia peered at me over her spectacles and Willie arched a brow.

"Anyway, how do you know it's a false name?" I asked. "If Lord Farnsworth likes exotic women, she could be French."

"France is not an exotic country, India," Aunt Letitia said, returning to her book.

"All the whores back home have French names and some put on bad accents too," Willie said. "They think it makes them more sophisticated."

"Do the men fall for it?" I asked.

"The stupid ones do, and there are plenty of those."

Aunt Letitia turned the page with a vigorous swipe of her finger. "Do change the subject. Preferably to something that doesn't involve prostitution."

"Can't," Willie said. "Lord Farnsworth's got himself a mistress and now we have her address. Want to call on her, India?"

"No!" Aunt Letitia cried before I could respond. "India is not going to call on a whore."

"Courtesan," I corrected. "And you're right, Aunt Letitia. I'm married to the future Lord Rycroft and shouldn't be paying calls to women like Angelique L'Amour."

"Thank you." She shot Willie a triumphant smile.

Willie slumped in the chair and inspected her fingernails for five minutes. When she finally looked my way again, I winked at her and jerked my head in Aunt Letitia's direction.

Willie sat up straight. "I'm going to pay a call on Jasper."

"Marvelous," I said. "Can you give him an update on the progress of our investigation into the missing coronet? I know he's not in charge of the case but we ought to involve him, considering it's related to magic."

Willie screwed up her nose. "I don't know if I can remember everything to tell him. There's a lot of suspects and a lot of information."

"Then I'll come with you."

Aunt Letitia was none the wiser as Willie and I exited the sitting room together.

"Well done," I said as we headed down the stairs. "You understood what I wanted you to say perfectly."

"That's because you and me are alike. Different but alike." She hooked her arm through mine. "Like peas and pods. Wood and nails. Bullets and guns."

"Those are the worst analogies I've ever heard."

"What do you expect from an uneducated, sharpshooting, rough riding cowgirl?"

* * *

ANGELIQUE L'AMOUR's rooms were located above a butcher in a Pimlico street lined with shops. The busy thoroughfare was alive with activity on this sunny Thursday as pedestrians passed the plain black door without even glancing at it.

"It's locked," Willie said after trying the doorknob. "Told you she was a prisoner."

"Of course it's locked," I said. "What woman living alone would keep her front door unlocked?"

She knocked but there was no answer.

"Perhaps she didn't hear it," I said.

She knocked again, louder, but there was still no answer. "I'm right, India, and you know it. She's being held against her will by the toff. I'm going to break the door down."

"You are not," I hissed, glancing around.

A few people stared as they walked past, but it was hard to tell if that was because we were lingering or because Willie was a woman dressed in men's clothes. A young man in a bloodied apron peered out of the butcher's window. He rearranged the display of meat and sausages then rearranged them again, slowly.

"There are too many witnesses," I said. "We'll come back later. Oh, wait a moment."

A woman with ebony skin approached from the south. She was very pretty, with sensuous lips and large, chocolate colored eyes set in a delicate heart-shaped face. Her purple outfit strained to contain her bust but showed off her tiny waist. Her proportions defied nature, and I wondered how she could even breathe with her corset laced so tightly. She held a key in one hand and a fully laden basket in the other. The end of a loaf of bread poked out from beneath a cloth.

"Good afternoon," she said in a thick accent. "May I help you?"

"Are you Miss L'Amour?" I asked.

"*Oui*. And you are?"

"My name is Mrs. Glass and this is my friend, Miss Johnson. We're from the Pimlico Female Protection Society, a charitable institute that seeks to reclaim young women who have fallen from the path of virtue. We want to help you." It had been my idea to pretend we were from a charity, but Willie hadn't liked it. From the way Miss L'Amour's spine stiffened, perhaps I should have listened to Willie.

"I am not in need of your help," Miss L'Amour said.

"Perhaps we can have a chat over a cup of tea."

"Step aside, *s'il vous plaît*."

Willie moved to block the door. "Are you being held here against your will?"

"*Pardon*?"

"Against your will, by your keeper?"

Miss L'Amour spoke rapidly in a language that sounded French to me, but could have been made up words. I wished I'd asked Fabian along.

"That fake accent might fool Farnsworth but it don't fool us," Willie said.

Miss L'Amour's lips pressed together. "Your fake clothes do not fool me. You are a woman. A stupid woman."

Willie tilted her chin forward. "How do you figure that?"

"Because you do not see what is before your eyes." She clicked her tongue. "Come inside. You are making a scene."

She unlocked the door and led the way up the steep stairs to the parlor above. It was a cozy space, large enough only for a sofa, armchair and occasional table. The thick brocade curtains, deep burgundy upholstery and dusky pink cushions gave the room a homely yet elegant feel.

Miss L'Amour deposited the basket beside a small gas burner on a table in an adjoining room that seemed to be used as a larder. A second door led to a bedchamber containing an enormous four-poster covered with sea green velvet blankets and several pillows. It was unmade. Such a large bed couldn't have been brought up the narrow stairs. It must have been assembled in the bedroom.

Miss L'Amour caught us peering into the bedroom and shut the door. "What do you want?" she asked mildly.

"We want to know if your master treats you well," Willie said.

Miss L'Amour bristled. "*Davide* is not my master. Or my keeper. He is my lover." She had no qualms admitting it. If anything, she was defiant, daring me to gasp or show shock. If only she knew the sort of household we kept, she would realize it took quite a lot to shock me nowadays.

"Gentlemen don't pay their lovers," Willie said. "They pay their wh—"

"Courtesans," I cut in. "They pay their courtesans. We know what you are, Miss L'Amour, and it's of no concern to us. You may live your life however you wish. We will not judge you."

She regarded Willie from beneath thick lashes.

"I was only making sure you weren't held against your will," Willie muttered.

Miss L'Amour suddenly laughed, a deep, joyous sound that brought a smile to my face. Even Willie blushed and almost smiled. "It is very sweet of you to worry, Miss Johnson. I see where the mistake is made. Let me assure you, I am quite well and not a prisoner here. I am cared for." She indicated the room with an elegantly languid lift of her hand. "I live better now than I did in *Paris* where *Davide* found me two years ago. I am luckier than most."

"Aye, but you're still at his beck and call," Willie said. "You have to be here for him whenever he wants you."

"As does any member of staff, *non*? Or a shop girl? A governess? We must all be in our place of work when it is required. I am no different." She took Willie's hand and clasped it between both of hers. "*Merci*, Miss Johnson. I thank you for your concern, but it is not necessary. I am very content. *Davide* is a good man. A little, how do you say, *excentrique*, and a *romantique*, but he is kind. Now, does that satisfy you? Are you content that I do not need your charity?"

I wanted to drop the charity ruse, but could think of nothing else on the spur of the moment. She didn't sound like a woman who would betray her lover to spite him or to extract herself from their arrangement. Making promises to help free her from his clutches would only result in another of those throaty, joyous laughs. But the truth wouldn't work either. She needed Lord Farnsworth's patronage and wouldn't assist us if he were guilty of the theft.

"We're satisfied," I said. "We're also relieved to know no one is taking advantage of you." I scrambled to think of something else, but it was useless. This woman unnerved me. She was so confident, so sensual and lovely. I felt like an unsophisticated frump next to her.

Willie coughed and rubbed her throat. Her coughing increased until she was bent over, making awful choking sounds. "Water," she gasped out.

"I have wine," Miss L'Amour said with alarm.

Willie nodded and hustled her toward the room used as a kitchen. With Miss L'Amour's back turned, Willie jerked her head at the bedroom door.

I hurriedly opened it and looked around. Far more attention had been paid to decorating the bedroom than the parlor. It was very feminine with its sprigged muslin bed curtains festooned with bows and tassels. Matching tassels hung from the window curtains, and a lace cloth adorned the dressing table. A green and gold Oriental rug covered part of the floor. I raced on tip toes around the room, checking under the bed, in the dresser and night table drawers. I tried the large trunk at the foot of the bed but it was locked. Damnation. It would be the perfect place to store stolen objects.

Willie coughed again, loudly.

I returned to the parlor where I sat on the sofa and settled into a position that I hoped made it seem as though I'd been there the entire time. Willie clutched Miss L'Amour's hand, a glass of wine in her other. Miss L'Amour's back was still to me, but she seemed to be listening intently to something Willie whispered in her ear.

When Willie joined me in the parlor, Miss L'Amour

watched her go, her smoky gaze on Willie's derriere. I pretended not to notice and hoped I didn't give away my surprise.

"We better go, India," Willie said.

Miss L'Amour's gaze snapped to mine then she dipped her head coyly, embarrassed to have been caught.

"Thank you for your concern," Miss L'Amour said. "Your charity is kind, but it is not for me."

"We're glad to hear it," I said.

She gave Willie a small knowing smile. "Goodbye, Miss Johnson. I will see you later, yes?"

Willie blushed and nodded.

I waited until we reached the pavement, but I couldn't contain my curiosity any longer. "Are you two meeting up?"

Willie headed toward Woodall and our waiting carriage, her strides long and purposeful. "I asked her to meet me down at the docks tonight."

"Why?"

"She was making cow eyes at me."

"Cow eyes?"

"Fluttering her long lashes. Cows have long lashes."

"I've never noticed."

"I asked her if she wants to see me again and she said she did, but not here." Willie opened the carriage door and practically dived in, so quickly did she want to leave. "Angelique thinks—"

"Angelique? You're already on first name basis?"

She shrugged. "Angelique thinks Lord Farnsworth pays the butcher's boy to report any callers she gets. You visiting today ain't so bad. She can tell him you're a whore friend."

I groaned.

"But if someone dressed like a man comes on his own at night, Farnsworth wouldn't like it," Willie went on. "Told you she was a prisoner."

"She's not a prisoner. No woman should have gentlemen

callers at night, anyway. You know, you could negate the problem by wearing a dress."

She pulled a face. "No one's worth that. Besides, I think she likes me in this."

Going by the heat in Miss L'Amour's gaze as she watched Willie walk off, I tended to agree.

Willie settled into the corner of the cabin with a smile. "You got to admit, I did well in there. Not only did you get a chance to look through the bedroom, but I organized to get her out so Matt can break in tonight."

"Oh! *That's* why you're meeting her at the docks."

She frowned. "Why'd you think I did it?"

I shrugged. "You like beautiful women; she's a beautiful woman. She's, er…available for the right price."

Willie tipped her hat forward to cover her eyes, crossed her arms, and smiled. I doubted her only reason for meeting Miss L'Amour at the docks was to get her out of the apartment.

* * *

MATT AND DUKE returned home some time before the dinner gong sounded, which gave us an opportunity to exchange reports before we headed into the dining room. With Aunt Letitia dining with us this evening, all talk of investigations would be banned. Besides, Matt wouldn't want to tell her he'd been breaking into houses, and I didn't want her knowing Willie was meeting a courtesan at the docks later. With Aunt Letitia changing for dinner, the rest of us took the opportunity to meet in the library. Only Cyclops was absent.

Despite saying he would investigate Mrs. Rotherhide again, Duke had, in fact, stayed with Matt all day and watched Sir Charles Whittaker's residence. "Whittaker left first thing," Duke said. "Just after the housekeeper arrived."

"I thought she was live-in," I said.

"It doesn't appear so." Matt handed Duke and Willie a glass

of brandy each. That was another thing Aunt Letitia wouldn't like—drinking liquor before dinner. In honor of her I refused, and Matt abstained too.

"It was an age before she left again," Duke went on. "But by then the char woman had arrived. So we waited until she finally left too. Not knowing how long we had before the housekeeper returned, we got in and out real quick."

"We didn't need much time anyway," Matt said. "There was only one locked drawer in Whittaker's writing desk and that was easy to get into. It contained the purchase papers for the carriage and horses he recently bought, as well as other receipts for furniture. There were no keys, no deposit box numbers, no paperwork for other properties where he could have hidden his collection. No signs of a collection at all."

"What about hidden rooms?" Willie asked.

"We checked for loose floorboards and hollow wall panels, we looked for false drawers and compartments. We upturned furniture, measured for unaccounted spaces… We looked everywhere."

"Could be a mechanism you've never come across," she said. "Maybe a trigger that opens up a slim panel or something."

Matt shrugged.

Duke swirled the contents of his glass. "It was real strange. He had no personal things there except for a picture of himself and an older woman. Could be his mother."

"There were no banking details," Matt added. "No deeds for shareholdings, not even letters."

"How odd," I said.

"He could just be real private," Duke said.

"And have no friends or family," Willie added.

"That's quite sad," I said. If I had not found Matt when I did, I too would be without family, and my only friend would be Catherine. The thought left a hollow feeling in my gut. Poor Sir Charles.

"What did you two get up to today?" Matt asked. "Did you go

for a walk in the park? A drive? Did you meet with Charbonneau?"

Willie stretched out her legs and crossed them at the ankles. "We did our own investigating. We ain't letting you boys have all the fun."

"Fun?" Duke barked a laugh. "Standing on your feet all day waiting for a house to become empty ain't fun."

"I wish you'd tell me when you're going investigating," Matt said to me.

"You weren't here when we decided to go," I told him. "And I left a message with Bristow."

"And she had me." Willie raised her glass in salute.

Duke grunted. "That's why he worries."

Willie poked her tongue out at him.

"We visited Lord Farnsworth's courtesan," I told them.

"What's she like?" Duke addressed his question to Willie.

"She's a real beauty," Willie said with a tilt of her lips.

"She seems nice," I added with a pointed glare for Willie. "Why are women always judged by their looks first? Beauty doesn't matter."

"It does for the whores of rich men."

"*Courtesans*. Anyway." I turned back to Matt who was watching us with a smirk. "Willie managed to distract Miss L'Amour long enough for me to have a quick look around the bedroom, which is probably the only room where Farnsworth could hide a coronet. It was a very small place."

"What did you find?" Matt asked.

"There's a locked trunk at the foot of the bed. You should look in there first."

"We arranged it so you can break in tonight," Willie added.

"How?" Duke asked.

"By getting Angelique out of her apartment. I'm meeting her at midnight at the docks."

"Are you mad? She's a whore!"

"Courtesan," Willie said with a sniff. "And I can afford her."

"Why the docks?" Matt asked.

"I can't bring her back here, can I? Anyway, it was all I could think of at the time."

"What if Farnsworth visits her and she's not there? He'll get suspicious. If he's paying for her lodgings, he won't share her."

Willie smirked. "He won't share her with a man. I bet he ain't even considered sharing her with a woman."

"Be careful down at the docks," Duke said with a shake of his head. "It's rough at night."

"It's well lit and bobbies keep an eye out for thieves but ignore the whores as long as they don't cause a ruckus. The rich merchants ain't taking any chances with their goods getting stolen from the warehouses."

"Duke and I'll look around the apartment while she's out," Matt said. "We'll start with the trunk."

"That's if he did hide the coronet at Angelique's place," Willie added. "It could be in his own house. We've got to wait for Cyclops to get us inside."

"I'm quite sure we decided we weren't breaking into Lord Farnsworth's house," I said. "There are too many servants. It's too dangerous."

"How else are we going to know if he's hidden it in there? Tell her, Duke."

Duke looked disappointed but he managed a shrug before draining the rest of his glass.

"Is something wrong?" Matt asked.

"I was going to have supper with Mrs. Rotherhide later then spend the night. S'pose I better let her know I can't make it."

"Again?" Willie scoffed. "She's not tired of you yet?"

"You can still go," I said. "I'll be Matt's lookout. I've done it before. It'll be fun."

Matt narrowed his gaze. "Fun?"

I waved a hand in dismissal. "More entertaining than waiting here worrying about you. You go and see Mrs. Rotherhide,

Duke. Enjoy yourself. You too, Willie. Be sure to keep Miss L'Amour occupied for as long as possible."

Willie grinned into her glass. "I reckon I can do that."

"Oh, there's something else," I said quickly, in an attempt to distract myself from Willie's gloating. "Mrs. Delancey asked Mrs. Landers to invite me to her soiree tomorrow. The invitation arrived in the last post of the day. You're invited too, Matt."

* * *

AFTER DINNER, Duke headed out to Mrs. Rotherhide's, while Matt and I sat with Aunt Letitia in the sitting room. Willie had retreated to her bedroom. Bristow entered at ten past nine and announced that Cyclops was outside and wished to speak with us. Matt and I met him at Lord Farnsworth's carriage, where he stood by the horses, alone.

"I just took Farnsworth to his club where he's going to dine with friends," Cyclops said. "I've got an hour and a half before I have to collect him."

"Where is he going after that?" I asked.

"I don't know yet, but I know it ain't home. According to the other staff, he's out every night, even Sundays."

"We do know he's not seeing his mistress tonight," Matt said. "She told Willie she's available. They're meeting at the docks. I'm going to check inside her apartment while she's out."

Cyclops chuckled. "Willie doesn't waste any opportunity."

"Come inside out of the cold," I said. "Peter will watch the carriage for a while. You should eat something."

"I ate before I left. Farnsworth's cook's good, but not as good as Mrs. Potter."

"I'll be sure to tell her you said that. No doubt there'll be extra helpings for you when you return."

He flashed a grin. "I'll get going and drive around for a while. But I came to tell you what I learned today about Farnsworth. According to the footman, his lordship has been out every night for the last two weeks, and comes home real late, sometimes at dawn. Farnsworth being out 'til all hours ain't unusual, but what was unusual about one particular night this week was what happened the next day. The coachman was dismissed without warning or explanation. When I asked which night that was, the footman said Monday."

"The night Cox's townhouse was broken into and the coronet stolen," Matt said.

"I reckon Farnsworth had his coachman drive him to Cox's and wait while he burgled it. Later, he got scared that the papers would report it and the coachman would read about the theft and realize that's where he took his master. Farnsworth didn't know at the time that Cox wanted to keep it out of the papers."

"But dismissing the coachman wouldn't have stopped him reporting it to the police," I said. "In fact, he'd be more likely to report the man who dismissed him."

Cyclops shook his head. "According to the other staff, the coachman can't read. If he'd stayed in Farnsworth's employment, he might have heard something about the theft from the others if they read about it. But being unemployed, he wouldn't be around servants who gossip about their masters and mistresses. It ain't easy to get another job in the city if you don't have a reference from your last place. He might be without work for months. He might not even get back into service."

"We should look for the coachman," Matt said with a nod of approval.

"I'll see if any of the servants know where he went."

"What about the keys to get into Farnsworth's townhouse?"

"Matt," I warned. "You're not breaking in."

"I'll see what I can do," Cyclops said.

"Be careful," I told him.

* * *

THE STREETLIGHTS GLOWED SOFTLY, like faraway moons. The cool air was still, the night silent except for our footsteps on the pavement. Walking after midnight with my husband would be quite romantic if not for the task ahead of us. Despite having broken into houses before, my heart pounded, my skin felt cold. I would never get used to it, but I was determined not to show Matt my fear.

I led him to the butcher's shop and indicated the door to Miss L'Amour's apartment. He gave a single nod and checked the vicinity. We were alone. The street that had been a hive of activity during the day was now empty of people and traffic. I took particular note of the butcher's shop. If Miss L'Amour was correct, and the youth reported all comings and goings to Lord Farnsworth, I'd have to create a diversion so Matt could enter undetected.

The butcher's shop was shrouded in darkness, the nearest streetlight reflecting in the window like an eerie, disembodied orb. There was no sign of anyone inside or outside the shop.

"Keep your knife in your hand," Matt whispered. "Be prepared."

I took the small blade out of my pocket and clutched it firmly. Then I sank into the shadows near Miss L'Amour's door.

Matt went to work on the lock and quickly had it open. He slipped inside and disappeared, leaving the door slightly ajar. I scanned the street, straining to hear into the deep darkness.

A dog barked in the distance; a night bird cawed; carriage wheels rumbled like low thunder at the end of the street before fading.

Silence again.

My palms became clammy, my fingers cramping as I clutched the knife tight.

A light breeze caressed my cheek and dust swirled in the gutters. I scanned the street, left and right, opposite. The shadows were thick, the light cast by the lamps pathetically thin.

Still, there was no sound. Not even from inside Miss L'Amour's residence.

Not even when Matt emerged. My heart leapt into my throat at his sudden reappearance.

He simply shook his head and took my hand. The steady stroke of his gloved thumb over mine soothed my nerves. We were safe. It wasn't a trap. Miss L'Amour had not somehow guessed we were going to break in tonight and tricked us. She really had gone to the docks for a rendezvous with Willie.

Matt and I left, hand in hand like forbidden lovers sneaking away for a tryst.

***

A VISITOR just after dawn was never welcome. Even less so when it was a policeman.

Bristow was already awake and answered the door, sending Peter to fetch Matt. We both threw on housecoats, me over my nightgown and he over nothing, and hurried down the stairs.

The hulking form of a large constable stood in our entrance hall, red faced and unable to look either of us in the eye. I clutched my housecoat at the collar but it was tightly buttoned up. Matt wasn't showing any flesh either, except for his feet and ankles. So why the blushes?

"I'm sorry for this, sir, madam," the young constable said, still not looking up from the floor tiles. "But your name was given and I was ordered to fetch you."

"My name was given by whom?" Matt demanded.

"The woman we arrested last night. She insisted we come get you. Made an almighty fuss until my sergeant gave in and sent me as soon as it was light."

Dread settled into the pit of my stomach.

"What woman?" From the heavy tone of Matt's voice, I sensed he'd guessed the answer too.

"Her name's Willemina Johnson. She says she's your cousin. If she's not, I'll tell my sergeant—"

"She is." Matt sighed. "What did she do?"

The constable shifted his weight from foot to foot and his face grew redder. "I'd rather not say, sir. Not in front of your wife."

"Out with it," I snapped at him. It was too early for games. I didn't know what Willie had done, but I was already furious at her for dragging us out of bed at this hour.

The constable cleared his throat. "She—er...she was soliciting—"

"I doubt that," Matt growled. "Whatever Willie is, she's not a prostitute."

"That may be, sir, and soliciting is awful hard to determine with certainty. I can assure you she wasn't arrested for that."

"Then what was she arrested for?" I asked.

The constable chewed on his lower lip.

"Well?" Matt prompted.

"Gross indecency."

CHAPTER 10

The sergeant on duty at the Leman Street police station was a fool. He wouldn't believe Matt when he informed him that gross indecency only applied to sexual activity between men, not women.

"Course it applies to two women being…intimate," the sergeant said. "It's indecent."

I rolled my eyes for what must have been the hundredth time since arriving. The thick-necked, pock-marked sergeant refused to release Willie even though the charges were made up. The night shift weren't the smartest, I'd quickly realized. They were the burliest policemen, the ones unafraid to go out at night into London's rotten core. They were employed for their formidable size, hard fists and firm jaws, not for their knowledge of the finer points of law. To be fair, I doubted this particular predicament arose often, if ever.

"If my cousin hasn't been arrested for soliciting then she has to be released," Matt said. "What about the other woman? Did you arrest her too?"

"She got away." The sergeant returned to his ledger. "You should go home and get her a lawyer, sir. That's why you were notified, at your cousin's request."

"My lawyer is in bed," Matt said through clenched teeth. His temper had risen when the conversation with the sergeant began, but it had remained at a simmering, civilized level. I suspected it wouldn't be long before it boiled over.

The sergeant's gaze flicked up to me then back down to his ledger.

Matt blew out a breath like a bull just before it charges. "If I bring my lawyer down here and he explains the law to you, will you release her?"

"On the say-so of *your* lawyer?" The sergeant scoffed. "No. You have to wait for the prosecution office to get back to me."

"And when will that be?"

The sergeant flipped open the case of his pocket watch. "The office doesn't open for another two hours. That'll coincide with a change of shift here. I'll wait for one of the new constables to come in then by the time he reaches the office, waits to speak to one of the prosecutors, then gets back here...I'd say another three hours or more." He slipped the watch back into his pocket with a slow move that I suspected was deliberately done to frustrate us. Just like Brockwell.

Brockwell! If anyone knew the finer points of the law it would be the man who wrote down every word in an interview, whose moral compass never deviated, and who liked to lecture anyone who would listen about the law.

"Will you believe a detective inspector from Scotland Yard?" I asked.

The sergeant narrowed his gaze. "If he can prove he's from Scotland Yard, I'll have to do as he orders."

Matt and I looked at one another and wordlessly left the station. Matt gave Woodall Brockwell's home address. At this time of day, he was more likely to be there unless he was investigating an important case.

The carriage leapt forward as Woodall urged the horses to make haste. My hair tumbled over my eyes. I'd not taken the time to arrange it after hurriedly dressing. Aunt Letitia would be horrified to see it flowing about my shoulders like a schoolgirl's.

Matt didn't seem to notice. He seethed on the seat opposite, his glare focused on the scene rushing past the window. I didn't dare say a word.

We arrived at Brockwell's residence, and I was very glad that we didn't have to wake him. He answered the door with a piece of toast in hand.

"Blimey! It's only you two. I thought it was someone from the Yard come to fetch me for a murder. To investigate one, I mean." He invited us into the small entrance hall, out of the drizzling rain. "Is something wrong?"

"It's Willie," Matt said. "She's been arrested—falsely—and the moronic sergeant on duty won't release her. He thinks he's in the right and won't take my word for it. Will you come and set him straight?"

The mention of Willie's name had seen Brockwell tense, his gaze sharpen, but by the end of Matt's speech, he had relaxed again. "Sometimes the night sergeants can be a little too enthusiastic."

"I don't mind enthusiasm in the police force, but I would like them to know the law."

"To be fair, it's quite an obscure law," I said.

Brockwell reached for the coat hanging on the stand by the door. He slotted the piece of toast into his mouth, drew on the coat, and removed the toast again, leaving behind a bite-sized chunk. He followed us outside, chewing loudly, and locked the door.

He finished the piece of toast as he settled into the carriage and wiped his mouth with his sleeve. I watched him, wondering when he was going to ask. Wondering what his reaction would be when he found out. I wasn't sure whether to worry or be amused.

"So," he finally said when he finished his mouthful. "What was the obscure law she's supposed to have violated?"

"Gross indecency," Matt said, also watching Brockwell intently.

Brockwell's lips twitched. He was smiling. I thought he might be jealous at the thought of Willie being with another man, but he seemed to accept it. He scrubbed his sideburns. "I see the problem. The sergeant refuses to believe she's a woman and Willie refuses to, er, prove it, so the sergeant thinks he arrested two men."

"That's not it. The sergeant knows Willie is a woman, and the other person caught in the act wasn't a man."

Brockwell's hand stilled. He stared at Matt then suddenly looked away. He shifted on the seat and resumed scratching his sideburns. "I see." He cleared his throat. "I'll inform the sergeant of his error. You're correct, Glass. Gross indecency applies only to men. There is nothing in the law that mentions women. Perhaps the lawmakers never considered two women would…" He drifted off, his face reddening.

"Or perhaps they don't consider it to be indecent when they do," Matt said.

Brockwell blushed, and I felt my own face heat. I wished Matt wouldn't say things like that to shock. Not to a man like Brockwell, who was not only straight-laced but quite possibly in love with Willie.

* * *

"Come home and have breakfast with us," I urged Brockwell. We stood in the reception area of the Leman Street police station, waiting for the duty sergeant to escort Willie from the holding cell. The detective inspector had flashed his Scotland Yard identification and ordered Willie's release after giving a swift, no-nonsense lesson in the precise legal meaning of gross indecency.

The sergeant had wasted no time in acting. He seemed worried about the repercussions of the false arrest. It was difficult to tell if he was more worried by Matt's thunderous expression or Brockwell's cold one. Neither man looked as though he would tolerate incompetence.

"Thank you, Mrs. Glass, but I ate breakfast before your arrival," Brockwell said. "I must get to work."

"But it's still early."

He slapped his hat on his head. "Even so. Good morning."

"You're leaving now? Don't you want to see Willie?"

For the first time since entering the station, he looked uncertain. "I think it's best if I don't."

I moved to block the exit. "Stay. She'll want to thank you."

He hesitated. That hesitation cost him moments in which he could escape before Willie arrived.

She didn't seem too ruffled from a night spent in the holding cell. Her clothes were crumpled and her hair resembled an abandoned bird nest, but that wasn't out of the ordinary. She didn't even look particularly tired.

"You didn't both have to come," she said to me.

With his back to her, she didn't realize Brockwell was standing there until he turned around. She froze.

Brockwell touched the brim of his hat. "Good morning, Miss Johnson."

"Jasper," she began. "I—I… What are you doing here?"

"I came to explain the law to my colleague." Brockwell nodded at the sergeant, now back behind the counter. "He understands his mistake and won't make the same one again."

The sergeant studied his ledger intensely.

Willie swallowed. "Right. Well. Thanks. I s'pose I owe you a favor."

"You owe me nothing. I must go. Good morning, all."

He stepped around me and left.

"Willie," I hissed. "Go after him."

"Why?"

"To thank him properly, of course."

The sergeant asked her to sign the ledger and returned her few belongings to her, including the gun.

She strode past me and we followed her out. By the time we reached the pavement, Brockwell had departed.

"Visit him later," I said to Willie. "I think he's upset. He didn't accept my invitation to join us for breakfast, and Brockwell never misses an opportunity to eat for free."

She climbed into our waiting carriage and threw herself into the corner, arms crossed. "I knew he'd be like this. He's fine that we ain't committing to each other, but me being with women... that's different. He's a prude, India, just like you. "

"Then he'll come around, just as I did. Even Aunt Letitia accepts that part of you now, in her way. Brockwell will accept it too, if you give him the opportunity."

"I don't think so. It's different for you and Letty. You're friends, family. You ain't intimate with me."

I appealed to Matt as he sat beside me, but he put up his hands. "I did my part. I got her out. How was it in there, Willie? Did they treat you well?"

"As well as can be expected," she said morosely. "Don't fuss, Matt. It ain't my first time in prison."

"Try to make it your last," he muttered.

* * *

I SPENT most of the day with Fabian, attempting to create spells to make objects fly. None worked, which only confirmed that we needed an actual magician for each type of object we were trying to float.

"I asked Mrs. Delancey if her husband had any distant cousins on his father's side," I told Fabian. "She claims not."

"Pity," he said on a sigh. "But she may not know of his entire family. You should ask Mr. Delancey."

"Perhaps he's going tonight. Mr. and Mrs. Landers are hosting a soiree and have invited Matt and me. It seems there'll be some other members from their so-called collectors club there."

"I have been invited too," Fabian said. "I declined, but now that you say you are going, perhaps I will change my mind. I can engage Mr. Delancey in conversation and ask him about his magic family."

"An excellent idea. Do come, that way I know I won't be the only magician there and the focus of their attention. It's draining. Oh, I think Oscar might be going, since Louisa is a member of the club. That makes three magicians."

Fabian's lips flattened at the mention of her name. When Fabian arrived in London, she was the first person he turned to. Their fathers had been great friends, and Louisa and Fabian had sent one another letters over the years. She had proposed marriage to him within weeks of his arrival, but when it came to light that she was marrying him purely because she wanted to marry a magician and have magical children, he'd turned her down.

Indeed, he would have refused her anyway, even if that wasn't her motive. He wanted to marry a magician too, to strengthen his magical lineage.

"You two have not repaired your friendship?" I asked him gently.

"We have not spoken since her betrothal to Barratt. I am pleased for her, but the last time we met, it was tense between us. She was angry with me. Does Barratt know?"

"She told him. He knows she's marrying him for his magic bloodline, but he doesn't care." I smiled wryly. "He's marrying her for her money, so I suppose they're even."

He laughed softly. "They make a good couple." His eyes turned sad and his smile faded. "But I worry for their future. There must be some feeling between husband and wife, *non*? Some affection. Marriage is for a lifetime." He sounded a little melancholy. Perhaps his own decision to marry for magic instead of love was weighing heavily on him.

"Sometimes I wonder if Louisa rushed her proposal to Oscar," I said. "If she'd taken her time, she might have genuinely fallen in love with a magician. Ah well. Perhaps the affection between Oscar and Louisa will deepen over time." I hoped Fabian connected my suggestion to his own situation and continued to look for a magician to love rather than give up on love altogether.

Going by his sorrowful eyes, he didn't think the notion possible.

* * *

THE DRAWING ROOM AT THE LANDERS' house was filled with members of the collectors club. It seemed that upon my acceptance of her invitation, Mrs. Landers had sent out numerous others to people she had not previously bothered to invite.

"It's a rare thing to have a private audience with a magician such as yourself," she told me. "I wanted to share my good fortune with my like-minded friends so I added one or two other guests at the last moment."

"One or two?" her husband muttered, glancing around.

Mrs. Landers laughed. She had a light, delicate laugh that suited the fine-boned woman. She was everything I was not. Small, fair-haired, with the tiniest waist and hands I'd ever seen. Even her facial features were delicate, giving her a childlike quality. Standing beside her husband, with his receding hair, the twelve-year age gap seemed larger.

"We are even more fortunate that Mr. Charbonneau changed his mind and came too," Mrs. Landers said as she gazed upon Fabian as he spoke to Louisa and Oscar. "Aren't we, Mr. Landers?"

Mr. Landers smiled blandly. "Yes, m'dear," he said with equal blandness. His gaze was directed toward the refreshment room where the food and wine had not yet been laid out.

"Tell me about your collection," I said to Mrs. Landers. "Will we have the opportunity to see it tonight?"

"Patience, dear Mrs. Glass." She laughed again. "For a magician, you are quite impatient to see magical objects. This must be the third or fourth time you've asked."

I looked toward the refreshment room too. It was going to be a long night.

"My wife likes to draw out the theatrics," Mr. Landers said.

"It will be worth it," she said. "We have such a fabulous collection, don't we, Mr. Landers? It's small but very unique."

Mr. Landers' gaze shifted to the dark wood cabinet with the gilded moldings and green marble top, situated on an occasional table. The single door was marked with gilded roses in the corners and a golden, semi-naked cherub holding a bowl of fruit stared out from the center. It was a fine piece of furniture. Fit to hold a magical coronet.

"You can feel it, can't you, Mrs. Glass?" Mrs. Landers asked, excitement edging her voice.

"Feel what?"

"The magic in that cabinet. It was made by a magician. I understand you can feel magic heat, so you must be responding to it. Or perhaps you can feel the magic inside. Yes, that must be it. We have some fine pieces, all with strong magic infused through them."

"How do you know it's strong? Are you a magician?"

Her hand fluttered at the diamond pendant at her throat as she laughed. "Lord, no. How I wish I was, don't I, Mr. Landers? It was the magician craftsmen themselves who assured me. The prices I paid—well, we don't discuss money. Do tell us, Mrs. Glass, can you feel the magic?"

"I have to touch an object to feel the magic." I indicated the room. "The other furniture has been moved to the side to allow space, but that cabinet takes pride of place in front of the arranged chairs. I suspected it's part of your evening's entertainment. That's why I was looking at it."

"My, you *are* clever. Mrs. Delancey did say as much, didn't she, Mr. Landers?"

At the mention of her name, Mrs. Delancey broke away from

Matt and Mr. Delancey and joined us. "What a delight this evening will be. We're so fortunate to have not one or two magicians, but *three*. This is a coup, Mrs. Landers!"

Mrs. Landers flipped out her fan and covered her mouth with it. "How you do go on, Mrs. Delancey. We are greatly honored, and I have you to thank for suggesting I invite Mrs. Glass."

"And Mr. Glass," I added, loud enough for Matt to hear.

He looked up, saw the plea in my eyes, and joined us. "We were just discussing the magical coronet," he said to Mr. and Mrs. Landers. "Did you read about it?"

"Oh, yes, we certainly did," Mrs. Landers said. "If only we knew the name of the lord who owns it! How I'd dearly love to see it."

"Buy it, you mean," Louisa said in a voice that commanded attention. All conversations stopped and everyone in the room looked at her. "That's what all of you want: ownership. You want to lock away the magical pieces and wait for their value to rise before offloading them to someone else in the club who will do the same. You ought to *share* them with the world."

Oscar stood beside his fiancée, nodding.

Mrs. Landers gave a small gasp.

Her husband stiffened. "This is the collector's club," he said to Louisa. "We collect magical objects, in case you've forgotten. If you don't agree with it, perhaps you ought to leave."

"Dear Mr. Landers," Louisa said, smiling sweetly. "You are entirely correct and I apologize. I am delighted to be in your house tonight with such wonderful company. Please don't send us away because of my silly outburst. I promise to bite my tongue before I speak next time."

It would have been a pretty speech if not for the complete lack of contrition in her tone.

"He is not talking about sending you away tonight, Louisa," Lord Coyle piped up. "He means you will be banned from the club altogether. You're only in it by the skin of your teeth anyway, considering you do not collect magic."

"Ah, but I collect something far more valuable." She smiled at Coyle as she looped her arm through Oscar's.

Oscar's gaze dropped to meet hers, but he didn't match her sly smile.

"No one will be offering to buy the coronet from the lord anyway," Sir Charles Whittaker announced. "You have to find out who stole it and make an offer to the thief."

"Stolen!" Mrs. Landers cried. "Dear lord, no. How diabolical."

"That's the problem with announcing these things in the papers," Mrs. Rotherhide said. She wasn't as pretty as Louisa or Mrs. Landers, or as fashionably thin, but she had lovely warm eyes, rosy cheeks and generous curves. I could see why Duke liked her.

"It isn't the fault of the newspapers," Louisa said defensively. "It's the thief who stole it, not the author of the article."

"It was a gossip piece," Oscar pointed out. "Not a proper article."

Nobody seemed to be listening. All were a-twitter about the theft.

I looked at Mrs. Delancey who was looking at Sir Charles. He, in turn, glared at Matt.

"Be careful," Sir Charles said with a spark in his eyes. "Or Mr. and Mrs. Glass will accuse you of stealing it."

Everyone in the room looked at us. Then Mr. Landers barked a laugh. "Don't be absurd. None of *us* would steal it. We're not stupid enough to attract the attention of the police for a trinket."

"It's hardly a trinket," Lord Coyle said. "It's a magical golden object."

"It's exceedingly rare," Mrs. Rotherhide added.

"Forgive my husband," Mrs. Landers said with a light tap of her fan against Mr. Landers' arm. "He doesn't understand the value of all the different magic. If only he'd spend a little more time studying them."

"You ought to come to more meetings, Landers," Mr. Delancey said. "They're enlightening. You might find your wife's collection is valuable. When shall we get to gaze upon it?" he asked Mrs. Landers.

"Soon, soon," she said cheerfully. "We're not all here yet."

Conversations began again, but I could still feel the simmering anger being thrown our way by Sir Charles. He didn't appear to be listening to Louisa and Mrs. Rotherhide, quietly talking beside him.

Mrs. Landers swept closer to us, the full skirt of her pale blue silk chiffon gown seeming to float across the floor with her light step. She was all smiles for Matt. "Mr. Glass, are you investigating the theft of the coronet?"

"We are," Matt said.

"Then you know who originally owned it."

Matt remained silent.

Unperturbed, Mrs. Landers forged ahead. "Do tell us who it is. Everyone in this room is very discreet. No one would tattle."

"Why do you wish to know?" I asked.

"If the owner comes from a family of gold magicians, then I'd like to meet him. Wouldn't it be exciting? It doesn't matter how weak his magic is, all that matters is that it's *gold* magic. Isn't it thrilling, Mrs. Glass?"

"What my wife is trying to say," Mr. Landers said, "is she won't tell anyone who it is. She just wants to know so she can invite him to things like this, and perhaps add a piece of his to her collection."

"We'll pay for it, of course." Mrs. Landers indicated the cabinet. "We've paid for everything in there."

Her husband's jaw hardened and I detected a slight wince. No doubt his recent financial troubles meant his wife could no longer indulge her whims like she used to. I wondered if she knew he'd been forced to sell off properties.

"The gentleman in question isn't magical," I said. "The coronet was given to his ancestor many years ago. He doesn't know who made it. Indeed, the magic felt so faint that I suspect it was put into the gold centuries earlier."

"But what if you're wrong?" Mrs. Landers said matter-of-factly. "What if there are gold magicians still in existence?"

"There are not," Fabian told her.

"And if anyone would know, it would be Fabian," Louisa added.

Fabian gave her a small bow of thanks. She returned it with a shallow curtsy and a smile. Beside her, Oscar's lips flattened.

"We'll learn who it is sooner or later," Mr. Landers said. "So you might as well do as my wife asks and tell us. Everyone in this room is very discreet. Well, I can't account for Charbonneau and Barratt, of course, having only just met them, but people like us, people of high society, are extremely cautious with gossip. It's the lower orders that spread it."

"Is that so?" Matt asked with ominous calm. "Then how does that explain why much of my information is gathered through gentleman's clubs?" It wasn't quite true, although we had found out about Lord Farnsworth's mistress that way. But Matt was right; gossip was the great social leveler. Everyone exchanged it, and everyone was, at one point or other, the topic of it, no matter their standing within society.

Mr. Landers sniffed. "The servants tattle."

"That's unfair," his wife scolded. "Our Wentworth is very discreet. He wouldn't share any of my secrets. Not for a thousand pounds."

"Do you have many, Mrs. Landers?" Mrs. Delancey asked. "Secrets, that is."

Mrs. Landers laughed, as did Mrs. Delancey, but no one failed to notice that she didn't answer the question.

As if he heard his name, the butler—a youthful fellow compared to the other butlers I'd encountered—entered and introduced the dandy with him as Lord Farnsworth.

Farnsworth surveyed the room with a broad, somewhat foolish grin. "What have I missed?"

Mrs. Landers greeted her latest guest, kissing him on both cheeks in the French way. "Do come in and meet our honored guests. We have three magicians in attendance tonight. Can you believe it? Three!"

Lord Farnsworth took her hand and rested it on his arm. "Lead me to 'em, dear lady."

The butler caught Mrs. Landers' attention with a mere shift of his stance. He arched a brow ever so slightly. She gave a single nod, and he bowed. She walked off and as he straightened, his gaze lingered on her, unwavering. He didn't depart until she joined Fabian.

According to Willie's informant among the staff, the butler was devoted to Mrs. Landers. He had been her family's footman and gained the promotion when she married Mr. Landers a year ago. That accounted for his youth. I'd never met a footman older than mid-thirties. This butler appeared to be about that age. It was still considerably older than Mrs. Landers, who couldn't have been more than twenty-two or three. She seemed to attract the attention of much older men.

I glanced at Mr. Landers. If he noticed the butler's interest in his wife, he didn't show it. He too was mid-thirties, although he wasn't aging well compared to the rather dashing butler.

Mrs. Landers steered Lord Farnsworth toward Matt and me. He was short and slim with ginger-blond hair parted down the middle. He smelled of lavender and musk and wore diamond cufflinks.

"This is Mrs. Glass, the watch magician," Mrs. Landers announced. "And her husband."

Lord Farnsworth took my hand and bowed over it. "What a delight to finally meet you, Mrs. Glass. I've heard so much about you from my friends. You're a lucky fellow, sir," he said to Matt.

"Quite," Matt said.

"I was just telling Farnsworth that he missed out on the news about the coronet," Mrs. Landers said.

"Dreadful shame, that," Lord Farnsworth said.

"What is?" Matt asked.

"The theft. Now it'll be some years before it comes up for sale on the magic market."

"Magic market?" I echoed.

"The trading market for magic objects." Lord Farnsworth indicated the room full of people from the club. "I can't imagine anyone with a stolen artifact in their collection will be too keen to show it off, even in private company. The jealousy will send anyone who catches wind of its whereabouts to the police in two shakes."

"Ah, but to *own* such a thing," Mrs. Landers said. "Wouldn't that be wonderful? There would be no need to sell it in a hurry. No need at all. One could keep it for decades under lock and key."

Lord Farnsworth pushed out his bottom lip as he considered her words.

"Not that anyone here is a thief," Mrs. Landers added emphatically. "I've already told Mr. Glass to look elsewhere for his suspects."

"The common classes," Lord Farnsworth muttered. "Can't trust a single one of 'em. I'm curious, though. Who was the fellow who owned it?"

"They won't say," Mrs. Landers said. "Mr. Glass doesn't want to divulge who the scandal is about." She leaned closer to Lord Farnsworth, and said in a loud, conspiratorial whisper, "How do you think we can get it out of them?"

"Blackmail."

Mrs. Landers laughed, which in turn made Lord Farnsworth laugh. The topic was abandoned and Farnsworth chatted to Matt about horses and gambling. It quickly became obvious that he was obsessed with both.

That gave me an idea. "Do you play poker, my lord?" I asked.

"Can't say I've tried it yet. You play, Glass?"

"I used to, back home," Matt said.

"And where is home?"

Matt hesitated, his head tilted a little to the side. "America," he said with a smile. A smile that I knew to be false. He thought Farnsworth a nitwit, but I doubted Lord Farnsworth realized.

"So you came here to marry one of our magicians, eh?" Lord Farnsworth winked at me. "Don't you have them in America?"

"None of India's quality," Matt said without missing a beat.

"Indeed. I believe she's very powerful."

"Speaking of wives," Mrs. Landers said, "that's what you need, Farnsworth. Tell him about the wonderful state of marriage, Mr. Glass. Tell him how a wife can bring him joy."

Lord Farnsworth's lips twitched as he tried to contain a smile. "I have quite a bit of joy in my life already."

Mrs. Landers blinked innocently back at him. "A wife will cure you of your need to seek joy elsewhere."

Lord Farnsworth and Matt went quite still.

She suddenly seemed to become conscious of the weighty silence.

"Cure you of going to gambling dens," I said. "That's what Mrs. Landers means."

"Yes," she said with a nervous little laugh. "That's what I meant."

Lord Farnsworth patted her hand, still resting on his forearm. "As it happens, I am on the hunt for the future Lady Farnsworth. Can't put it off any longer. An heir must be got and all that. I think I'd like being a father. I'll teach the lad how to pick a good foal from bad." He thrust out his chin in an attempt to make it appear more prominent, and failed. It was a very weak chin.

"Mr. Glass, you have eligible cousins, don't you?" Mrs. Landers asked. "Lord Rycroft's three daughters," she said to Lord Farnsworth.

I glanced toward Lord Coyle, expecting him to march over and declare that Hope wasn't a consideration as she belonged to him. But he was too far away to overhear our conversation.

"The eldest is recently married," Matt said. "The middle one is available, but I must warn you, she's odd. And the youngest is currently considering a proposal which I think she will accept."

Somehow, I refrained from glaring at him. It wasn't fair to cut off potential suitors yet. Hope hadn't given Coyle an answer.

"What a pity," Mrs. Landers said.

"How odd is the middle one?" Lord Farnsworth asked. "Absolutely barking or just a little soft in the head? I don't mind if she's not all there. I'm used to it. My mother thought fairies lived in the garden. She would leave little confections out for them by the lily pond. She fell in once. Had to be fished out by the gardener. We didn't let her out without a strong footman in tow after that."

"Something tells me you two might get along," Matt said, smiling.

I was beginning to agree. It was almost impossible to imagine this man with Angelique L'Amour. She could run rings around him with her intoxicating laugh, her beauty and grace. I supposed a courtesan must take her employers where she could, but this man was ridiculous. How she must long for someone more worthy. No wonder she jumped at the chance to have a clandestine rendezvous with Willie.

Lord Farnsworth wagged his finger at Matt, a slow smile creeping across his lips. "Speaking of families, I just had a thought. You're investigating the theft of the coronet, presumably on behalf of the owner. And who is most likely to ask someone of your caliber to investigate? Who would share such private, scandalous information about their illegitimacy?"

"A family member," Mrs. Landers said on a breath. Her eyes lit up. "It must be Lord Rycroft!"

Lord Farnsworth tapped his chin. "Not necessarily. Who did the older cousin marry?"

My heart sank but I kept calm and smiled benignly.

Mrs. Landers gasped. "Lord Cox!" She turned to Lord Farnsworth. "I know nothing about him. Do you?"

"Quiet chap," he said. "Doesn't own racehorses."

"It's not him," Matt said.

Lord Farnsworth tapped the side of his nose. "Course not." He winked. "We won't say a word."

"Mr. Landers!" Mrs. Landers called.

Her husband looked over at her, a little irritated at the loud interruption to his conversation with Sir Charles.

"We know who owned the coronet that was stolen," she said.

"It's not him," Matt said again.

She signaled for her husband to join her. The drawing room had gone quiet, all eyes on us. I felt cold through to my bones. How had this spiraled out of control so quickly?

"Who is it?" Mrs. Rotherhide asked, taking a step closer.

"It's a family member of Mr. Glass's," Mrs. Landers said with a superior air. "Most likely Lord Cox."

The collective gasp sucked all the air out of the room. Immediately, the murmurs began. Who was Lord Cox? How was he connected to Matt? Was he really illegitimate? Would he lose everything?

It was heart-breaking. We'd come here to gather information on the theft of the coronet, and we were going to leave a trail of destruction behind.

CHAPTER 11

"It's not Cox!" Matt snapped.

Lord Farnsworth grinned. This was just a game to him, and to Mrs. Landers too. The silly fools didn't care that they were ruining a good man's reputation. It was just gossip, a way to pass the evening. It was sickening.

"You doth protest too much," Lord Farnsworth chided. "So it must be him."

"I did not say it was him," Matt ground out.

Lord Farnsworth put on a serious air. "Your conscience is clear, Glass. If he ever asks me, I will assure the fellow you defended his honor to the bitter end."

"The poor man," Mrs. Landers said. "And his poor wife. She won't be able to enter decent society ever again. What will become of them? Where will they go?"

"Listen to me!" Matt snapped. "It is not Lord Cox."

"Tosh." Lord Farnsworth waved his hand. "It's all right, Glass. Your secret will not go beyond these walls."

Matt seethed. I could feel the anger vibrating off him. One more word from Farnsworth and the idiot lord might find himself at the end of Matt's fist. And that would only add fuel to the fire. The more Matt defended Lord Cox, the less Farnsworth and Mrs. Landers believed him.

The bang of Lord Coyle's walking stick into the floor silenced the whispers. We all turned toward him. "Glass is speaking the truth. I know who that article is about and it's not Cox. If I hear another word against him tonight or any day after this, I will personally seek out the rumormonger and cast him or her out of the club and spread my own rumors about them, true or not. If you think I am not serious, then by all means test me. I have more influence in this city than any of you will ever have, and my word is believed." He folded his hands over the top of his walking stick. "Have I made myself clear?"

Heads bobbed in a series of nods. Mrs. Landers let go of Lord Farnsworth's arm and clung to her husband's instead. Lord Farnsworth paled beneath the glare of Lord Coyle.

"Course it's not Cox," he said with forced cheerfulness. "I hear he's a fine fellow. Very upright. Solid stock, the Coxes. First rate pedigree."

A deafening silence filled the drawing room, broken only by the shuffling of feet and clearing of throats.

Mrs. Landers' forced smile stretched thin as she surveyed the sea of shame-faced guests. With every passing moment, she seemed to grow smaller, her eyes filling with panic as she realized her party was becoming a hostess's worst nightmare—a failure. She was too inexperienced to dig her way out of it. All she could do was stare at the door, as if willing the butler to enter with refreshments and rescue her. But it was too early for supper.

It was Mr. Landers who finally broke the silence with a clap of his hands. "Shall we look at your collection, my dear?"

"Yes!" she cried with relief. "An excellent notion. Mrs. Glass, you sit there, in the front as our honored guest. Everyone else, take a seat please."

I sat where indicated, Matt beside me, while the other guests chose a place in one of the three rows.

"This is exciting," said Mrs. Rotherhide, seated on my other side. "It's been over a year since we saw Mrs. Landers' collection. It was quite small at that point. She's been collecting aggressively since and claims to have some marvelous pieces now. I'm particularly looking forward to seeing the little drummer boy she bought from a magician toymaker last month."

Mrs. Landers stood beside the cabinet and waited as everyone settled. An eager smile had returned to her face, the gossip and Lord Coyle's admonishment already forgotten.

Once everyone was seated, she put out her hand to her husband. He removed a chain with a key attached from his pocket and handed it to her. She unlocked the cabinet, stepped aside, and opened the cabinet door.

The audience leaned forward to get a better look. Several objects were arranged across two shelves. The little toy drummer took pride of place on the top shelf at the front.

"I can't see," a woman behind me said. "It's too dark."

"Then I shall bring them out for you." Mrs. Landers removed a small wooden box without a lid and handed it to me. The silk cloth inside was trimmed with the most intricate, delicate silk birds in flight while the varying shades of white and blue background made it look like they were flying through fluffy clouds.

"It's exquisite," I said.

"Touch it, Mrs. Glass," Mrs. Landers said. "Feel the magic."

I touched the handkerchief. A throbbing warmth spread up my fingers. The magic in it must be quite new. I wondered if the magician could make it fly, then I remembered Abigail Pilcher, the former nun and silk magician. According to Abigail, she was simply able to work silk quicker than anyone else, and turn it into the most beautiful creations. Perhaps she'd made this.

"May I?" asked Mrs. Rotherhide.

I passed the box to her.

"No!" Mrs. Landers cried as Mrs. Rotherhide fingered the silk. "Only Mrs. Glass can touch, to vouch for the strength of the magic. I do apologize, but those are my rules."

"Quite understandable," Mrs. Rotherhide said.

"Tosh," Mrs. Delancey said from behind us. "If one can't touch the items, what is the point?"

"To see them, of course," Mrs. Landers said.

"You keep them locked away in that cabinet," Mrs. Delancey pointed out.

"I bring them out on occasions such as these."

Mr. Delancey looked over Mrs. Rotherhide's shoulder at the box. "Are you open to offers?"

"No," Mrs. Landers said. "Perhaps one day, but not now. Most of these things are new to me, and I want to possess them for a while yet." She reached into the cabinet and pulled out a plate with a slice of white bread on it.

"Bread?" I asked accepting the plate from her.

"It's four months old," Mrs. Landers said. "And look, not a speck of mold on it. The baker said the magic will last six months before the mold will set in, but I'll keep it until then. I'm very pleased to be able to share that one with you, Mrs. Glass."

"You lucky thing," Matt muttered beside me.

Mrs. Landers stabbed him with a sharp glare.

I went to pass the plate to Mrs. Rotherhide, but Mrs. Landers wouldn't let me. "Touch it first, Mrs. Glass, then pass the plate around."

I dutifully touched the crust. It was a little warm, but not overmuch. I handed the plate to Mrs. Rotherhide.

"It's not my sort of thing." She passed it on to Lord Coyle beside her.

"Good lord," I thought I heard Louisa mutter from two rows back.

Mrs. Landers handed me a small wooden wren on an olive branch next. It was quite lovely and she presented it to me with all the reverence of a maid handing the queen her crown. I was not allowed to pass it on, since it did not come on a plate or in a box.

She continued to produce items from the cabinet, and one by

one, I touched them. All held varying degrees of magical warmth. None were the coronet, although I knew she wouldn't hide it in there if she'd been the one to steal it. She might be silly but she wasn't that much of a fool.

Finally, she came to the last item, the little toy boy dressed in a soldier's uniform, a drum slung over his shoulder. At first I thought it was made of wood, then I realized the arms and legs were metal. She turned the key at the back and wound up the mechanism inside then set it on top of the cabinet. The toy's legs moved up and down, marching, and the arms rose and fell, banging the drumsticks on the drum. Most remarkably, the toy actually moved forward. The legs didn't just go up and down, they gave the drummer momentum.

"Remarkable," said one of the guests.

"The tune's a little off," said another. "Is it supposed to be God Save the Queen?"

"It's nothing like God Save the Queen," said Mrs. Delancey. "What is it, Mrs. Landers?"

"I'm not quite sure," Mrs. Landers said, catching the toy before it marched off the cabinet.

"It doesn't march in time to the beat," said Mrs. Rotherhide, sounding disappointed.

"But it does march splendidly. The legs get so high. Here, Mrs. Glass, tell me what you think. How strong is the magic?" Mrs. Landers handed it to me. "I bought it just last month off a fellow."

"Who?" Lord Coyle asked.

"No one you know," Mrs. Landers said, cheekily.

"You mean he's not officially on our list of magicians?" Mr. Delancey asked.

"Then you must add him," Mrs. Delancey declared.

"Perhaps she wants to keep the name to herself to ensure his prices are kept low," Lord Farnsworth said.

Mrs. Landers just smiled at them all then turned to me. "Well, Mrs. Glass? What do you think?"

"It's well made," I said. "The face is particularly fine. But I'm afraid it's not magical." I handed the toy back to her.

She stared at me. "Of course it is." She pressed the toy into my hands. "Touch it again."

I cradled the drummer boy for a moment then shook my head. "There's no magic warmth in it. I am sorry."

She fondled the diamond pendant at her throat. "That can't be! I bought it from a toy maker in Bond Street. He has very fine pieces."

"Unless he's on our list, he's not a magician," Lord Coyle said.

Mr. Landers stepped up alongside his wife. "There must be dozens of magicians not on your list, Coyle. Most are in hiding, like Mrs. Glass. If my wife says she bought this toy from a magician, then he was a magician."

"He could have lied to her," Mrs. Rotherhide said sympathetically. "Never mind, dear, it has happened to many of us."

Mrs. Landers blinked back tears and her chest rose and fell with her rapid, ragged breathing. She turned watery eyes to the back of the room. I followed her gaze and spotted the butler, standing with his back to the door.

"Refreshments will be served," he said smoothly. "If you could all make your way to the supper room."

It was the hostess's duty to make the announcement, but Mrs. Landers didn't seem in any state to do it. Even so, the butler should have remained quiet. Indeed, the refreshments hadn't yet arrived.

Although we all followed his orders, it was another four minutes before the train of footmen brought in champagne, hot chocolate, tea, lemonade, sandwiches, sugared fruit, and cake on silver platters.

Matt and I were separated. He was cornered by Mr. Delancey and two of his friends, while I was surrounded by Mrs. Delancey, Louisa, Mrs. Rotherhide, Lord Farnsworth and two others. They peppered me with questions while Mrs. Delancey and Mrs. Rotherhide made sure my plate was always full and my champagne glass exchanged with another as soon as it was empty.

Louisa was the only one not paying me much attention. She was distracted by Fabian and Oscar, talking quietly alone in the far corner. Sir Charles joined them and she soon peeled away and wandered over there too.

"Poor Mrs. Landers," Mrs. Delancey whispered. "She looks quite upset by your discovery, Mrs. Glass."

Mrs. Landers did indeed seem upset. She finished her second glass of champagne and immediately reached for another. Her husband spoke quietly to her, but upon her fierce glare, he moved off. She stood alone, fussing over the refreshments, moving platters back and forth and rearranging the sandwiches. She looked in despair.

"What do you know about her?" I asked.

"Not a great deal," Mrs. Rotherhide said. "She comes from money and married into money. Her family only came to London that one season to find her a husband. She succeeded and they returned to the country, never to be seen again."

"She's quite a little doll," said Lord Farnsworth. "Wish I'd beaten Landers to the punch, but I wasn't attending balls back then. Too busy with other things and not interested in marriage."

"I doubt she would have been interested in you," Mrs. Rotherhide said.

Lord Farnsworth looked offended. "Why not?"

"Too young." She winked and he laughed.

"Very true, Mrs. R, very true."

"How did her family make their fortune?" I asked.

"Trade, I s'pose," Lord Farnsworth said with disinterest.

"What sort of trade?"

He shrugged. "Finance?"

Mrs. Delancey shook her head. "Her husband is in finance, but her family isn't, or they would be in London more often." She leaned in. "India, are you suggesting they're magicians and made their fortune in manufacturing?"

"It's possible," I said. "It would explain her interest in magical objects."

"It would also explain how she knows about magic in the first place," Mrs. Rotherhide said.

"How did you become interested in magical collections?" I asked her.

"My husband was a collector. I took over his collection after he died, but I haven't added to it."

"Mrs. R doesn't see the value in trading," Lord Farnsworth explained. "Neither does Lord Coyle. They both hoard. Mr. and Mrs. D, and most others in the club, will trade if the price is right."

Mrs. Rotherhide smiled sadly. "I simply haven't got the inclination since my husband died. Perhaps one day."

"Let me know when that day comes," Lord Farnsworth said, quite seriously.

"Do you display your collectibles for all to see?" I asked Mrs. Rotherhide. "Or do you keep them in a locked cabinet like Mrs. Landers?"

"In a trunk in the attic with my husband's things."

"The attic!" Mrs. Delancey cried.

"Negligent," Lord Farnsworth muttered into his cup of chocolate.

"And what about you, my lord?" I asked him. "Are yours on display?"

"Also locked away. Got to keep 'em safe. Can't trust the maids not to knock 'em off their perches."

"Tosh," Mrs. Delancey said. "Don't employ clumsy maids."

"Do you trade frequently?" I asked him.

"Certainly. I'm a gambler, you see. Horses, cards, company stocks, art and collectibles. But I keep it all locked up somewhere safe. The collection only comes out when I want to trade. Don't want a thief coming in and stealing it, like poor old Lord —whoever."

"Quite right," Mrs. Rotherhide said. "You ought to be careful,

Mrs. Delancey. You wouldn't want the same thing to happen to one of your pieces."

Mrs. Delancey waved a hand. "Our house is very secure and our butler has excellent hearing. There's no possibility of someone sneaking in at night when he's on duty."

I sipped my champagne and watched Mrs. Landers again as she drained her third glass. Her husband ought to stop her. She'd begun to sway.

But Mr. Landers was paying her no attention, caught up in conversation as he was with Sir Charles Whittaker.

"What about Sir Charles?" I asked my companions. "Does he like to trade his collection?"

"Hoarder," Lord Farnsworth declared.

Mrs. Delancey agreed. "I've never seen it."

"He only has two items," Mrs. Rotherhide said. "A wooden statue of a dog and a cast iron candlestick. He doesn't hide them. The candlestick even had a half-burned candle in it. It was some months ago when he showed them to me in his parlor. He might have added to his collection since then."

Lord Farnsworth waggled his pale eyebrows. "Some months ago, eh? Why have you seen his collection and not the rest of us? What makes you so special?"

Mrs. Rotherhide sipped her champagne, ignoring him.

Mrs. Landers suddenly swayed rather violently. She caught herself on the edge of the table, thankfully. No one seemed to notice.

I made my excuses and joined her. "Are you all right?" I asked.

She gazed in my direction but didn't appear to see me. "Mrs. Glass?" Her words slurred. "Mrs. Glass, how kind of you to come tonight." She hiccupped then swayed again.

"I think you should sit down."

"Not here." She looked around. "They all pity me. They think me stupid. Even my husband." Her lower lip wobbled. "I want to go home."

She was on the verge of tears and people were beginning to stare. I had to get her out. "Will you walk with me to the ladies' dressing room?" I asked.

She nodded and took an uncertain step. I clasped her hand tightly. She gave me a wobbly smile and took another step forward.

"Are you from a magical family?" I asked as we headed out.

"No. Why?"

"I was curious about your interest in collecting magical objects. Your husband doesn't seem all that keen."

"It's my hobby. I was in love with a carpenter magician back home." She sighed. "I wasn't allowed to marry him, though. He was too poor. He didn't use his magic to enhance his woodwork. It was something he kept for himself and his loved ones." She smiled wistfully. "Shhh. Don't tell my husband."

"The carpenter carved that little wren for you, didn't he?"

"Isn't it lovely?" Her eyes filled with tears. "It's all I have of him. All I'll ever have. I was made to marry Mr. Landers, which I know is for my own good and I don't regret it. Truly, I don't. He indulges me, and puts up with my silliness. What more can a wife ask for?"

I thought it best not to add to her woes by telling her my opinion of marriage was the opposite. She was very close to bursting into tears already. "May I ask how your father made his fortune?" It was a terribly crass question. Aunt Letitia would be horrified.

But Mrs. Landers either didn't mind or was too drunk to care. "The railway. He speculated at the right time."

That solved that mystery.

We reached the door to the dressing room, flanked by potted palms. The butler hovered nearby, watching us. Or rather, watching Mrs. Landers.

"Why did you have to tell everyone?" she whined. "Couldn't you have waited until we were alone?"

I wondered when she'd remember and blame me for her

failed party. It was time to make my excuses. "I am sorry," I said. "You're right, I should have waited until we were alone to tell you about the toy drummer."

"Everything is ruined. I hate it here. I want to go home." She burst into tears.

I stepped toward her to comfort her, but the butler pushed me out of the way. He took her into his arms and she sobbed into his chest.

"Wentworth," she gasped out. "Oh, Wentworth, if it weren't for you, London would be unbearable."

I shouldn't listen to their private exchange. It wasn't kind to take advantage of Mrs. Landers in her inebriated state. I disappeared into the dressing room but put my ear to the door. It might be unkind, but eavesdropping was a necessary evil of investigative work.

"Don't cry, little one," the butler said in deep, sonorous tones. "I'll take care of you. Of everything." After a pause, he added, "I have something that will make you feel better."

"A present?" she asked weakly.

"A fine present. I'll show it to you later, but only if you dry your tears now. Good girl."

"What is it?" she asked. "What's my present?"

"Ah, now, I can't tell you or it won't be special. Meet me in your sitting room after everyone has gone. I'll give it to you then. Now, dash away your tears and join your guests. And stop drinking the champagne. Give me a smile. There's my pretty girl. Off you go and don't let them see you upset. "

I raced away from the door and just managed to slip behind a privacy screen before Mrs. Landers entered. She hummed through her ablutions then left again. Either she'd forgotten I was there or was pretending to forget.

I opened the door and checked the vicinity before leaving. As I closed the door behind me, I glanced at the staircase. Could the butler's gift be the coronet, stolen to win her affection? He was in love with her, that much was clear. And while she seemed to be fond of him, it was more of a daughter's fondness for a father figure. He might hope to win her over with a special gift, and nothing could be more special for Mrs. Landers than the magical golden coronet.

It must be hidden somewhere, but I couldn't bring myself to race up the stairs and search his room for it. The servants might all be busy downstairs, but it was too risky. I didn't know which room was his, anyway.

I re-entered the drawing room and joined Matt as he spoke with Lord Farnsworth. Soon after my arrival, guests began to leave. They left in great numbers, even though it wasn't late. Mrs. Landers plastered a smile to her face, but she must feel the slight keenly.

It was all my fault. She was right. I should not have told everyone her toy drummer held no magic.

Matt and I gave our leave, as did Lord Farnsworth. As we waited for our carriages to arrive, he tapped Matt on the arm.

"Don't s'pose you could put in a good word about me to your mad cousin, eh, Glass?"

Matt waited for more, or perhaps for Lord Farnsworth to admit he was joking, but Lord Farnsworth merely smiled back at him. "If you wish," Matt finally said.

Our carriage arrived and we climbed in. Lord Farnsworth saluted as we drove away. "Do you think he's serious?" Matt asked.

"He seems so," I said. "He wasn't laughing."

"I've met some odd people over the years," Matt said. "I'm even related to some. But he's got me baffled."

"He's just a cheerful idiot."

"How has he managed to keep his fortune? Cheerful idiots usually gamble it all away or get swindled. By all accounts, he's doing all right for himself."

"Well enough to keep a courtesan."

"I asked him about his coachman," Matt said. "I told him I was looking for a new one and heard he'd just dismissed a fellow. I lamented the difficulty of finding reliable staff and he lamented the difficulty of finding discreet servants. He said he dismissed the coachman for not keeping his mouth shut about Farnsworth's private business."

"A visit to Lord Cox's in the middle of the night, perhaps?"

We discussed the evening all the way home, and both came to the same conclusion. Aside from being a very strange night, we'd learned a little but not quite enough to narrow down our list of suspects. Neither of us could draw any definite conclusions. At least we had some ideas for where the coronet might be.

Upon our return home, Matt sent Bristow to bed and we stayed up with Duke in the sitting room. We were about to tell him everything we'd learned when Willie arrived.

"I was with Angelique again," she said, pouring herself a whiskey from the drinks trolley.

"You didn't get arrested this time," Duke noted.

She smacked the top of his head as she passed him. "We got a room at a hotel near Kings Cross. She had to get back to her apartment, on account of Lord Farnsworth was planning to meet her at midnight after the Landers' party. Find out anything?" she asked.

"Quite a bit," I said. "All of our suspects were there. Your Mrs. Rotherhide was the nicest person in the room, Duke."

He smiled. "I reckon I'll visit her tomorrow night."

"Don't get all soft on her, Duke," Willie said. "I know you, and you're the sort that falls in love with every woman you been with, and some you ain't."

"Do not," he muttered into his glass.

"She's a society lady, and you ain't got two bob to your name. You can't offer her anything."

"Can't I?" he said with a dimpled smile.

She rolled her eyes. "You know what I mean."

"It's just a bit of fun, Willie. You mind your business, and let me mind mine."

"Fine." She drained her glass and got up to refill it. "So you don't reckon it's Mrs. Rotherhide who stole the coronet?"

"She doesn't strike me as a thief," I said. "But my instincts haven't always proven reliable in the past, so I'll keep an open mind. What I did learn was that she keeps her magic collection in the attic. She never gets it out to show anyone. If she did steal the coronet, she probably stored it in there with the other pieces."

Willie pointed her glass at Duke. "So all you got to do is look around the attic."

"I ain't doing that. She trusts me."

"See! I knew you'd get all soft. She's your target, Duke. Investigation first, fun later."

Duke's shoulders slouched. "I don't want to betray her. I like her, and I don't think she did it anyway."

"Willie's right," Matt said. "If you get the opportunity to look in the attic, you should take it."

Willie shot Duke a triumphant look. He scowled back at her.

"On the other hand," Matt went on, "you most likely won't get the opportunity. There are too many servants, all of whom will live in the attic rooms. Sneaking around will be impossible."

"Aye," Duke said, nodding.

"Soft," Willie muttered as she resumed her seat.

"As to our other suspects," I said, "both Lord Farnsworth and Mrs. Landers seem very likely candidates. Or I should say, the Landers' butler." I told them how Wentworth seemed to be in love with her and had promised Mrs. Landers a special gift. "It could be the coronet," I finished. "He could have stolen it for her, as a love token."

"And you reckon *I'm* deluded," Duke said to Willie with a shake of his head. "Mrs. Landers ain't going to leave a comfortable life to run off with the butler."

"I don't think she's in love with him," I said. "It's more likely she relies on him, as a girl relies on her father. I'd say she has done so for much of her life."

"He's definitely a suspect now," Matt said. "But I don't see how we can find out if the gift he gave her is the coronet."

We fell into silence, each of us considering how we could learn more. I discarded every idea that came to me as being too risky.

"What about Farnsworth?" Duke asked. "You said he's still a suspect, India."

"Despite being one of the silliest men I've met," I said, "we can't rule him out. He seems to have a knack for gambling and trading. He'd know the value of a magical golden coronet the moment he read about it. The problem is, we don't know where he keeps his magical items."

"Hopefully Cyclops will have some news on that front," Matt said.

Willie tapped her finger against the tumbler, frowning, "What I want to know is, how did any of them find out Lord Cox had the coronet in the first place? The article didn't name him."

She was right. If we learned that, we'd learn the key to the mystery.

Matt suddenly sat forward. "If I were a collector of magic artifacts and I read that article, the first thing I'd do is approach the newspaper and bribe someone into telling me who gave them the information. That'll lead them straight to Longmire."

"You're suggesting we do the same," I said. "Only we'll ask the columnist the identity of the person who approached him."

He raised his glass in salute. "We'll visit the office of the newspaper tomorrow. India, shall we retire?"

I finished my sherry and rose.

"One more thing," Duke said. "What about Whittaker? Is he still a suspect?"

"Unlikely," I said. "For one thing, you and Matt had a good look around his place and found nothing. For another, Mrs. Rotherhide says he only has two magical items, a wooden statue of a dog and a cast iron candlestick. He leaves them out in the parlor. He doesn't sound like a serious collector and I suspect only a serious collector would steal the coronet."

"He and Mrs. Delancey didn't speak to one another," Matt pointed out to me as we left.

"Guilt, perhaps?" I asked. "Over their affair?"

"Guilt over something. Or a disagreement."

* * *

A LETTER from Lord Coyle arrived in the first post before we left the house. It was addressed to both Matt and me, and got straight to the point.

"'My protection of Cox's reputation was done for Hope, no one else,'" Matt read as we put on jackets and coats. "'It comes at a price. You know what that price is. The clock is ticking.'"

"Clock," I muttered as I buttoned my jacket over my dress. "He didn't give us a time for a deadline, just a day. Clocks have nothing to do with it. By my calculation, there are five more days for Hope to accept. Yes, I know I'm being pedantic." I clicked my tongue as I struggled with a too-tight button.

Matt gently pried my fingers off it. "Allow me. You're all thumbs this morning."

"Coyle's letter has rattled me. What shall we do, Matt?"

"We'll speak to Hope again."

"But it's Coyle!"

He finished the task and gently caught my chin. His warm gaze held mine, instantly calming my frayed nerves. "It will all work out, India. You'll see."

He sounded so confident, so composed, yet nothing was resolved. Coyle wanted an answer by Thursday or my debt would not be wiped, Hope hadn't made up her mind and didn't seem likely to before then, and I felt ill just thinking about encouraging her to accept him.

Matt kissed my forehead and drew me into his arms. I relaxed against his chest with a sigh. Worrying would resolve nothing. We should take action. The problem was, what action should we take?

CHAPTER 12

Being a Saturday, only a skeleton staff was in the offices of *The Daily Courier*. Fortunately one of them was the editor, Mr. Diamond, who was well acquainted with the gossip piece in question.

"We'd like to speak to the author of the article," Matt said. "Is he in today?"

"Or she?" I asked.

Mr. Diamond heaved a sigh that seemed to deflate his entire body, quite a feat considering he was a robust man whose girth didn't allow him to sit too close to the desk. "Another one," he muttered. "If I charged a shilling for each of you who asks, I'd be a rich man. No, you cannot speak to him," he said with exaggerated patience. "He doesn't know who the lord mentioned in the article is. His source didn't say."

"You don't understand," Matt said. "We don't care who the lord is. We want to know if someone successfully bribed the information out of him."

Mr. Diamond sat back and regarded us properly. "We don't accept bribes here."

"Perhaps it was a donation to the charity of his choice." Matt removed a bank note from his pocket. "Or was it your choice, Mr. Diamond?"

The editor's chair creaked with the shifting of his weight. He took the money from Matt and indicated we should sit with a wave of his ink-stained hand. He slipped the money into the top drawer of his desk and regarded us with his hands clasped over his stomach.

"How did you know I wrote it?" he asked.

"It was a guess," Matt said. "Having seen how newspapers work back home, I suspected there was no dedicated gossip columnist."

Mr. Diamond grunted. "So you don't want to know who the lord is? I must say, that's different to every other Tom, Dick and Harry who's strolled into my office since the article was printed."

"Have there been many enquirers?" I asked.

"A half dozen or so."

"Did any succeed in getting the information out of you?" Matt asked.

Mr. Diamond stroked the sparse whiskers sprouting along his jawline. "I told you, the source didn't say."

"Come now," Matt said. "There's no need to feign ignorance. We already know it's Lord Cox."

Mr. Diamond sucked air between his teeth as if we'd pressed on an open wound.

"We've been employed by Cox to help him track down who is spreading the malicious gossip. So tell us, Mr. Diamond, did someone succeed in getting his name from you?"

"One." Mr. Diamond leaned forward and pressed his palms flat on the desk. "You must understand, I didn't do it for money. I did it because he threatened me. He said he'd hurt my family."

I gasped. "Did you go to the police?"

"There's nothing they could do. I didn't see who made the threats, you see, and he left behind no evidence except for a handwritten note. I gave him the information he wanted, of course. I had to. I was scared."

"If you didn't see who left the note, who did you give Lord Cox's name to?" Matt said.

"I placed it between the pages of a book and left the book on a bench in Hyde Park, just as the note demanded. I watched from afar for a while, but whoever picked it up was very discreet. I never saw them." He looked to the ceiling and blew out a breath. "I'm relieved nothing has come of my indiscretion. I've been worried one of the other papers would report the lord's name."

"You thought it was a rival newspaperman?"

"It crossed my mind. But it was a few days ago, so now... I'm no longer sure." He frowned. "If you want to tell Cox who spread the gossip, why don't you want to know who gave me the information in the first place?"

"It's too late to stop him," Matt said. "We want to stem the flow of further leaks."

Mr. Diamond's jowls shook as he hastily reassured us, again, that he was blackmailed, that he was afraid for his family's safety. "Otherwise I'd never divulge such sensitive information. Our gossip pages are very popular, but I admit to being conflicted as to whether to write the stuff that comes across my desk sometimes."

"This one was too good to pass up?" I asked snidely.

He swallowed and looked down at the desk. "I'm relieved you don't want to know who gave me the damning information about Lord Cox. If it gets out that we don't protect our sources, then those sources would dry up."

Matt gave him a flat smile as reassurance. "Is there anything you can tell us about the person who blackmailed you? Anything at all?"

Mr. Diamond shrugged. "I think the note was written by a man. The handwriting was firm and bold."

"Who delivered the threatening note to you?" I asked. "One of your staff?"

"That's the thing. None claimed to have done it. The blackmailer must have delivered it himself. It was a busy time of day, just as we finalize for the overnight print run, ready for the morning's distribution. Everyone gets in each other's way. It's chaos. I stepped out of my office for a few minutes to speak to the head compositor. When I got back, the note was right here." He stabbed a finger in the middle of his desk.

"It must have been Monday," Matt said. "What time?"

"That's right, it was Monday. About a quarter past six."

We thanked him and left. Matt assisted me into the carriage then gave Woodall instructions to drive to Mr. Longmire's address.

"Why are we visiting him again?" I asked as the coach jerked forward.

"I want to make sure he stopped sending out those threatening letters to magicians."

"Surely the beating put an end to that."

"Longmire didn't strike me as someone who'd bow to threats."

"They could have killed him!"

"If they wanted to kill him, they could have done so." He took my hand. "You don't have to come in if you'd rather avoid him."

"It's not that. It's just…I don't like him, and I prefer not to give people like that the time of day. The more attention we give him, the more inflated his sense of self-worth becomes."

"Then we'll make the visit short."

* * *

As it turned out, Mr. Longmire was not at home. His valet, Mr. Harker, agreed to speak with us. He moved the newspaper and teacup off the table and invited us to sit.

"We won't be long," Matt said, remaining standing while I sat. "We'd hoped to speak with Mr. Longmire, but perhaps you can help." He placed some coins on the table.

Mr. Harker covered them with the newspaper. *The Times* was

opened to the advertisement page for domestic servants. "I'd be more than happy to assist you, Mr. Glass. What is it you'd like to know?"

"Does your employer still sneak out at night?"

Mr. Harker nodded. "I was surprised, after that incident in the alley. I thought he'd be more cautious. But he's not a cautious man."

"Do you know where he goes?"

"No, sir. Walking, I suspect. When he returns, he eases into the chair as if his feet ache."

"I take it there have been no more attacks?"

"Not to that extent, but Mr. Longmire was spat on only yesterday. It wouldn't surprise me if he is attacked again one of these nights."

"Are you worried for yourself, Mr. Harker?" I asked.

"No, madam. The thugs have no issue with me."

I indicated the newspaper. "But you're looking for other employment."

"Not out of fear for myself, you understand. It's the taint of working for a man like Mr. Longmire. I have high standards and —there's no other way to put this—he's crass, uncouth, and a bully." His spine stiffened even more. "I'm a gentleman's gentleman, madam. Emphasis on the first gentleman."

"I understand."

We returned to the carriage and this time Matt asked Woodall to take us home. "That wasn't terribly enlightening," I said as Matt closed the cabin door.

"On the contrary. Longmire is still delivering threatening letters to magicians. I suspect that's where he goes every night, walking around the city and leaving his poison behind at the workshops of successful craftsmen."

I rubbed my forehead where a headache was beginning to bloom. Mr. Longmire had caused nothing but trouble since arriving in London. "We can ask Oscar if he knows of any magicians receiving them."

"Don't bother Barratt," Matt said. "I need to catch Longmire in the act and warn him to stop."

"As much as I have faith in your capabilities, if he's still writing the letters after being beaten up, I doubt he'll stop simply because you order him to."

He removed his glove and rubbed the back of my neck.

I closed my eyes and leaned into him, enjoying the sensation of his hand on my bare skin. "Pampering me will not convince me that trying to catch him in the act is the best thing to do."

He said nothing.

"Neither will ignoring me." I sat up and lightly grasped his chin as he often did to me when he wanted to make sure I was taking him seriously. "Don't follow Longmire in the middle of the night. It's unsafe and quite pointless."

"I disagree."

I narrowed my gaze. "Are you doing it just for the sake of something to do? Is it because sneaking about at night is thrilling?"

"I can think of other thrilling things to do at night time." He waggled his eyebrows and grinned.

I wasn't going to get a straight answer out of him because I was right and he didn't want to admit it. I sighed and rested my head on his shoulder again. "You are *not* going alone."

"Of course not, but you're not coming with me."

"I don't want to. Take Willie. She loves pointless, thrilling tasks, and I feel better knowing one of you is armed."

* * *

After our conversation with Mr. Diamond, we had a very clear path ahead of us—finding out who of our suspects could not be accounted for at a quarter past six on Monday afternoon. Our thief was placing the threatening note on Mr. Diamond's desk at that time.

The problem was, how to question our suspects about their

whereabouts without making it obvious they were a suspect? Willie said she'd speak to the disgruntled Landers' maid about the butler while Duke offered to speak with Mrs. Rotherhide.

"I'll work it into conversation," he said as he drew on his coat in the entrance hall.

Willie snickered. "Before or after you get her into bed?"

"It's the middle of the day!"

"Ain't no rules about when you can do it."

"Some of us prefer to be discreet."

She rolled her eyes.

"Stop it, both of you," I hissed. "You're lucky Aunt Letitia isn't here. She'd be horrified."

"We wouldn't talk like this in front of her," Duke assured me.

Bristow handed Duke his hat, and I was reminded of Mr. Harker seeking alternative employment. Domestic servants were considered to be a reflection of their employers. A respectable, worthy servant wouldn't want to be tainted by a master with a tarnished reputation.

"I do apologize for their behavior, Bristow," I said. "You shouldn't have to put up with it."

"It's quite all right, madam," he said.

"No, it's not. You're the perfect butler with an excellent reputation to uphold and sometimes you must cringe at the vulgarities tossed around in this household."

"Vulgarities?" Willie snorted. "You ain't seen real vulgarity, India. If you did, your toes would curl."

I presented her with my shoulder. "Anyway, we appreciate you and Mrs. Bristow, and the other staff too."

"Thank you, madam." Bristow gave me a small bow then opened the door for Willie and Duke.

Matt, who'd stood silently throughout the exchange with a small smile on his lips, came up to me. "I pay them all very well," he whispered. "They're not going anywhere, no matter how vulgar Willie gets."

"Sir, a carriage is pulling up," Bristow announced. "It's Lord Farnsworth. Are you at home to receive him?"

"Certainly." Matt greeted Lord Farnsworth on the front steps, not because he was eager to see him, but because he wanted to signal to Willie and Duke to speak to Cyclops.

They understood his look and nod without a word exchanged, and waited for Lord Farnsworth to join us inside.

"What a welcome!" Lord Farnsworth declared, striking Matt on the arm with his fist. "You taking over butler duties, eh, Glass?"

"I happened to be standing by the door," Matt said jovially. "Come in, come in."

I'd been about to leave too, to spend the afternoon with Fabian, but decided to delay my departure and see what Lord Farnsworth wanted. Matt invited him into the library, where we wouldn't be disturbed by Aunt Letitia.

Lord Farnsworth went straight to the clock on the mantelpiece. "Does this have your magic in it, Mrs. Glass?"

"I've worked on it," I told him.

He stroked the glass cover over the face. "How much?"

"It's not for sale," Matt said.

"Everything's for sale! Name your price."

"It's not for sale," Matt said again. "My wife is very attached to all the clocks in the house."

I pressed my lips together to suppress my smile as Lord Farnsworth's face fell.

"Ah well, can't blame a chap for trying, eh?"

"Would you like tea, my lord?" I asked.

He waved a hand. The sapphire in the ring on his little finger flashed in the sunlight. "Can't stay. Must dash, people to see. I just wanted to tell you something." He stood with his back to the unlit fireplace, his hands clasped behind him. He looked quite serious. "After the Landers', er, interesting little party, I got to thinking. And then I had a very clever thought. So clever, that I knew I had to share it with you, Glass."

"I'm intrigued," Matt said.

"Of course you are! It's a very intriguing matter, the theft of the coronet, and you, sir, have been trusted with the investigation. I envy you. I'm always up for an intrigue, but alas, I must seek them out. They never find me."

"Your clever thought?" Matt prompted.

"Right, yes." Lord Farnsworth frowned again, all seriousness. "Did you notice when Cox's name came up that someone in that room didn't blink an eye? Not even a single lash! Not that Cox *is* the owner of the coronet—or rather, the owner who may not be the owner because his newfound older brother is the rightful owner. I assure you, I will never mention the poor chap's name in connection to the rumor again. But." He lowered his voice. "Someone showed no shock when Cox's name was mentioned. Indeed, he defended him!"

"You're talking about Coyle," Matt said.

"Don't you think his behavior last night odd?"

"No," Matt said tightly. If Lord Farnsworth continued to walk this path, he'd better know when to stop before Matt threw him out. "Is that all?"

Lord Farnsworth looked from Matt's scowling face to me then back again. "Have I offended you?"

"Not at all," Matt said. "It's just that I thought we put the matter to rest last night. The lord in question is not Cox. He's a good man."

Lord Farnsworth's lower lip protruded as he nodded. "Very well, but I still think Coyle knows who it is. Or perhaps *he* is the thief."

"Perhaps," Matt said.

"You going to confront him?"

"I might."

Lord Farnsworth nodded again. "Good, good. Well then, I'm off. Good afternoon to you both."

"Just a moment," Matt said. "I'm glad you came by today, as I've been thinking about joining a club, but I don't know which one. I visited two today and dropped a few names of gentlemen of my acquaintance. Yours was one. I hope you don't mind."

What was Matt up to? He hated those clubs.

"Course I don't mind! I'd be delighted to nominate you for membership. A first rate chap like yourself *must* belong to a club. There's nothing like it for good company and good food. I often dine there."

"So I was told. Apparently the last time you were there was Monday afternoon."

"Monday? That's odd. I've been there this week but not Monday. Who'd you talk to?"

"The fellow was adamant you were there, but I can't remember his name. Are you sure you weren't?"

"Course I'm sure. I know exactly where I was on Monday afternoon. Checking out the goods at Tattersalls."

"Tattersalls?" Matt asked, even though he knew all about it.

"Blood-stock auctioneers. Best in the country. Carriage horses and off-course betting," he clarified when Matt gave him a blank look. "If you speak to the right people, you can stake an interest in a racer too. I placed some wagers and spotted a fine creature but she went for too much. Never mind. It's always a good day out, Tattersalls."

I smiled to myself. All we had to do now was verify if anyone saw him there.

"You in the market, Glass?" Lord Farnsworth asked.

"I am," Matt said. "But I don't know the local scene here."

"Come with me to Tattersalls. There's another auction this Monday. Meet me at three out the front." He winked. "Bring a bank draft. Now, I must dash. Good day, Mrs. Glass. See you Monday, Glass."

He let himself out of the library and was met in the entrance hall by Bristow, who had to rush to the front door before Lord Farnsworth got to it first. Matt and I watched him leave.

"He doesn't improve on further acquaintance," Matt said. "I

thought he might be different during the day, before imbibing champagne, but it seems he's always an idiot."

"An idiot who's going to show you around Tattersalls where you can verify his whereabouts for last Monday."

* * *

I'D PROMISED Matt I wouldn't wait up for him, but I couldn't help it. I couldn't sleep while he was out following Mr. Longmire. Parts of London were dangerous enough after dark, but Mr. Longmire added a measure of unpredictability to the mix. Unpredictable because Matt didn't know where he was going, who he was meeting, and whether he carried a weapon.

The later the hour, the more I worried. I shouldn't have sent Willie with him. She was too volatile, too quick to draw her gun. But Duke hadn't returned from visiting Mrs. Rotherhide and Cyclops was unavailable.

I sprang up the moment I heard the front door and raced into the entrance hall.

"I need a drink," Willie said, heading to the library.

"Well?" I asked Matt. "How did it go?"

"Don't get mad," he said, touching his forehead at the hairline.

I held the candle higher. "You're bleeding!" I grabbed his arm and bundled him into the library. "Pour another drink, Willie."

"For him or you?" she asked.

"Both. Sit," I ordered Matt.

He sat and I checked the wound. It was a small cut but there was also a bruise forming around his eye. I frowned at him and he gave me a sheepish shrug.

"What happened?" I asked, accepting the glass of sherry from Willie.

"We met with trouble," Matt said, taking the whiskey tumbler that Willie offered. "Longmire was set upon by two men near his lodgings. Willie and I intervened."

I fixed him with a glare then turned it onto Willie. "You should let Longmire fight his own battles."

"I can't stand by and watch that," Matt said. "Not two against one."

I sighed. He was right. He wasn't the sort of man who could look the other way when someone was in trouble. Not even if the victim was a man he disliked.

"They ran off after throwing a couple of punches," Matt said.

"Lucky punches," Willie cut in. "Matt got there before me. By the time I reached the fight, it was all over. If he'd waited for me, that pretty face of his wouldn't be all knocked about now." She glared at him.

He smiled back. "At least you didn't draw your Colt."

"Only because I was worried I'd hit you in the dark."

"Thank goodness you were there, Willie," I said. "Your presence helped even up the numbers and probably scared them off."

"You're welcome, India. I'll protect Matt any day. You just ask."

Matt cleared his throat. "I think it was my capabilities that made them abandon the fight. I got in several good punches. I doubt they even noticed Willie."

"Didn't notice me? I was hollering like a stuck pig!"

"What did Longmire do while you two were fighting and squealing?" I asked.

"Not squealing," Willie pointed out. "Hollering. You ain't never been around pigs, India, so you don't know the difference."

I took a long sip of my drink, hoping to find some patience in the bottom of the glass.

"He was receiving the blows of one of the thugs," Matt said.

"He didn't even thank us afterward." Willie shook her head. "We shouldn't have bothered, Matt. He ain't worth it. He was dropping off more of them nasty letters," she told me. "That's where he goes every night, to deliver another."

"We confronted him after we saw him slip one under a door,"

Matt said. "He didn't care. He headed home, we followed at a distance and saw the men come out of the shadows and attack him."

"Did you get a good look at the men?" I asked.

Matt nodded.

"Then you should see Brockwell tomorrow and report the incident. Give him the names of the two magicians Oscar gave me. He should start by questioning them."

"I'm not sure it's wise to interfere," Matt said.

"It ain't a case for Jasper anyway," Willie added.

"It involves magic, and he's the resident expert on magical crimes in Scotland Yard," I said. "I'm sure he'll look into it. You must go too, Willie, to give an identification."

She scratched her head, messing up her wild hair even more. "He don't want to see me."

"This is work, not pleasure. He won't refuse. Anyway, I'm sure he does want to see you again. He must be missing your company by now."

"I disgust him, India."

"Nonsense. He just needed time to get over his surprise, that's all. I'm sure he has come to realize your—er—broad tastes are not so shocking."

"It still shocks you."

"No, it doesn't."

"Then why are you blushing?"

"It's the candlelight. You're going to see him tomorrow, Willie, and that's that. Even if I have to drag you there myself."

She grunted into her glass. "I'd like to see you try."

"Don't test me. I know where you keep your gun."

"You'll shoot me?"

"I'll confiscate it." I shot her a smile. "That'll hurt you more."

* * *

Detective Inspector Brockwell was off-duty on Sunday afternoon. We waited for him at his home, but it was some time before he returned. He had probably taken advantage of the spring sunshine and gone for a walk. He invited us inside upon his return.

"Is this about your arrest?" he asked Willie as he showed us into the parlor. "You have nothing to worry about. I made sure it wasn't recorded."

"It ain't about that," Willie said, not meeting his gaze.

He gathered up the newspapers covering one of the armchairs. He looked around for somewhere to put them, but all the spare surfaces were taken up by other newspapers, files, sketches, notes and what appeared to be a box of evidence. Two dirty cups, a plate and bowl had been stacked on one of the occasional tables. The crooked pile looked as though the vibrations from our footsteps would send it tumbling to the floor.

"Do you mind if we talk in the kitchen?" he asked. "Sundays are my housekeeper's day off. I think she left some cake in case I had visitors. Not that I get many visitors. In fact, the only visitors I ever get are you three." He chuckled but it quickly faded.

He led the way down the hall to the kitchen, scratching his sideburns the entire time.

"Is your visit here to do with that bruise around your eye and the cut on your forehead, Glass?" he asked as he pulled a tin off a shelf. He opened the lid, sniffed the contents then set it on the table. "She already sliced it. Help yourselves while I make the tea."

Willie shook her head. "You're hopeless without the housekeeper." She took a plate off the buffet and placed slices of fruitcake from the tin on it. "Can you make the tea or is that too difficult?"

"I'm capable of making tea," he told her from the range where a kettle rested over the low heat. "I have to make it every morning before she comes and every Sunday."

I watched the scene of comfortable domesticity with a smile on my face. Until Willie noticed and scowled at me.

"So what happened, Glass?" Brockwell asked. "Did you annoy someone?"

"Willie and I were set upon—"

Brockwell spun around, teapot in hand. "Are you hurt, Miss Johnson?"

"Do I look hurt?" Willie snapped.

I wanted to shake her. He cared about her, that much was certain from his reaction.

He tried to hide his concern with a grunt. "I suppose you scared them off with your gun."

"I didn't draw it."

"Good. We can't have women going about brandishing guns in the streets of London. We don't want to turn into the Wild West."

"What's wrong with the Wild West?" she shot back. "And do you think men are better handling guns? Or just that women shouldn't be allowed to have 'em?"

"That's a loaded question," Matt warned him.

"Thank you, Glass," Brockwell said with heavy sarcasm.

"Let's discuss the assault," I said cheerfully.

"You should report it at your local station," Brockwell said as he touched the side of the kettle. Satisfied it was hot enough, he poured it into the teapot.

"It's magic related," Matt said. "We thought you would prefer to investigate. Commissioner Munro won't want us to take it to the local constabulary."

"Don't bring my superior into this. He doesn't trouble himself with day to day cases."

"He does if it's related to magic. The thing is, a man called Longmire was assaulted a second time, most likely by the same attackers. Willie and I can describe them, and India has the names of two likely suspects, both magicians. Longmire sent them threatening letters, calling them cheats for using their magic in their businesses. We'd like you to interview them and see if our descriptions match their appearances."

"And if they don't?" he asked.

"Then we'll provide you with the names of other suspects."

Brockwell set out teacups and saucers, the sugar bowl and teaspoons. "You have to have it black, sorry," he said.

We drank tea at the kitchen table since the range warmed the room. Awkward silence quickly descended, however, until Matt broke it by asking Brockwell about his latest case. Brockwell refused to answer and that was the end of that.

I nudged Willie's leg with my foot under the table. She scowled back and remained silent. It would seem it was up to me to rescue this little tea party.

"We're still searching for the stolen magical coronet," I told Brockwell. "We have some suspects. All of them are wealthy and well connected."

He listened as I told him about our suspects, without naming names, and what we planned to do to unmask the thief. "Would you like to help us?" I asked. "It would be much easier if you could question the suspects in an official capacity. For one thing, we wouldn't have to spend so much money bribing servants." I laughed.

No one laughed with me.

Brockwell finished his tea and set the cup down. He toyed with it for a moment then pushed it away. Willie watched him from beneath lowered lashes, her fingers gripping her teacup tightly.

"I've already told you, I can't interfere in another detective's case," he said.

The conversation stalled again. We finished our tea and got up to leave. Willie said an awkward goodbye, Matt shook Brockwell's hand, and I caught the detective inspector by the elbow as he went to lead the way to the front door.

I let the other two go on ahead then rounded on him. "Speak to her," I hissed.

"I can't," he whispered back. "It's awkward between us now."

"It doesn't have to be. She likes you, a lot. She doesn't want your liaison to end. She told me so."

He stood there, blinking back at me with a rather stupid, vacant expression. It was impossible to read his thoughts.

"Does it bother you so much that she also likes women?" I asked.

He stretched his neck and scrubbed the patch of hair beneath his chin. "I let her go when she wanted me to. I didn't mind. Spending time away from each other can be good. Besides, we're both set in our ways and neither of us wants marriage. I've been patient and understanding, Mrs. Glass, but this...this is something I didn't see until it struck me in the face. I don't like surprises."

I stabbed him in the shoulder with my finger. "You need to get used to it or you'll both be miserable." I went to walk off but returned. "You were patient and understanding because what she wanted suited you. Now there's a new challenge in your relationship, one you weren't prepared for, and you're throwing up your hands in surrender. Just because something is new and different doesn't mean you ought to back away from it." Something Willie said to me a few days ago seemed appropriate now. "Not everything in life is methodical and clear-cut. Sometimes it's messy. Embrace the mess, Inspector, or you will lose her altogether."

I strode along the corridor, leaving the detective inspector staring after me.

"What were you two talking about?" Willie asked when we were in the carriage.

"I gave him some advice that someone once gave me," I said.

"How did he take it?" Matt asked.

"Only time will tell."

CHAPTER 13

Duke returned late in the afternoon after spending the previous evening and entire day with Mrs. Rotherhide. "Her servants had the day off," he said with a secretive smile.

"Let me guess, it took you all that time to find out where the merry widow was last Monday in the early evening," Willie said snidely. She'd been in a bad mood ever since returning from seeing Brockwell. Nothing had cheered her up, not even a game of poker. She'd constantly glanced at the clock and commented about Duke not being back yet. I wasn't sure if she was jealous that he was spending time with someone other than her or because she had no one when he did. Usually it was the other way around.

"She didn't want to be alone," Duke said.

Willie snorted.

Aunt Letitia entered the sitting room and asked me to play cards with her before dinner. "Not poker," she said. "Something more civilized."

"Of course," I said. "But I must hear what Duke has to say about our suspect. If you can't abide hearing about the investigation then you may not want to stay."

"Thank you for considering my sensibilities, but it's quite all right. If we must discuss such things as work..." She wrinkled her nose. "...then now is the time to discuss it, before dinner."

"It's not really work," Matt said. "I'm not being paid for this investigation."

"Then discuss it all you want. Perhaps I can help. Start with telling me about the crime and the victim."

"There was a theft and we've been tasked with retrieving the object. I can't tell you who the victim is because I've assured him privacy."

"It's that lord mentioned in the gossip column, isn't it? The one with the magical coronet, who suddenly found himself with an older brother." She clicked her tongue. "Dreadful business."

Sometimes her cleverness surprised us all.

"Don't look so shocked," she went on with a superior air. "It's not hard to deduce since you specialize in crimes involving magic. Duke, what do you have to report?"

Duke stood by the fireplace, his hand resting on the mantelpiece since he wasn't tall enough to rest his elbow on it like Matt. "Petronella—Mrs. Rotherhide—"

"You're on a first name basis with your suspect?" Aunt Letitia clicked her tongue. "I understand if Willemina makes the mistake of getting too close to a potential murderer—"

"Thief, in this instance," Matt said.

"But I expected better from you, Duke."

Duke slunk into a seat at the card table. "Sorry, Miss Glass."

Willie rolled her eyes. "Did you finally get to see her magic collection?"

"I did. There was no coronet. I also found out more about her movements on the Monday. She dined with friends that night and returned home at eleven-thirty. By my reckoning, she would have been dressing for dinner at a quarter past six in the afternoon."

"That's true," Aunt Letitia said. "It can take some time to

prepare, as you well know, India. Willemina, you wouldn't understand."

"Nope," Willie agreed, shuffling the cards. "I don't see the point of dressing for dinner."

Duke huffed out a laugh. "You don't see the point of dressing during the day. That outfit ain't fit to be called proper clothes," he added, waving a hand at her buckskins.

"It takes me a full five minutes to do my hair like this," Willie said.

"It shows."

She moved the cards to her left hand and was about to give him a rude gesture with her right, but Matt caught her fist and shook his head at her.

She snatched her hand free and continued to shuffle. "So the merry widow *claims* she was getting ready. Did you check with her maid?"

"She didn't claim anything, I just assumed," Duke said. "It's not something you can just put into the conversation. It wasn't easy asking her what she was doing last Monday without raising suspicion."

Willie dealt the cards, tossing Duke's carelessly in his direction. "So she could have been out at a quarter past six."

"Not if she had to get ready for dinner," Aunt Letitia said. "It takes at least an hour and a half. Longer if she had something elaborate done to her hair or if her maid is inexperienced."

Duke snatched up his cards. "But just to ease everyone's minds, I thought you could speak to her maid, Willie."

"Why me?"

"You're good at getting the maids to talk."

"True."

"Not as good as Matt, but good enough."

Matt's narrowed gaze slid to me. "You're overstating my abilities, Duke."

"What about the Landers?" Duke asked Willie. "Did you find out what they were doing on Monday at quarter past six?"

Willie had already informed us and it took some encouraging from Duke before she'd repeat herself. "The Landers were out all day and into the evening at a friend's house just outside the city. I checked with the coachman and he says he took them there and brought them back and they didn't leave in between."

"That's a solid alibi," Aunt Letitia said.

Willie nodded her approval. "You've picked up some of the lingo, Letty. Good for you."

"I might be old but I can still listen. It seems you can strike these Landers people off your list of suspects, Matthew."

"Not quite," Willie said and explained about Wentworth, the butler. "India found out he's in love with Mrs. Landers and gave her a special gift the night of the party. It could be the stolen coronet. Turns out, Wentworth took advantage of his employers' absence and left the house at the time in question on Monday. The other staff don't know where he went."

"Did he return with anything?" Matt asked.

"A box." She spread her hands apart. "About this big."

"Large enough for the coronet."

"He wouldn't tell anyone what was in it."

"Did you tell the maid that he gave Mrs. Landers a gift on the night of the soiree?" I asked.

Willie nodded. "The maid knew nothing about a gift. She reckons none of the staff knew or it'd be the talk among the servants."

"So the butler is still a suspect," Aunt Letitia said. "What will you do, Matthew?"

"Confront Mrs. Landers," he said. "I can think of no other option open to us. We have to find out what the butler gave her."

"I'll do it," I said.

"I was hoping you'd say that. Visit her tomorrow while I'm with Farnsworth at Tattersalls."

"I'm coming with you to Tattersalls, Matt. I'll visit Mrs. Landers in the morning. We're not meeting Lord Farnsworth until three."

One side of his mouth curved up. "There won't be many women there."

"Probably none," I agreed.

"You'll be a rose among thorns."

Willie snorted. "More like a cat among pigeons. Or a mouse among the horses."

"It's sweet of you to think of me as a mouse," I said. "But there's nothing mousey about me."

Matt just grinned.

* * *

MONDAY DAWNED COOL, wet and windy, the sort of day that kept ladies of Mrs. Landers' station indoors. Unless one had to go out to work or perform errands for an employer, it was best to keep warm and dry.

"How delightful," she said, with genuine enthusiasm upon receiving us in the drawing room. "I'm so pleased to see you again, Mrs. Glass."

I had expected a less amiable greeting after I ruined her party and devalued her magical collection. It was an enormous relief to be received with friendship. I probably didn't deserve it.

She invited me in and asked Wentworth to serve tea. Unlike his mistress, the butler's reception was cool. Not that he addressed me directly, but there was certainly a frostiness in the room that vanished when he left to fetch the tea.

"I just wanted to clear the air after the other night," I said. "I'm truly sorry about the toy drummer. I should not have spoken in front of everyone."

"It's quite all right," she said with a hint of steel in her tone. "It's in your nature to be honest."

"I still should have saved the truth for later. It wasn't my intention to crush your spirit."

Tears welled in her eyes but she rapidly blinked them away.

"To make up for it, I wanted to give you a gift," I said.

"Oh, that's not necessary, Mrs. Glass." She laughed, scanning me from head to toe. She spotted my black and silver beaded reticule.

"My gift is not a physical item," I said. "Not precisely anyway. It's words."

Her brow wrinkled. "Words?" Her forehead cleared. "Oh! A spell! Oh, Mrs. Glass, do tell me you're going to speak a spell for me."

"I am. Would you like it in a watch or clock?"

She clapped her hands. "Marvelous. Just marvelous. I'm thrilled and honored." She leapt to her feet. "Let me see. The old long case clock in the hall is too big. My husband's watch is with him and mine has sentimental value." She gave me an apologetic look. "I keep my magic items locked away, as you saw, and I'd rather have my watch on me. How about this clock?" She indicated the exquisite gold mantel clock with bronze classical figures representing Study and Philosophy bracketing the white enamel dial.

I checked the time against my watch. "It's running on time."

"Please do the spell anyway," she begged.

The clock was too heavy to lift safely so I left it in situ and rested my hand over the top. I quietly spoke the spell. A warm flare shot through me and burst out of my fingertips into the clock.

I removed my hand.

Mrs. Landers blinked at me. "Is it done?"

I nodded.

"I expected sparks."

"There's nothing to see," I told her. Only Matt's watch glowed when he used it. I assumed that was because the magic was being withdrawn. None of the other magical objects I'd encountered had their magic used in such a manner.

Mrs. Landers stood back and admired the clock. "Wait until I tell Mr. Landers. Thank you for your special gift, Mrs. Glass."

"Will you lock it away with the others?" I asked as I sat again.

"Of course. It must be protected."

Wentworth brought in the tea and set the tray down on the table between us. He didn't leave immediately but hovered by the door.

"That will be all, Wentworth," Mrs. Landers said.

He hesitated. "Are you sure, Madam?"

"Of course."

He retreated but left the door open. Mrs. Landers poured the tea and handed me a cup.

"He seems very dedicated to you," I ventured.

"He's a marvel. He was a footman in my father's household, you know. When I married and Mr. Landers said we needed a butler here in London, I suggested him. We're lucky to have him. It's terribly difficult to find reliable staff in the city, so Mr. Landers tells me."

"You are very fortunate indeed," I said with a sly little smile. "I noticed at the soiree just how dedicated he is to you."

Her face froze in a tight smile. "Pardon?"

My suggestive overture made me feel somewhat dirty. Although relationships between staff and their employers must go on behind closed doors, it was quite a different matter to accuse one's hostess.

I forged on anyway. "He comforted you when you were upset. Indeed, he even gave you a gift."

"I have no idea what you mean." She sipped her tea, her face flushed.

"Come now, Mrs. Landers," I said, mimicking the tone that Louisa used when about to make a snide remark. "It was clear that he's in love with you."

"No!" The word burst out of her mouth like a bullet.

"Of course he is. I witnessed how he was with you."

She glanced at the door. "He's good to me. Nothing more."

"It seemed like more." I loathed myself at that moment. The more I pushed, the more horrified Mrs. Landers became. Because the thought was abhorrent to her, or because I had discovered their secret? "He gave you a lover's gift," I went on. "It was a magical object, wasn't it? He knows how much you value them."

"Lord, no! Nothing like that." She turned away, her face glowing.

I waited, hoping she would dig her own grave. But she suddenly got to her feet. "Come with me," she said. "I'll show you what he gave me that night."

We passed Wentworth on our way out of the drawing room. "Madam?"

"Stop fussing, Wentworth," she snapped. "I'm not a child."

The butler sank back against the wall.

Mrs. Landers lifted her skirts and led the way up two flights of stairs to the level that was reserved for the family's private chambers. She marched down the corridor and into a bedroom, startling her ladies' maid as she inspected a dress hem by the window. Mrs. Landers asked her to leave.

Once alone, she stood in the middle of the room. It was a feminine bedchamber with floral curtains. Colored perfume bottles and pots for creams were arranged neatly on the dressing table. The bedspread was embroidered with roses and vines, and against the pillows was a yellow-haired doll dressed in a blue and white gingham dress with a white apron.

Mrs. Landers pointed to the doll. "Would a man give the woman he loved a doll she cherished as a child?"

"I…don't know. Mrs. Landers, I'm sorry—"

"You're not leaving here until you understand, Mrs. Glass," she said primly. "That doll was my constant companion as a child. I had no friends. My company consisted of my parents, some elderly neighbors and the servants. And that doll. When I came to live with Mr. Landers in London, I didn't think I'd need my childish toy. But it wasn't easy for me here. I missed home. Wentworth knew that, and he thought my beloved doll would once again be a comfort. He wrote to my family's housekeeper asking for the doll to be sent here. It arrived last Monday afternoon, but he waited for the right time to give it to me."

"Monday afternoon?" I said weakly.

"Apparently he had to rush to get to the post office before it closed at six, but then he didn't have the courage to give it to me straight away. He worried he'd overstepped. On the evening of the party, after you—after my toy drummer was proven to be a fake—he felt it was the right time. Perhaps you still think we are lovers, even now, but I can assure you, we are not. He is merely concerned about me."

I could have pointed out that wanting her to be happy was a sign that he loved her, but I'd done enough damage for the day. He might be in love with her, but she wasn't in love with him.

My task was not yet complete, however. "May I take a closer look at her?" I asked. "I do so love dolls."

"Go ahead," she said, a little softer. "She's nothing grand."

"I can see she's special to you, and well loved." I picked up the doll. She wasn't warm to touch. I ran my hand over her hair. It felt real but not warm. Her arms and torso didn't hold magical heat either. Wentworth had not sought out an expensive magical gift for his employer, just a sentimental one. That wasn't the act of a man who would steal to please her.

I put the doll back, nestling her against the pillow where she smiled at us with full, pink lips. "I'm sorry for my ridiculous behavior," I said. "I've been cruel. I do hope you can forgive me."

"Of course, Mrs. Glass. You are always welcome here."

I doubted it. I suspected I would never be invited back. What I did know for certain was that neither Mrs. Landers nor her butler stole the coronet.

* * *

LORD FARNSWORTH STOOD at the stone archway of the horsey capital of London, as Tattersalls was called by many. The auction yard in Knightsbridge was responsible for the sale of most of the city's riding and carriage horses, and attending auction day at Tattersalls was one of the great gentlemanly pleasures, so Matt told me. He'd heard all about it from Lord Cox whom he'd visited that morning.

Lord Farnsworth spotted Matt first but his gaze soon settled on me as we approached. He eyed me coolly. "You'll grow bored out here, Mrs. Glass," he said after greetings.

"I don't plan on waiting out here," I said. "I'm going in with you."

He laughed. When I merely smiled back, he turned to Matt. "A fine joke, Glass. Very amusing. But I wouldn't want my wife hanging about outside Tattersalls. Is your conveyance near?"

"She's coming inside," Matt said.

Lord Farnsworth's brow plunged. "She can't!"

"There's no law against it, is there?" I asked.

"Should be," he muttered.

I took his arm. "Come along, my lord. Time is a-wasting."

"You won't like it."

"Why not?"

"It smells of horse."

"Every street in London smells of horse."

He sighed. "Most unprecedented, this."

"I'll try not to embarrass you."

"My dear Mrs. Glass, it's not me who shall be embarrassed if you get ahead of yourself. If you so much as raise an eyebrow during the auction, your husband will find himself with stock he might not want."

"I'll try not to buy the pretty horses. Only the fast ones."

"Very amusing." His frown continued as we entered the auction yard.

The spacious area reminded me of London's railway stations with its grand glass roof overhead letting in an abundance of light. In the middle of the yard was a magnificent colonnaded structure that looked like a classical temple, but I soon realized was a fountain.

"Sorry," Lord Farnsworth said to a gentleman who stepped aside to let us pass. "I'm very sorry," he said to another.

I thought he was apologizing for muscling through the crowd, but after several more apologies, I realized they were for me. Not only did he not want me there, but none of the others seemed to, either. They stared at me as if I'd grown two heads. There were no other women present among the hundred or so gentlemen.

"All around the perimeter are the stables," Lord Farnsworth said to Matt. "There's a viewing gallery up there, where I suggest Mrs. Glass stands. Down here amongst it is more fun but not appropriate for a lady."

"And who do I speak to if I want to find out about the quality of today's offerings?" Matt asked.

"The quality is for you to judge. There'll be someone on hand to answer any questions about sires, that sort of thing. Want to take a look?"

"I prefer to go alone," Matt said. "Do you mind escorting my wife to the gallery?"

Lord Farnsworth looked as though he minded very much. "Don't you want help, old chap?" he asked, somewhat desperately. "I'm very good at picking out a mudder. Got a knack for it, in fact. I don't want you making a poor decision at your first Tattersalls auction."

"I'll be better without my wife's influence." Matt shot me an apologetic shrug.

"Then why's she here?"

"For the thrill," I said, tightening my grip on his arm so he wouldn't follow after Matt. Lord Farnsworth's glare drilled into Matt's back as if willing him to return and take charge of me. "Don't worry about him. My husband is quite good at choosing the right stock."

Lord Farnsworth sighed. "Come along, then. I'll find you a nice spot to stand where you can see the action from a safe distance."

He directed me through the crowd, apologizing all the way.

"This isn't the place for a woman," he said, for what seemed like the hundredth time.

"Oh, I don't know." I took up a position in the gallery, overlooking the auction yard where a horse with a gleaming black coat was being taken through its paces. "Lots of women like horses. I never learned to ride but I can appreciate a fast racehorse."

"Perhaps when you move to the country you can learn."

"Move?"

"When old Rycroft fertilizes the daisies and your husband installs himself in the family pile. There'll be opportunity aplenty to learn to ride then." He was too short to see the proceedings from behind me so maneuvered himself into position on my right. "Lots of new clocks too, I s'pose. You'll have a grand time in the country." He sniffed. "Not my thing, of course. Too many matrons, not enough gambling hells."

"You do like horses, I see, and gambling. And magic objects, of course," I added, steering the conversation in a direction that would serve my purpose. I turned to him suddenly, startling him. "Tell me, now that we are alone, who do you think stole the coronet?"

"Dear lady, I don't have so much as an inkling."

"I suspect it's someone from the club."

He looked over his shoulder. "Where's Glass got to? Perhaps I should go and find him, see how he's getting on."

I caught his arm. "He won't appreciate the interference."

"Interference?" he spluttered. "I say, my opinion is worth something around here."

I hugged his arm in case he decided to leave anyway, and giggled into my hand like a silly girl. "I have to confess that I thought *you* had taken it."

"A horse?" he asked, still looking for Matt, or perhaps just an escape route.

"The coronet."

He swung around to face me. "Me?"

I gave a little shrug. "You're a gambler and gamblers like taking risks. Theft is an enormous risk."

"Gambling doesn't land a fellow in prison. I'm not a thief, Mrs. Glass."

"No, of course not." I laughed lightly. "As I said, it was just a passing thought when I first met you."

The auction of the first horse began and we both turned our attention to the yard. The auctioneer stood on a wooden rostrum, the horse and its handler beside him. Someone placed an opening bid but I didn't see where it came from. I soon got caught up in the auction and assumed Lord Farnsworth did too.

"You can look through my house," he said, proving his thoughts were elsewhere. "Today. Right after the auction."

"My lord?"

"I want to prove I didn't take the coronet." He looked serious, not at all like the jovial idiot I was used to.

"There's no need. I believe you." I could have kicked myself. My manners had stopped me accepting his offer and searching his house. Perhaps that was precisely what he'd hoped and he was bluffing, poker-style. There was one way to rectify my mistake. "I'm sure if you did take it, you wouldn't store it at home." I lowered my voice and leaned closer. "You would hide it elsewhere. At your mistress's apartment, for example."

He went very still. Only a vein pulsed high in his throat. "My what?"

"Don't blame my husband," I said. "It wasn't he who told me about her."

His nostrils flared.

"While I don't approve of women like that, I do want you to know that I don't blame either her or you," I went on. "You are not married and she is quite possibly better off with your arrangement. That is neither here nor there." I bit the inside of my cheek before I talked myself out of the opportunity that had just presented itself.

"I beg you, don't tell any of your friends about her," he whispered.

"Of course not. I have no friends among your set anyway."

"You know the Rycrofts. Anyway, ladies gossip." He screwed up his nose. "They've got nothing better to do."

"That's because all the interesting endeavors are reserved for the men." I indicated the auction yard. "If we could come to Tattersalls, we wouldn't need to pass the time gossiping in parlors."

His lips flattened. "Please, Mrs. Glass, for the sake of my future wife, do not tell any of the Rycrofts about Angelique. It wouldn't be fair."

"For your future wife?"

He cleared his throat. "Yes, of course. That's what I meant. Not fair for the girl I eventually marry to know someone came before her. Wives don't like that sort of thing."

"So I hear."

"It's going to end, anyway."

"When?"

He stared down into the yard and applauded along with the crowd as a filly was sold.

"My lord?" I prompted.

"Soon. I've got my eye on a prospective bride. Good breeding, pleasing face, not too much of a bore. I think we'll get along."

"Have you told Angelique that it must end?"

"Not yet."

"You really ought to. That way you can propose to this girl with a clear conscience."

Shadows darkened his eyes. "The problem is, I'm finding it hard to give her up. Wish I could have both. Some men do."

I touched his arm. "But you are not that sort of man, are you?"

As if he just remembered that he was speaking about his mistress to a woman he hardly knew, he became quite agitated, fidgeting with his tie and cuffs, and clearing his throat over and over.

To the relief of both of us, Matt appeared. I waved and he approached, smiling. It froze upon seeing our faces. I suspected Lord Farnsworth and I looked rather stunned by his intimate admission.

"I think we should go, India," Matt said. "There's nothing here that interests me today."

"Eh, what?" Lord Farnsworth asked, returning to his jovial self. "Not going to make a bid?"

"Not today."

"Pity. I was looking forward to testing your mettle. Think I'll stay a while longer, anyway." He took my hand and raised it to his lips. "Good day, Mrs. Glass. It has been rather… er…interesting."

Matt steered me out of Tattersalls onto Brompton Street with his hand at my lower back. It wasn't until we climbed inside our waiting carriage that he finally spoke.

"It wasn't Farnsworth who left that threatening note for the editor," he said. "He was here at that time, just as he claimed. I spoke with two attendants who saw him around six last Monday."

I sighed. "So if he's not the thief, who is? The Landers were at a friends' house at that time, their butler was fetching the doll from the post office, and Mrs. Rotherhide was getting ready for a dinner party. All of Lord Coyle's suspects can be accounted for."

"Except for one," Matt said thoughtfully. "We dismissed Whittaker after searching his place, but what if he keeps his collection elsewhere and the coronet is with it?"

"According to Mrs. Rotherhide, he keeps his two magical objects in the open," I said.

"She might not know if there's a secret collection."

"Are you sure your search was thorough?" I asked. "It was rather rushed."

"We didn't know how long we'd have," Matt agreed.

"You should look again. Tonight. I'm coming with you."

He arched his brows at me. "Was being the only female at Tattersalls not enough of a thrill for one day?"

"You have a strange notion of what thrills me. Tattersalls was a bore and Lord Farnsworth is a cowardly scoundrel as well as an idiot."

"Why cowardly?"

"He hasn't told Angelique that their arrangement must end soon." I rested my hand on his thigh. "So can I come tonight?"

"We don't even know if we can enter Sir Charles's house tonight. He might be home."

"I'm sure we'll think of something to get him out."

"Yes, you can come." He kissed my forehead. "Not that I could stop you."

* * *

DUKE TOOK Mrs. Rotherhide to the theater, and Cyclops was still spying on Lord Farnsworth, so Willie agreed to watch Sir Charles's house while we were inside and whistle if she saw him return. She grumbled about it all the way there.

"Why do I have to be watch?" she whined. "Why can't India?"

"Because it was my idea to go and Matt's my husband," I said. "Besides, you're a better whistler."

"And where's Duke, anyway? Out having a good time, that's where, leaving me stuck being lookout for you two." She took out her watch and checked the time. She couldn't see the dial in the dark so tried to catch the light as we passed a streetlamp, only to click her tongue when the light wasn't strong enough.

"It's ten to nine," I told her. "Or thereabouts."

She pocketed the watch. "Duke owes me. Cyclops too. I bet he's sneaking off with Catherine and not doing his duty watching that prissy lord."

"Catherine doesn't sneak about with men in the night," I said.

She grunted.

"Speaking of sneaking off at night," I added, "have you arranged to meet Angelique later?"

"Nope."

"Is she spending the evening with Lord Farnsworth?" I hadn't told Willie about Angelique soon becoming free. Matt advised me to wait. Willie might want to become Angelique's new benefactor in an attempt to rescue her, but she couldn't afford to keep her. He didn't want her to rush in only to get rejected. If Angelique wanted to be with Willie without making it a financial arrangement, then she could approach her without interference from us.

"I don't know what she's doing," Willie said. "She can do what she wants." She looked out the window, her arms crossed. "Is it far?"

We parked around the corner from Sir Charles's house and waited in the shadows across the street. At nine o'clock, Sir Charles's carriage rolled up. Five minutes later, Sir Charles climbed in and drove away. No one had seen him off and he'd locked the door himself. Our trick to get him out had worked. It felt like a victory.

It had been Matt's idea to write a note to Sir Charles asking him to meet at Sam's Chop House in South Kensington at nine-thirty. The chop house would still be open and South Kensington was far enough away that he would be gone for some time, even though he would probably leave when the author of the note failed to arrive. We had not signed it, but had hoped he would assume it was Mrs. Delancey and that he wanted to see her.

Matt quickly picked the lock on the front door with his tools and we slipped inside, leaving the door open a crack so we could hear Willie's warning. The house was dark and I carefully traversed the stairs, worried about tripping. Matt went on ahead and entered the parlor. He'd lit a lamp and turned it down to keep the light dim. He handed it to me and began tapping the walls, listening for hollow spaces where Sir Charles might keep his artifacts.

I held the lamp aloft. The fireplace and chimney seemed like good hiding places. The coals glowed in the grate like rubies in the sunshine. Perhaps it wasn't a good place, after all. Sir Charles wouldn't want to burn his collection.

The candlesticks on the mantelpiece caught my attention. One or both of these were magical, according to Mrs. Rotherhide. I touched one. Nothing. The same with the other.

I looked around the room and found the dog statuette on a side table. I rubbed the head. It held no magical warmth.

"Matt," I whispered, brandishing the statue. "It's not magical. Nor are either of the iron candlesticks."

He joined me. "Are you sure?"

"Yes. He lied to Mrs. Rotherhide. Do you think he didn't want her to know where he kept his real items so showed her these to satisfy her curiosity?"

"Perhaps, but why?"

I didn't have an answer to that.

Matt inspected the dog. "I think it's more likely he doesn't have a magical collection at all. He simply picked two items in here that he could tell her were magical. She wouldn't know any better."

"But he belongs to the collectors club! He must have a collection."

Willie's whistle pierced the air. Matt extinguished the lamp and peeked out the window down to the street. He swore under his breath. "His carriage is pulling up. We have to leave."

Leaving wasn't so easy when we were one floor up. We couldn't go out the front door or Sir Charles would see us. We had to head downstairs and leave through the back.

"The service stairs," I hissed and shoved him toward the corridor. The service stairs would be hidden in a wall panel and lead directly to the kitchen and other service rooms. From there, we could escape through the rear door to the courtyard.

We tiptoed across the corridor and pushed on wall panels. I prayed there were no loose, creaking floorboards.

The rumble of wheels on the street was the only sound. They were not arriving, but going. Sir Charles had already alighted. He would have noticed his front door ajar.

He would be alert for any sounds we made.

I glanced over my shoulder toward the staircase. Silence. There should be some footsteps at the least. If I'd come home and noticed the door ajar, I would have called out or made my presence known somehow to warn the burglars to leave and avoid a confrontation.

But I was not Sir Charles.

Matt found the door and pushed it open. He hustled me inside. With my heart in my throat, I clutched the handrail and raced as quickly down the narrow stairs as I dared. At the bottom we paused to take stock of our location and to listen.

It was dark. I could just make out the shape of the doorway leading to the kitchen. A corridor led to our left and disappeared into the bowels of the house.

The way out.

The shadows near the kitchen moved. Something clicked.

I knew that sound. I'd heard Willie cock her gun enough times to know it. To dread it.

"Come out," said Sir Charles. "Or I'll shoot."

CHAPTER 14

Matt stood so close in front of me that I felt his body tense. If Sir Charles fired, the bullet would hit him. I couldn't risk him being shot, not even with his watch to save him. There was a very high chance that he would die instantly and no matter how quickly I placed his magic watch in his hand, I wouldn't be quick enough.

But knowing Matt, he wouldn't reveal our identities either. I was quite sure Sir Charles couldn't see our faces in the dark, just as we couldn't see his.

"What do you want?" Sir Charles snapped.

We remained silent.

"Tell me what you want and I won't shoot."

Matt's fingers found mine and squeezed. A warning to remain silent? Or to prepare to flee?

Hell and damnation, what should we do? If we revealed ourselves, surely Sir Charles wouldn't shoot us. But how to explain what we were doing there? I felt sick and hollow at the same time, and my nerves stretched to breaking point. I ran through every scenario in my head, but came up with only one way forward.

"Money," I whispered to disguise my voice.

Matt's fingers twisted with mine.

"No, you're not simple burglars after my silver," Sir Charles said. "You sent me away with an anonymous letter. I didn't fall for it, of course. I simply made it look as though I did. Your lookout is a good whistler, although he wasn't quick enough. He fled, by the way. Don't expect rescue from that quarter."

Matt's thumb rubbed mine, reassuring. I was anything but reassured.

The shadow that was Sir Charles stepped toward us. "Who are you and what do you want?" I could just make out his raised arm and the gun pointed at us.

How long could we remain silent before he shot us?

How long dare we remain silent before revealing ourselves?

Matt wouldn't do it. He would rely on the bullet not hitting him true in the heart and me placing the watch in his hand. I would not take that risk. Not ever.

I drew in a breath to speak.

The click of another gun cocking filled the dense silence. Willie! I knew she wouldn't abandon us.

"Put down your weapon," she commanded in a deep voice with a Cockney accent. I had not heard her approach.

Sir Charles hesitated.

"I said, put it down!"

His silhouette placed the gun on the floor.

"Kick it away," Willie said in that same masculine voice.

Sir Charles did so. "What do you want?" he pressed.

Matt took my hand and we raced along the corridor, away from Sir Charles and Willie. I didn't know how he could see in the dark. He'd only been this way once before, but somehow he found the back door. He slammed the bolt back and pushed the door open.

We raced across the courtyard, out of the gate and headed toward the street where Woodall waited with the carriage. Our footsteps pounded on the cobbles, giving away our position. I couldn't tell if Sir Charles followed us.

"Willie?" I gasped out between deep breaths.

"She'll be fine," Matt said.

We didn't break stride until we reached the carriage. Matt bundled me inside and I landed face-first on the seat. He helped me sit up.

"Are you all right?" he asked.

"Yes." I pressed a hand to my rapidly beating chest and tried to catch my breath. Matt sat opposite, his hands on my knees, watching me. His breathing was regular. In the dim light cast by the nearest streetlamp, I could just make out his ruffled hair, his bright eyes.

As my breathing steadied, I peered out the door. "Where is she?"

"She had further to run than us," he said.

She also had to escape from Sir Charles's house through the front door without him turning around and shooting her as she retreated. What if she had not escaped?

"We didn't hear a gunshot," Matt said, guessing the path my thoughts took.

He was right, and it was a small comfort, but there were other ways Sir Charles could stop her from leaving.

A figure overshot the corner, almost fell, and sprinted toward us.

"Thank God," I muttered, feeling light-headed with relief.

I flung the door wide open and Willie dove in.

The carriage took off at speed as Matt managed to wrangle the door closed. I peered through the rear window, but no one followed. Thank God. I sat back and blew out a breath.

Willie whooped, her teeth flashing white. "I needed that," she declared.

"I did not," I told her. "I'm still struggling to catch my breath."

"Lucky you didn't lace your corset tight or Matt would've had to carry your unconscious body." She laughed.

I crossed my arms, but I couldn't stay mad at her. She'd just saved us.

"You took a risk following him inside," I said.

"Calculated risk. It was dark in there. I don't think he guessed I was a woman."

"You were very convincing," I assured her. "You mimicked the Cockney accent perfectly."

"I've been practicing."

Matt leaned forward, elbows on knees, and raked his hand through his hair. "He guessed the letter was a fake. It was a bad idea. I should never have relied on it."

I cradled his face in my hands, forcing him to look up at me. "It was a good idea. I'm as surprised as you are that he guessed."

Willie slapped Matt on the back. "Don't worry. He won't figure out it was you two. Neither of you seem like the sort to break into houses, so I reckon you're safe. But now he's alert to intruders, it's going to be real hard to get in again."

Matt took my hands, kissed the back of one, and sat up straight. "We're not going to try again. If he has a magical collection, its location will have to remain a secret for now."

"If?" Willie echoed.

"According to India, there was no magic in the two objects he told Mrs. Rotherhide were magical. Either he didn't want her to know about his real magical items, or he doesn't have any."

Willie considered this with her arms crossed. At least, I thought she was considering it, but it turned out that she was thinking about our narrow escape. "There ain't nothing like a close-call to get the blood pumping. Duke and Cyclops'll be disappointed they missed all the fun."

"I'm glad it made you feel better," I said. "You seemed upset earlier."

She sighed. "You going to pester me, India?"

"Until you give in and tell us what's wrong."

"Ain't nothing wrong, it's just…it's Angel."

"Angelique L'Amour? What about her?"

"I like her. The problem is, even though she says she likes me, I don't think she does. Not the same way. Not the way I want."

"Don't worry about her," Matt said. "There are others who do like you the way you are."

"I know. I just don't like that she's trying to dupe me."

"Why would she try to dupe you?" I asked, all innocence. I didn't want her knowing Matt and I had already discussed this matter.

"To get me to be her benefactress," Willie went on. "She hasn't come out and said it, but I think that's what she's hoping. I can tell she's not used to being with a woman, and I can also tell she don't partic'ly like it. So I asked myself why she would pretend, and that's all I can think of."

"You haven't confronted her?"

"I want to be sure before I do."

"She must think you can afford her," Matt said.

"It ain't a matter of affording her," Willie said. "After our first time, she wouldn't accept my money. I just don't want to pay for something I can get for free. I don't like her *that* much."

Matt's low chuckle was almost lost amid the rumble of wheels on the road.

"What's so funny?" Willie spat.

"I'm just glad you're immune to her charms," Matt said.

Willie gave an amused grunt. "Men might fall for her sweet talk, but not me."

"If she's shopping for another benefactor," I said, "that means she knows Lord Farnsworth is giving her up soon. He *has* told her. He lied to me. And that begs the question, what else has he lied to us about?"

* * *

THE ENCOUNTER at Sir Charles's house had shaken me, but I didn't want Matt to know. He would forbid me from going with him on such adventures ever again. I awoke late, after tossing most of the night, to find I'd missed breakfast in the dining room. Polly Picket brought up a tray with eggs, toast and coffee to the small chamber off the bedroom. Matt joined me just as I was finishing.

"I sent Duke to Farnsworth's stables to fetch Cyclops home now that we know he couldn't have left the letter in the editor's desk," he said, sitting on the other chair. "He sent a message back to say he'll see out the day. He doesn't want to leave Farnsworth short-staffed."

"He's so thoughtful," I said. "Mr. and Mrs. Mason would be lucky to have him as a son-in-law. I do hope they come to see that."

"So do I. Cyclops doesn't say much, but I think he's in love with Catherine."

"And I think she's in love with him." I smiled and reached for his hand. "I'm so glad one of your friends is settling down here. Hopefully Willie and Duke will be just as content to stay and not long for California. I've been worried they would want to return to America."

He tilted his head and regarded me levelly. "You were worried they would want to go home or that I would want to follow?"

I picked up the coffee cup with both hands. "Do you like it here, Matt? I mean, not just because I'm here, but do you really like it?"

"I do. Have I ever said otherwise?"

"No, but I don't want to keep you from your home, from the place you love. You used to talk about returning to California."

"In the very early days. But London grew on me, as did the people." He smiled. "I like to find out what secrets they're hiding behind their manners and aloofness."

I smiled back; but of course Matt would say he wanted to stay in England. For one thing, he knew it was what I wanted to hear. And for another, he could not leave. Not while Gabe Seaford lived here. Matt needed the medical magician just as much as he needed me, the watch magician. Without us, he could not survive when his watch began to fail again.

* * *

We decided to visit Lord Coyle after breakfast and ask him some direct questions about Sir Charles Whittaker. If anyone had answers, it would be him.

Whether he would reveal them to us was another matter. I suspected he would want something in return. Lord Coyle never did anything for free. At least this time we knew what he would ask of us—convincing Hope to marry him.

"Make it quick," Lord Coyle said when he greeted us in his study. "I'm on my way out." He'd hardly looked up from his desk when we entered and simply waved us to the chairs opposite. The distinctly masculine room matched the rest of the distinctly masculine house, with the dark wood paneling, the lack of feminine frills and decorative items. Paintings framed in thick gold depicted hunts and cows rather than flowers and cottages.

"We have a question about Whittaker we hoped you would answer," Matt began.

Lord Coyle continued to write. "You still haven't solved the mystery of the coronet's theft?"

"Not yet," Matt said tightly. "We dismissed Whittaker as a suspect almost immediately, but—"

Lord Coyle looked up. "Why?"

"Because he didn't seem to have a magical collection of particular note. He didn't seem to display it nor were there any locked trunks or other hiding places for it. He has not asked India to add anything either."

"Those are not good reasons to strike him off your list completely."

"He's back on the list, as it happens," I said. "Tell us, my lord, have you seen his collection?"

Lord Coyle dropped the pen in the stand and flipped the lid on the inkpot closed. "He doesn't show it to anyone. Nor does he keep it on display like the Delanceys, as you pointed out. But that doesn't mean he hasn't locked it away in a well-kept hiding place, or even in a safety deposit box."

"We found no evidence of such hiding places," Matt said. "But there's more. According to one source, he has two magical objects that he does display. He just doesn't advertise that they're magical."

"There you have it. He has a small collection. Everyone has to start somewhere."

"I have touched both items, but neither contain magic," I said.

Lord Coyle stroked his moustache with his thumb and fore-finger. "I suspect they're a ruse to put others off. If one of the other collectors covets his items enough to steal them, he will only lose two worthless objects. It's a clever security measure. I wish I'd thought of it."

"And the real magical collection?" Matt asked. "Where does he keep it?"

"I don't know."

"Why has no one seen it? Not even you?"

"He showed me two items some months ago when he requested to join. I assumed they were magical."

"Why accept his word for it?" Matt was like a hammer, relent-lessly pounding away with his questions, not giving Lord Coyle a chance to think—to connive—in between.

"The truth is, no one in the collectors club has any way of knowing if any items are magical. Membership is based on an interest in magic, more than anything. Our collections are a vehicle for those with a mutual interest to come together."

"*You* value your collection," Matt said.

"I never said we don't value our collections, Glass. We all do. We trade or purchase items. They have value to us. A value that we alone set. What I'm saying is, if Whittaker doesn't have a collection, he can still belong to the club. Lady Louisa doesn't have a collection, either. As long as they abide by the rules of secrecy, they can stay." He placed his hands flat on the desk and pushed himself to his feet with a grunt. "Now, if you don't mind. I must be off."

I rose too. Matt did not.

"We haven't finished," he said. "Why is Whittaker seeing Mrs. Delancey in secret?"

"I don't know," Lord Coyle said. "But I can think of one good reason that should not be discussed in the presence of a lady."

"My wife doesn't mind hearing unpleasantness," Matt shot back.

I narrowed my gaze at him.

"What is the real reason you're here, Glass?" Lord Coyle said. "Is it because there are only two days left before you must convince Hope to accept my proposal if you wish to wipe away your wife's debt? Because I will not change my mind. I will not extend the timeframe."

"That is in hand," Matt said. "As you say, there are still two more days. Leave it with me."

My gaze narrowed further.

"We're here because we have no suspects in the coronet's theft, Whittaker notwithstanding," Matt said. "Someone bribed the identity of Cox out of the newspaper editor but all suspects have an alibi for the time the note was left on his desk."

"Alibis can be bought, Glass. You of all people should know that." Lord Coyle gripped his walking stick hard and stamped it into the floor. I imagined the sound must send a shudder through the house that could be felt all the way down in the service rooms. It probably acted as a warning to the servants to prepare to be summoned.

Matt stood slowly. I could see him considering which of our suspects could easily bribe someone, and whose alibis would be the most susceptible. Not the post office, but maids and other servants, certainly. But the most likely in my opinion were the attendants at Tattersalls.

"Farnsworth," I said to Matt.

Not only was Lord Farnsworth a valued Tattersalls client, he had led us there without much prompting on our part. He'd offered up the alibi quickly and easily.

"I have no evidence to the contrary," Lord Coyle said, "but I suspect Farnsworth is not as stupid as he seems."

"If you have no evidence, why do you think that?" I asked.

"Because nobody can be that idiotic." He walked past us and opened the door. "Fetch the conveyance," he ordered the waiting footman.

The footman hurried off without a word.

"I hear he's fishing around for a wife," Lord Coyle went on, leading the way across the landing. "That will cause his mistress some distress."

It didn't surprise me that Lord Coyle knew about Angelique. "What does that have to do with Farnsworth stealing the coronet?" I asked. "Or do you think *she* did it?"

"I'm merely suggesting she is a weak link for you to exploit." Lord Coyle regarded me fleetingly before dismissing me and turning to Matt. "I see *you* understand, Glass. Explain it to your wife. She's too innocent to think like us."

I arched my brows at Matt.

Matt's lips flattened. "If Angelique does know about Farnsworth's hunt for a wife, she'll know her days as his mistress are numbered. With no benefactor and no prospect of one, she will have to live the life of a prostitute in the slums to make ends meet. It would be a hard life."

"Courtesans are a dying species in England," Lord Coyle agreed. "It's our prudery. I blame the queen. They're still in demand in France, however, but Farnsworth's girl won't return there unless she's desperate. Her brother is in Paris and he was cruel to her, I believe. She was forced to work for him and his gang. Farnsworth took her away from all that by bringing her here." He stopped and leaned heavily on the walking stick.

"What Coyle is suggesting is for us to use Angelique's dire future to our advantage," Matt went on. "By putting pressure on an already desperate Angelique, she might spy on Farnsworth for us."

"I don't know about spy for you," Lord Coyle said. "But she will certainly give you answers. I'd wager she knows Farnsworth's movements better than anyone."

He had an excellent point. It might be worth asking her if she knew where Lord Farnsworth was last Monday at a quarter past six. I wasn't so sure about putting pressure on her, however. It seemed unnecessarily heavy-handed. Hopefully a bribe would convince her to speak up. After all, she wasn't going to lose Farnsworth over it; she'd already lost him.

Lord Coyle signaled to a footman. "See Mr. and Mrs. Glass out." As we headed down the stairs, he called after us, "Two days. Don't waste them."

* * *

WE ALIGHTED FROM the carriage outside the butcher's shop and were about to knock on Angelique's door when I asked Matt to wait.

"The butcher's boy," I said, nodding at the window. "He's watching. According to Angelique, he's always watching. Perhaps he can tell us something."

Matt signaled for him to come outside. The lad spoke to someone over his shoulder then joined us on the pavement. He wore a bloodied apron but his hands were excessively clean.

"What do you want?" he asked. He wasn't as young as I first thought. I guessed him to be about twenty. He still had the gangly limbs and spotty face of youth, but the direct gaze of someone used to talking to those older than himself.

"We just want a few words with you," Matt said. "About your neighbor, Angelique L'Amour. How well do you know her?"

"Not well."

"You spy on her for Lord Farnsworth."

"No!" he cried. As if he surprised himself with the volume of his vehement reply, he ducked his head and looked around to see if anyone overheard. "No, I don't," he said, quieter. "I would never do that to her, and I wouldn't do it for *him*."

"Why not him?" I asked.

"Because he's a...a turd." I suspected he was going to say something more vulgar, but stopped himself. "I hate him."

"Why?" I asked again.

"The way he is with her...it's not right. He lords it over her."

"Do you understand their arrangement?" Matt asked.

The youth flushed and nodded.

"Does Lord Farnsworth treat her poorly?" I asked. "Is that why you dislike him so much?"

He shuffled his feet and wiped his hands down his apron. "I heard them arguing once. Over a week ago, it was."

"Just the once?" Matt asked. "They don't usually argue?"

The youth shook his head.

"What did they argue about?"

The lad hesitated. "I shouldn't say. It's their private business."

"We're worried about Miss L'Amour," Matt said. "If Lord Farnsworth is mistreating her, we can help."

"I don't think he's cruel to her."

"And yet you don't like him," I added.

"It ain't right, what she is to him. It ain't decent."

It was interesting that he blamed Lord Farnsworth for Angelique being a courtesan. He didn't see it as her fault. Perhaps, in a way, he was right. Women didn't become prostitutes because they wanted to, but because it was the only course left for them to take. Angelique was luckier than most to be housed in an apartment and have only one...customer.

Matt pulled out some coins from his pocket. The lad's eyes widened and Matt dropped the coins into the apron pocket. "What was their argument about?"

The butcher's boy checked inside the pocket. His lips moved as he counted the coins and when he looked up, there was a satisfied gleam in his eyes. "The lord told her he couldn't keep her much longer because he had to get married."

"Are you sure?" I asked.

He nodded.

So Lord Farnsworth definitely lied to us about not informing Angelique of his plans. "What else did they say?" I asked.

"She yelled at him in French, mostly, and he spoke back to her in French, only he can't be real good at it because he changed to English. He suggested she go back to Paris and she said she can't because of her brother." The youth shrugged. "She said she liked it here and wanted him to keep their arrangement the same. Then they spoke quieter for a bit before she started shouting again. She said she hated him for abandoning her."

We thanked him and waited until he'd returned inside the shop before knocking on Angelique's door. She opened it wearing a pink and green dress with pink ribbons in her hair. The outfit would be far too lurid on most, but looked fetching on her.

"Mrs. Glass, how delightful." She looked past me. "Is Willie with you?"

"Not today," I said and introduced Matt. "May we come in?"

Her smile tightened. "May I help you?"

"We're investigating the theft of a family heirloom," Matt said. "We suspect Lord Farnsworth may be involved and hoped you could answer a few questions for us."

She went to close the door but Matt blocked it. She spat a few words at him in French and he responded in the same language, startling her. He took the opportunity to enter, forcing her back.

"I think you'd prefer it if we asked our questions away from prying eyes," he said.

Angelique glared at me. "You lied."

"Yes," I said. "I am not from a charity. We're private inquiry agents tasked with finding a stolen artifact, as my husband explained."

She lifted her skirts and stomped up the stairs. "You think *Davide* stole it? Bah! He is not a thief. He is rich!"

"The artifact in question is priceless," Matt said. "He would steal it just to possess it."

She showed us into the small parlor where a chemise and sewing basket were laid out on the table. The door to the bedroom was closed. "I do not know how I can help. *Davide* has not said a thing about a theft."

"We know he's releasing you from your arrangement," I said. "You don't have to protect him anymore."

She descended gracefully onto a chair and folded her hands on her lap. "It will be very hard for me. I will need a new benefactor. It will take time to find one."

Once again, Matt removed money from his pocket. This time it was bank notes, not coins. He placed them on the table as if casually setting them aside. Angelique's gaze followed the movement of his hand from beneath her lush lashes.

"Was Lord Farnsworth here with you Monday before last at about a quarter past six?" he asked.

She considered this then shook her head. Her fingers twisted together.

Matt and I exchanged glances. "Do you know where he was?" Matt pressed.

"*Non*."

"Come now, Angelique," I said. "Please tell us if you know."

"I do not."

I wasn't sure I believed her, but I suspected she was too loyal to Lord Farnsworth to betray him, or too frightened.

Matt wasn't prepared to give up as easily, however. "Last Monday, at a quarter past six, someone left a very nasty note on the desk of the editor at *The Daily Courier*. The letter threatened to hurt the editor's family if he didn't reveal the name of a man alluded to in an article printed the day before. That man is the owner of the stolen artifact. As you can appreciate, the person who left that letter might be dangerous. He is almost certainly a thief."

Her chest rose and fell with her deep breath but she did not look up.

"Lord Farnsworth is a suspect, but we need to know what his movements were last Monday at that time to be certain. We suspect you know where he was, Miss L'Amour."

"Please, do not ask this," she whispered.

"He is releasing you, Angelique," I said gently. "You don't have to protect him anymore."

Her thumb pressed into the flesh of her other hand. "Please understand, he is still my benefactor."

She wasn't going to answer. We couldn't get the information we wanted from her, but perhaps there was a question she would answer. It didn't implicate him directly. "He's not what he seems, is he?"

The question seemed to take her by surprise at first, but she shook her head.

"He's quite intelligent," I went on. "Someone you like to be with. Someone worthy of your love."

She nodded and pressed her fingers to her lips. Tears welled in her eyes.

Matt handed her his handkerchief. She dabbed at the corners of her eyes then handed it back. She picked up the bank notes and gave them back too.

"He is still my benefactor," she said with a lift of her chin. "I cannot accept this."

We let ourselves out and returned to the carriage. Matt gave Woodall instructions to drive us to Lord Farnsworth's house.

"Are we going to confront him?" I asked. "With what? We have no evidence against him."

"I'm hoping inspiration will strike when we get there."

"That doesn't seem like a particularly clever plan. Speaking of clever, are we in agreement that Lord Farnsworth is not as stupid as he pretends to be?"

"We are."

"Do you think Angelique lied to protect him?"

"I do."

An idea came to me. One that might get us some answers from Lord Farnsworth. I told Matt my plan and he kissed me thoroughly on the mouth. I took that as a sign that he liked it.

CHAPTER 15

Lord Farnsworth had just got out of bed, according to the gentleman himself, despite it being nearly lunchtime. He greeted us in the drawing room wearing a purple and red housecoat with gold dragons embroidered through it and matching indoor shoes. He liked lurid clothing as much as his mistress.

"Bring tea and cake for the Glasses," Lord Farnsworth ordered his butler. "And a chocolate for me. I haven't had my morning cup yet," he said for our benefit as the butler retreated. "So, tell me what this is about. Does Mrs. Glass wish to come to my club now? Or sit in parliament?" He laughed.

I no longer believed that laugh. This man was no fool, I was quite certain of it. I didn't know why he pretended to be one. The act had been going on for years, apparently, so it had nothing to do with the theft of the coronet. He wasn't hiding a cunning mind behind a mask of stupidity for nefarious reasons.

Unless the coronet was the latest theft of many.

"You lied to us," Matt began.

Lord Farnsworth hesitated barely a moment before scoffing. "About horses? Come now, Glass, if you knew your stuff, you'd have recognized that colt as a potential winner when you inspected him. It's not my fault you can't recognize a dasher from a disaster."

"You lied about Angelique L'Amour."

"What's she got to do with Tattersalls?"

"You told me you hadn't informed her about your pending marriage," I said. "But we've just been to see her and she said she knew."

"Ah."

"You argued about it, according to the butcher's boy," I went on.

Lord Farnsworth clicked his tongue. "The spying little prick."

"Between him and Angelique, we learned quite a few things about you," Matt said.

Lord Farnsworth's Adam's apple bobbed above the collar of his housecoat. "And what might those things be?" His eyes sharpened, no longer hidden behind lazy, hooded lids, and his lips no longer curved into that perennial, good-natured smile. The mask was slipping. He was worried.

"Angelique says you sent her to bribe the editor of *The Daily Courier* to learn the name of the peer mentioned in the gossip piece," Matt said.

I watched Lord Farnsworth carefully to gauge his reaction to our lie. He seemed surprised and perhaps annoyed. A muscle in his jaw bunched momentarily before flattening again. His eyes resumed their lazy heaviness and his jaw slackened.

"I wonder why she said that," he drawled. "I didn't send her anywhere. The theft of the coronet is nothing to do with me. Besides, was the theft Monday night? I was with Angelique all night."

"She didn't mention it."

The creases at the corners of Lord Farnsworth's eyes deepened ever so slightly.

"Why would she lie?" Matt pressed.

"I don't know."

A moment passed, two, three, in which Matt and Lord Farnsworth glared at one another. His lordship seemed to be considering his options, contemplating what to say. Now that I knew him to be smarter than he let on, I could tell he was trying to work through the different scenarios before him, as I often did.

"Did you pay her to say such a thing?" he asked.

"I tried to pay her," Matt said, "but she wouldn't accept it."

"She's still loyal to you," I said. "She's in love with you."

Lord Farnsworth barked a laugh. "No, she's not, or she wouldn't have claimed I sent her to bribe the newspaperman. Or is that just something you made up to get me to talk?" His gaze slid to me.

I remained calm, composed, but it wasn't easy when my heart hammered violently.

Lord Farnsworth lifted a hand in a dismissive flourish. "I'm not in love with her either, in case you were wondering. Loyalty and love are not the same thing. Be careful not to confuse the two, Mrs. Glass. Ah, my chocolate," he announced as the butler brought in a tray.

He set it down and retreated upon Lord Farnsworth's dismissal. Lord Farnsworth poured the tea himself and handed me a cup and saucer. He didn't immediately let it go.

"You're right, I lied about Angelique not knowing my future plans for matrimony. I'm sorry, Mrs. Glass. I don't like discussing personal matters." He let go of the saucer. "Back to your rather tenuous claim that Angelique says I sent her to bribe a newspaperman on my behalf…consider how she looks. She's very distinctive, wouldn't you say?"

"There are disguises," Matt said.

"Do you think a disguise could obscure a jewel like Angelique?" When we didn't answer, he added, "Search this place. Top to bottom. I'll inform the staff to allow you access. You won't find the coronet because I didn't steal it. Nor did I send my mistress to steal it on my behalf." He smiled. His lethargic tone had returned, along with the indolent gaze. He wasn't concerned in the least.

That made me even more suspicious.

But I could see no way forward. My plan, to let Lord Farnsworth think Angelique had told us everything in the hope he would confess, wasn't working. Unless Matt thought of something, we would have to admit defeat. That galled me. Lord Farnsworth deserved to squirm a little.

Matt rose and I set the teacup down. Lord Farnsworth smiled at me as I stood too.

He picked up his cup of chocolate. "No search? Is that because you realize that I didn't do it and I didn't get Angelique to do it either? We're innocent, Glass. Both of us. Now kindly leave her alone. She had a difficult life before coming to England and just wants to be left in peace. Unless you know of a good chap to take her off my hands, I must ask that you not see her again. Good day. My butler will see you to the door."

I marched out of the house, my steps brisk. "The more I get to know him, the more I dislike him," I said. "He's guilty. I'm sure of it."

Matt's face looked like thunder as he assisted me into our carriage. "As am I. And I'm going to prove it."

"How?"

"By confronting the Tattersalls attendants. Coyle was right. Farnsworth must have bribed them to lie to me. He knew I'd ask around about him that day so he conjured up an alibi. Woodall," he said to the coachman. "We'll take Mrs. Glass home then drive to Tattersalls."

* * *

MATT DIDN'T ENTER the house after driving me home, so he didn't see that we had guests. Lord Cox and Patience sat with Aunt Letitia in the drawing room. Aunt Letitia was as pale as a summer cloud and her vacant gaze stared into space.

"Aunt Letitia?" I asked. "Are you all right?"

"Oh dear," said Patience. "I'm afraid we've upset her."

"Veronica?" Aunt Letitia reached out a hand to me as I sat beside her. "Veronica, take me to my room, please. I feel a little faint."

Lord Cox helped me take her upstairs to her bedchamber. He looked concerned as he gently eased her onto the bed.

I sent Peter to fetch Polly and sat with Aunt Letitia until she arrived. Then I returned with Lord Cox to the drawing room and a pacing Patience.

She raced to me and grasped my hands in hers. "India, I'm so sorry. I thought she was better."

"She still has a turn from time to time," I said. "Usually when she's had a shock or something upsets her."

"Oh dear. I'm afraid it was probably both." She looked to her husband. "We told her about Mr. Longmire."

"She had to find out eventually, I suppose."

I asked them to sit and poured myself a cup of tea. They already had a cup each, and a slice of cake. I took a long sip to gather my wits. It had already been a tiring morning and threatened to be a very long day.

"We came to speak to you and your husband," Lord Cox said, glancing at the door. "Do you expect him soon?"

"I'm afraid he didn't know you were here. He dropped me off then left. We didn't see your carriage."

"We caught a hack," Patience said with forced cheerfulness. "We think it wise to start economizing."

My teacup suddenly felt heavy and I almost dropped it. It clattered into the saucer, spilling tea over the sides. "What has happened?" I asked on a rush of breath.

Lord Cox swallowed. "My lawyer says the case is hopeless. Longmire has proof. Nothing can be done." He picked up his teacup, the picture of a dandy gentleman, but he was as white as Aunt Letitia.

"What if you offer Mr. Longmire more money to forget it?" I asked.

"I have offered him everything short of the title and lands. He has refused it. He wants everything, Mrs. Glass, and nothing less." He stared down into the tea. "One can hardly blame him. If I were in his shoes, I'd want what was mine too."

Patience touched her husband's arm. She looked close to tears as she regarded the man she'd married. Mere weeks ago, he'd been proud and aloof. Almost too proud and aloof to marry the woman he loved because of her past indiscretion. Now he was the one whose reputation hung by a thread. It was somewhat poetic, and I ought to rejoice that he was getting a taste of his own medicine, but it felt awful to enjoy his misfortune. Despite his cool attitude to Patience after learning of her encounter with a rogue, he didn't deserve this. This was simply awful.

"We'll fight it in court," Patience said.

Lord Cox shook his head. "No, we won't."

"But—"

"My dear." He turned to face her. I suspected this was the first time they'd truly sat down together and discussed the disaster and what to do about it. "My dear," he said, more gently, "I've known this day would come for years. Ever since I found out, I've been waiting for Longmire to discover it too. Somehow, I knew he would. It's almost a relief that the wait is finally over."

"What are you saying?" she hedged.

"When I received Longmire's letter, it felt like my world had come crashing down. I thought this was it. I should end it all."

Patience gasped.

"I'd let you down, and my children. I didn't know how to face you all."

Tears slipped down Patience's cheeks. "Don't talk like that. You haven't let anyone down, least of all me. We *will* get through this."

He patted her hand, his face tight. I suspected he was close to tears himself and might break down if he spoke.

"Whatever happens," Patience forged on, "I will love you. Your children will love you. That is all that matters."

"But if I am no longer a baron…what will I be?"

"A dedicated man who always did the best for his tenants. A considerate son who protected his father's secret and his mother's heart. A wonderful, doting father who continued to keep that secret for the sake of his children. A loving husband who has been forgiving and indulgent. No one can fault you, and if anyone does after this, shame on them. But be assured, your true friends will come to your defense."

He caressed her cheek and whispered, "Thank you."

"It won't be easy," she said. "But I will be by your side every day. We'll face the world together."

He pressed his forehead to hers and gave her a weak smile. She kissed him lightly on the lips. When she withdrew, they both seemed to remember where they were, and that I was watching on, albeit pretending the magazine on the table beside me was thoroughly interesting.

Lord Cox cleared his throat. "I'll speak to my lawyer. I don't want this dragged through the courts. It will only upset the children and the outcome is inevitable anyway."

Patience clasped his hand. "If Mr. Longmire covets the title and estate so much, let him have it. He will always be a nasty man with a shriveled heart. He will have what he covets but he will never have what you have, my dearest. He will never have people who love and respect him."

* * *

ACCORDING TO MATT, the two Tattersalls attendants who'd mentioned seeing Lord Farnsworth at the auction on the previous Monday did not change their stories.

"Farnsworth is a good client," he said as we ate a light

luncheon of sandwiches in the sitting room. "Too good. They'll lie for him if it keeps him happy. Damn it," he muttered.

"Perhaps they're not lying," I said. "Perhaps he really did send Angelique to the newspaper office in disguise while he remained at Tattersalls. It's true that she is distinctive, but a hooded cloak will hide her face and hair."

He nodded thoughtfully. "Have you seen Willie?"

"Not today."

"I'll ask her to question Angelique some more. She might be able to get answers that we couldn't."

I set down my sandwich, not particularly hungry anymore. I'd told Matt about the visit from Lord Cox and Patience, but it still played on my mind. Lord Cox looked so vulnerable, so distressed. Patience had surprised me, however. She'd become her husband's anchor in an increasingly turbulent sea.

"I don't know if I see the point in pursuing the thief anymore," I said on a sigh. "The coronet is going to Longmire, along with the title and everything else. Perhaps we should just give up."

"I'm not giving up."

"You don't like letting Farnsworth win, do you?"

"Is it that obvious?"

I smirked. "I just know you well."

He put down his sandwich too. "I don't like that he duped me. I also don't like that Cox's maid is getting the blame. He hasn't dismissed her because he doesn't believe she did it, but that fool of a detective inspector thinks she did and might arrest her anyway."

"Thankfully he hasn't found any evidence against her," I said. At his questioning look, I added, "So Lord Cox informed me. But you're right. Doubts about her will continue unless the real thief is uncovered. So what do we do now?"

The answer arrived after lunch in the form of Cyclops. We met him on the pavement where he stood with the horses and Lord Farnsworth's carriage.

"Any chance there's leftovers from lunch?" he asked Bristow who stood at the top of the steps.

"Lunch consisted of sandwiches, sir," Bristow said. "I'll check with Mrs. Potter to see if there are any left."

Cyclops pouted. "I hoped for more than sandwiches."

"I can ask her to make up a parcel of biscuits."

Cyclops rubbed his hands together and smiled. "That'll keep me going for the rest of the day." After Bristow disappeared inside, Cyclops said to us, "Farnsworth's cook ain't a patch on Mrs. Potter. Do you know what she's cooking for dinner tonight?"

"Roast chicken, game pie, followed by pastries, a trio of jellies and creams," I said. "I thought she was cooking a special meal just for us, but now I recall her asking when you'd be back."

"You can count on me being here for dinner."

"You're determined to finish out the day with Farnsworth?" Matt asked.

"It's only right. Glad I didn't leave yet, I've got some news. Are you still interested in speaking to the last coachman?"

"Certainly."

"I had to return some of his belongings this morning while Farnsworth was still abed. Seems he dismissed the coachman without notice and he left some things behind in his hurry." He removed a piece of paper from his coat pocket and handed it to Matt. "I wrote down the address."

Bristow returned and passed a paper bag to Cyclops. Cyclops checked inside and licked his lips. "I best be off. Tell Mrs. Potter she's a gem."

Matt extended his hand to me as the carriage rolled away. "Shall we speak to the coachman together?"

I placed my hand in his. "Do you have to even ask?"

* * *

I NEVER ENJOYED VISITING the East End slums, and today was no exception. The sun never reached the ground in the crooked, narrow lanes of the Old Nichol, and there were no flowers or any color amid the endless gray stone walls of the tenements, poor houses and work houses. Even the windows were gray with soot.

I stood close to Matt as we entered a secluded court. It was the sort of closed-in, airless space where vice could easily fester at night amid the dark recesses. During the day, however, there was nothing more sinister than the putrid smells that seemed as ingrained in the surrounding walls and cobblestones as the soot.

Matt nodded to a woman as she hung out her washing. She looked as though she'd never seen the likes of him and stared, open-mouthed. I smiled too but she hardly noticed me.

"Good afternoon," he said. "I'm looking for James Grundy."

She pointed at a nearby door.

Matt knocked and the door was opened by a stocky man with a hooked nose and protruding brow. I would have thought him a bruiser, but he was cleanly shaved and well dressed, although his clothing was a little long in the legs and tight across the shoulders.

"Mr. Grundy?" Matt asked. "I'm Matthew Glass and this is my wife, India Glass. We're private inquiry agents investigating the theft of a valuable item. We have some questions about your previous employer, Lord Farnsworth."

James Grundy had listened placidly enough until Matt mentioned Farnsworth. Then he spat into the ground near my feet. "Did he steal it?"

"We don't know."

"I hope he did, and I hope he swings for it. He's a prick. He dismissed me without warning. Did you know that? He didn't even give me time to get all my things. They came this morning, delivered by his new coachman. Lord Fuck didn't waste time replacing me. It's easy to find staff, but it's hard for a fellow to find work. I'm still looking."

"Why did he dismiss you?" Matt asked.

"Because I know too much, and I threatened to go to the newspapers if he didn't give me something to keep quiet. That were my mistake. Asking. I shouldn't have asked, I should have just told him the information was in the hands of the papers and I just have to give my word unless he paid." He spat again.

I didn't want to look down to see if it landed on my shoe. "You blackmailed him?" I asked. "That's why he dismissed you?"

"Like I said, I knew too much. I still do. I still might go to the papers if I don't get another job soon."

"But you haven't yet because Farnsworth said he'll claim you were disgruntled over your sudden dismissal and that will discredit you," Matt said. "Is that why you're holding off?"

Mr. Grundy ran his tongue over his top teeth beneath his lip and regarded Matt as if he were trying to determine if he was on Lord Farnsworth's side or not. Matt might be dressed like a gentleman, but after our questioning, Mr. Grundy must suspect he was here to find evidence against his lordship.

"I want to find work as a coachman again," Mr. Grundy said. "It's good work, pays well. But I've got no references from my last position thanks to that turd, and none of them toffs will take me on if they hear I blackmailed Farnsworth. I'll wait a bit longer before I go to the papers. That what you want to hear?"

Matt retrieved some money from his pocket and dropped the coins onto Mr. Grundy's palm. "Tell us the sensitive information you know about Lord Farnsworth."

Mr. Grundy pocketed the money and glanced around. We were alone. "He keeps a mistress. She has her own rooms in Pimlico where he visits her. Now that he's looking for a wife, he doesn't want anyone to know about his whore."

"Her name's Angelique L'Amour," Matt said.

Mr. Grundy shrugged a shoulder. "So you already know. Sorry I can't be more help." He went to close the door, but Matt stopped it.

"I paid for answers."

Mr. Grundy hesitated then crossed his arms and leaned against the doorframe. "That you did."

"What were Lord Farnsworth's movements on Monday last, late afternoon?"

Mr. Grundy rubbed his tongue over his top teeth again as he tried to recall. "Monday would have been Tattersalls. He always goes to Tattersalls for the auctions. I drove him there at two-thirty and we left about six. I remember the bells of St. Gabriel's ringing as I drove him home."

So Lord Farnsworth couldn't have been the one to deliver the note to the editor if he was at Tattersalls at a quarter to six. "Did you ever meet Miss L'Amour?" I asked.

He shook his head. "Never even saw her. He didn't take her out. Not with me driving, anyway. He only ever visited her in her rooms." He winked at me.

Matt stepped between us, blocking my view.

"Sometimes he stayed all night," Mr. Grundy said, sounding amused. "Sorry if that's too vulgar for you to hear, Mrs. Glass, but it's the truth. Gentlemen of Farnsworth's class keep mistresses. It's just a fact."

"Not all gentlemen keep mistresses," Matt growled.

Mr. Grundy snickered, but I wasn't interested in their little verbal tussle. Something he'd said reminded me of something Lord Farnsworth had said. Indeed, he'd tossed it out when we saw him this morning, but it now seemed rather pertinent.

I nudged Matt aside and regarded Mr. Grundy. "What about later that Monday night?" I asked. "Did you take Lord Farnsworth anywhere?"

"Just to Pimlico at about ten, it was. It was a cold night. He ordered me to wait for him, said he wouldn't be long. But he didn't come out till almost three in the morning."

Matt straightened. "Three? And he didn't leave Miss L'Amour's house in that time?"

Mr. Grundy shook his head.

I realized why Matt had wanted to make sure of the time.

The footman in the Cox household had heard a noise at ten to two. If Lord Farnsworth was at Angelique's house, he couldn't have stolen the coronet. He'd said as much just this morning, but I'd dismissed it as a lie. Angelique hadn't mentioned it when we'd asked her about Monday afternoon. Granted, we hadn't specifically asked her about the night of the theft, only the late afternoon visit to the newspaper office. Still…

"Did Miss L'Amour leave the apartment?" I asked.

Mr. Grundy shook his head again, but stopped suddenly. He frowned.

"Did you doze off?" Matt asked.

"No," Mr. Grundy spat, offended. "I was awake the entire time, watching and waiting. It ain't so bad. I like the peace and quiet in the middle of the night. No, sir, I saw every coming and going from that apartment above the butcher's shop. Farnsworth didn't leave until three, but someone else left earlier then came back about forty-five minutes later, all before Farnsworth came out. A man."

"Are you sure?" Matt asked.

"He weren't tall but had a barrel of a chest so I knew it wasn't his lordship. He stopped and spoke to someone in the doorway of the butcher's shop, but I couldn't see who. Then he left."

"Did you catch a glimpse of his face?" Matt asked. "Did he have a beard or whiskers?"

Mr. Grundy shrugged. "It was too dark."

"The moon was out that night," I said, remembering what Lord Cox's footman had told us. "You saw nothing of the man's features?"

"Nope."

Matt huffed out a frustrated breath. We thanked Mr. Grundy and left. "Damn it," Matt muttered as we passed beneath the arched entrance. "Do you think he's lying about not seeing the man who left Angelique's in the night? He might be tempted to blackmail him now that he knows the information is valuable to us."

"Could it be the butcher's boy? But why would he be in the room with Farnsworth and Angelique. Oh. Don't answer that."

"He doesn't have a barrel chest," Matt pointed out.

"He could have stuffed something down his shirt."

Matt stopped suddenly and rounded on me. He was grinning.

"What's so amusing?" I asked.

"Next time you come out with me to sneak into someone's house in the middle of the night dressed in Willie's clothes, look at yourself in the mirror before you leave."

"Are you telling me I look as though I have something stuffed down my shirt when I dress in men's clothes?"

"As it happens, you do have something stuffed down your shirt. Two somethings." He opened the carriage door for me, still grinning.

"It was Angelique! *She* left in the middle of the night, leaving Lord Farnsworth asleep in her bed. That's why Mr. Grundy didn't see her face; her darker skin made her features harder to make out in the night. *She* stole the coronet. And Lord Farnsworth knows nothing about it."

"I think he does. He's been protecting her even while she has been subtly implicating him."

So she had. She'd never told us he was at her place during the night and she had suggested that he wasn't as foolish as he seemed. He might be her benefactor, but she didn't care for him. She was quite happy for us to accuse him.

"Shall we confront him or Angelique?" I asked.

"Angelique. But before we speak to her, I want to ask the butcher's boy a few more questions. He knows more than he let on."

CHAPTER 16

The butcher's boy refused to join us on the pavement, signaling through the window that he had to work. Matt entered the shop and spoke to the butcher and returned with the lad. He looked sheepish, hunched over, as if he knew the interrogation he was about to face and wished he could be anywhere else but here.

"Is that your father?" Matt asked, indicating the butcher serving a customer.

The lad nodded.

"He told you to answer me truthfully. Does he know what this is about?"

The youth nodded again. "He asked me after the last time you were here. He wouldn't let me out until I told him what you wanted. He says I could be in a lot of trouble if I don't tell the truth."

"He's right," I said, taking a gentler tone. "You could go to prison."

"Prison!"

"I'll put in a good word for you with the police," Matt assured him. "But only if you co-operate."

"I don't want to go to prison."

"What's your name?" I asked.

"Terrence."

"My husband is friends with the police commissioner, Terrence. You won't go to prison if you tell us what you know about Miss L'Amour."

He swallowed. "I'm not a tattler."

"This isn't tattling," Matt said. "This is self-preservation. Where were you Monday evening last week?"

Terrence looked relieved at the innocuous question. "Here, all night."

"Were you standing in the doorway of your father's shop at any point?"

Terrence nodded. "Ain't no crime in that."

"Did you speak to someone?"

Terrence hesitated then nodded. "Angelique."

"What time was that?"

"I don't know. Well after midnight."

"What was she wearing?" I asked.

"Men's clothes."

"Do you know where she went dressed in men's clothes?"

Another hesitation.

"I know you like her," I said. "That's why you were outside her place that night, watching, perhaps hoping to catch a glimpse of her as Lord Farnsworth left. I know she acts like she likes you too, but she's using you, Terrence. She said what you wanted to hear so you would lie for her. Don't believe her trickery. If you don't tell us everything you know, you *will* go to prison."

He swallowed heavily and glanced at Angelique's door then through the window of his father's shop. His father glared back from behind the counter.

"I don't know where she was going," Terence said. "She wouldn't tell me. When she came out, I got the surprise of my life to see her dressed in trousers. She made me promise not to say a word to anyone, including the lord."

"Did you see her return?" Matt asked.

Terrence nodded. "It was a while later, maybe a bit less than an hour. She went straight past me."

"Was she carrying anything?" I asked.

"She had something wrapped up in a cloth, tucked under her arm."

"What about Lord Farnsworth?" Matt asked. "When did he leave?"

"Maybe thirty minutes after that. He was yawning and he smelled drunk. He didn't see me."

Matt clapped him on the shoulder. "Thank you, Terrence. I know this wasn't easy for you." We went to leave, but I hesitated. Terrence chewed on his lower lip.

"There's something else, isn't there?" I asked. "You must tell us, Terrence."

He released his lip. "Earlier that day, Angelique asked me to deliver a message to a newspaperman but to make sure no one saw me. So after the shop closed, I took the note and waited for him to leave his office. I pretended I was an errand boy and left it on his desk where he'd see it."

So that was how Angelique had sent the threatening note without being seen. Lord Farnsworth was right; Angelique was too beautiful to go unnoticed. Even in disguise, she would have turned heads. But Terrence was ordinary. There was nothing unique about him. He looked like many other youths in the city, and I suspected *The Daily Courier* employed several errand boys who came and went from the office, invisible to the senior staff.

"Did you also pick up a book for her in Hyde Park?" Matt asked.

"I don't know nothing about a book."

Angelique must have retrieved it from the park bench herself. The editor said his vision had been obscured and with her back turned and wearing a cloak, Angelique could go unnoticed among the busy Hyde Park paths in the late afternoon.

We waited until Terrence returned to the shop then knocked

on Angelique's door. She opened it with a broad smile but, upon seeing us, went to close it.

Matt stepped in, forcing her back. Her ankles hit the bottom step and he caught her arm before she fell. She shook him off and spat something at him in French. He didn't respond.

"What's this?" came the laconic voice of Lord Farnsworth behind me.

I spun around and edged inside, closer to Matt, but Lord Farnsworth merely stood there. I glanced past him to his carriage where Cyclops had jumped down from the driver's seat. He watched, alert.

"Miss L'Amour stole the coronet," Matt announced.

"Preposterous!" Lord Farnsworth spluttered. "Outrageous!"

"Enough acting, Farnsworth. We know that you know everything. You lied to us."

"*Oui*!" Miss L'Amour blurted out. "Yes, he lied. To me also. *He* is the thief. You cannot believe him when he says I did it."

Lord Farnsworth's body sagged with his heavy sigh. "I lied *for* you, Angel. I tried to save you. But it seems you are your own worst enemy. If only you had trusted me, I would have found someone else for you. Someone good and kind."

"Someone fat and ugly." She sniffed. "You are not that at least."

Lord Farnsworth sighed again. "Shall we go upstairs and discuss this like gentlemen, Glass?"

I wasn't sure how that would make a difference, but Matt agreed.

The parlor felt crowded with the four of us in it. Nobody sat, and as much as I wanted tea to help soothe everyone's frayed nerves, I didn't suggest it. Angelique stood with a defiant glare that she directed at the three of us.

Matt told her what we'd learned from Terrence. When he finished, she said something in French again, which I was beginning to think was an obscenity. "That stupid boy," she said in English. "I should not have trusted him."

"You should not have stolen the coronet," Lord Farnsworth said. "Then you wouldn't be in this corner."

"Why did you steal it?" I asked. "Are you interested in magical objects?"

"Magic?" she said. "Ha! You English and your silly fantasies. I took it for him."

Matt and I turned to Lord Farnsworth. He put up his hands in surrender, but didn't look alarmed at the accusation. He expected it. "Her English is a little raw," he said, apologetically. "I didn't ask her to steal it for me. I was here when I read about it in the newspaper and told her it would be a valuable piece that I'd pay a fortune for in order to add it to my collection. She knew I collected magical things." His lips flattened. "Although I didn't realize she thought magic wasn't real until now. She's a very good actress. Missed your calling, my dear."

Angelique rolled her eyes.

"I didn't know she decided to steal it," he went on. "I didn't find out until the following day."

"You didn't notice she'd gone out on Monday night?" I asked.

"I was asleep. Too much to drink, don't you know."

"Did she tell you she stole it the next day?" Matt asked.

"She offered to give it to me in exchange for keeping her on as my mistress. I refused. Too difficult to keep a girl holed up in here with a wife at home. Too expensive. So then she tried to sell it to me, for a very high sum, I might add."

"Only enough to keep me in a nice house for a few years," Angelique said. "You have money."

"Yes, but owning a distinctive stolen object like that is almost worthless to a collector. I couldn't resell it to other collectors and I couldn't show it off. Some of them are far too prudish. They'd think *I* stole it. I'd be cast out, banned. Best to steer clear of it. That's what I told her."

"And then?" I asked.

"And then nothing. She didn't mention it again."

We all turned to Angelique. "Did you sell it?" Matt asked.

Angelique tipped her chin even higher. Then with a click of her tongue, she gave in. "It is in there." She pointed to the tiny room she used as a kitchen. "There is a loose board in the floor under the table."

Matt pressed the boards until he found the loose one and pulled it up. He reached into the cavity and removed a bundle wrapped in cloth. The cloth folded back, exposing the golden coronet we'd seen at Lord Cox's house.

"I was going to take it to France and sell it," Angelique said. "I need the money now that he is leaving me."

"Speaking of leaving." Lord Farnsworth pulled out a small paper bag from his inside jacket pocket. "I came here to give you this. There's some money in there and a one-way ticket to Antwerp on a steam packet."

Angelique sniffed and was about to turn away, but thought better of it. She snatched the bag. "Thank you, *Davide*."

He caressed her jaw and smiled sweetly. "How many times do I have to tell you? You don't have to thank me. Everything I did for you, I did because I cared. You're a wonderful girl when you're not thieving or lying."

Tears welled in my eyes, but not Angelique's. She lightly kissed Lord Farnsworth on the lips. "I will pack now."

"You'd better," Lord Farnsworth declared. "The steamer leaves in two hours."

"Wait a moment," Matt said. "You both seem to be under the assumption we're letting her go."

I took his arm and held on lest he try to physically stop her. "No one was harmed in this crime, Matt."

"What about the maid? And how will you explain suddenly finding this?" He held up the coronet.

He was right. We couldn't just turn up with the stolen item without answers. And if we told the truth, Angelique would be hunted by the police and stopped from leaving the country. I didn't want her to go to prison.

"I will write a letter to your police," Angelique said. "I will admit everything. But please, I beg you, do not give it to them until I am safe."

I squeezed Matt's arm to convince him to agree, but it wasn't necessary. I could tell he thought it a good idea too.

"We'll hand over your confession to the detective assigned to the case tomorrow," he assured her. "I suggest you employ some sort of disguise to board the packet as they will check all ports once they realize you've fled."

"They will assume she has gone to France," Lord Farnsworth said. "They won't look toward Antwerp until it's too late." He took Angelique's hands in both of his. "Well then, dear girl. It's time to part. I'm going to miss you."

"And I you, *cherie*."

Lord Farnsworth leaned in to kiss her, but she swayed back, and he was left kissing the air.

She withdrew her hands. "You are no longer my benefactor. My kisses are not for you. Goodbye, *Davide*. And thank you for the adventure. It was fun sometimes."

Lord Farnsworth offered her a deep bow and turned away. Unlike his former mistress, tears pooled in his eyes. "Sometimes," he muttered as he headed down the stairs. "It was more than just *sometimes*."

Angelique wrote her confession, signed it, and gave it to Matt. I wished her well, but she merely nodded. I wasn't going to get gratitude from her after uncovering her lies.

We followed Lord Farnsworth outside. Cyclops looked relieved to see us. While he knew Lord Farnsworth and Angelique were suspects, he couldn't have known they were harmless. He climbed back up to the coachman's seat, ready for orders. Farnsworth didn't seem to notice that he'd got down from his perch in the first place.

"Makes sense that it was her," Farnsworth said with a forlorn gaze at Angelique's door. "She was an excellent thief, by all accounts."

"Pardon?" Matt asked.

"In Paris. Her brother's gang began as child pickpockets and grew up to become master thieves. They stole the jewels off the necks of ladies and silver from their dining tables. Angelique was forced into that life by her brother. He was cruel to her, turned her into…" He waved a hand at the door. "That's how we met. I stopped in Paris on my way home from a tour of the continent. She charmed me then tried to steal from me. I convinced her to give up that life and come to England as my mistress. I'm much fairer than a prison guard." He smiled sadly. "I thought she'd left that life behind, but it seems thieving is in her blood."

"She was just trying to secure her future," I told him. "She knew you were leaving her."

"Ah, yes, the Wife Plan." He laughed but it sounded grim.

"Marriage isn't so bad if you find a woman you get along with," Matt said cheerfully.

"I thought I had found her. She just wasn't the *right* woman."

Matt clapped him on the shoulder. "Next time you give your heart to a woman, don't pay her to be with you."

"Very droll," Lord Farnsworth said. "That reminds me. Is that cousin of yours still available?"

"I thought you had someone else in mind," I said.

"She found a richer man."

"I advise you to look outside my family," Matt said. "My cousin's unique charms are not for the faint-hearted."

Lord Farnsworth shrugged then gave Cyclops directions to take him to his club. "Oh, and Glass?" he said before shutting the door. "Do try to leave my name out of this when you talk to the police."

We watched him go then headed to our carriage, parked on the opposite side of the street. Matt took my hand and assisted me up the step. Once he'd settled beside me, I crossed my arms and glared at him.

"What?" he asked.

"'Marriage isn't so bad?'" I echoed.

"Ye—es," he said carefully. "Why can't I say that?"

"If you were selling matrimony, I wouldn't buy it based on that statement."

His lips quirked with his impish smile. "But you're not Farnsworth. To him, 'not bad' means it's the most amazing thing in the world. Trust me, I know men like him."

I narrowed my gaze, not quite sure whether to believe him or not.

We turned a sudden corner and I slid into his side. He trapped me in his arms. "I do like it when Woodall goes too fast around corners. Kiss me, Mrs. Glass."

"I suppose I will," I said on a theatrical sigh. "Your kisses are not bad, I suppose."

* * *

WE DECIDED to give Angelique the entire day to get as far away from England as possible, so Matt did not go to the police in the morning. The police, however, came to us. Not the young Detective Inspector Walker, but Brockwell. I suspected it wasn't just us he came to see, however, but Willie.

"I should go," she said, upon his entry. "I've got to do something."

Both Duke and Cyclops moved to block her exit from the library. Cyclops was installed back home after finishing his assignment as Lord Farnsworth's coachman, and Duke had returned after spending the night with Mrs. Rotherhide. He was not on assignment, and he planned to visit her again. We'd been telling them how the case of the stolen coronet had ended with Angelique handing it over to Matt. It was currently tucked between my unmentionables in my dressing table drawer.

"I won't be staying long, Miss Johnson," Brockwell said. "No need to leave on my account."

"It ain't on your account," she said huffily. "Like I said, I got something to do."

"What?" Duke asked.

Willie pursed her lips and tapped her finger on her outthrust hip. "Well, I got to see someone. About something."

"What something?"

"It's my private business, Duke. Don't you have a merry widow to pester?" She pushed past them and stormed out.

Brockwell watched her go. I took that as a sign that he was disappointed and that he still cared for her. I would be sure to tell Willie later, and ask her to give him another chance.

Matt pulled out a chair and patted the back. "Bristow, bring tea and biscuits for the detective inspector."

"Is there any cake?" Brockwell asked.

Matt nodded at Bristow and the butler left without a comment on the early hour or Matt's eagerness to feed the detective inspector. I suspected Matt felt sorry for Brockwell.

"Mrs. Potter baked a sponge especially for me," Cyclops said, resuming his seat. "She knows it's my favorite."

Duke rolled his eyes. "There's always cake here. It ain't nothing to do with her welcoming you home."

"You've been away, Mr. Cyclops?" Brockwell asked.

Cyclops looked to Matt. If he explained that he'd been watching Lord Farnsworth but was no longer needed there, Brockwell might wonder why and ask questions. We couldn't risk him coming to the conclusion that we already knew who'd stolen the coronet. Not yet. Angelique needed a little more time.

"A brief visit to the countryside," Matt said smoothly. "For the air."

"The air in London does get foul. Where did you go, precisely?"

Cyclops's eye widened. "Er…"

"Brighton," I said. "The same place we went on our honeymoon."

"Brighton," Cyclops repeated. "Matt and India talked about it so much, I wanted to see it for myself."

"I thought you said the countryside, not the seaside."

"Same thing," Duke said.

"No, it's not. One is in the country, the other is by the sea."

Brockwell frowned. "It is a curious time for you to go on holiday, Mr. Cyclops. Aren't you in the middle of an investigation, Glass? Don't you need all hands on deck to find the coronet?"

"The investigation is drawing to a close," Matt said. "I'm sure we'll have a culprit for your colleagues to arrest shortly."

Bristow entered, wheeling the tea trolley. Brockwell's eyes lit up at the sight of the sponge cake, taking pride of place on a cake stand. He rubbed his hands together as Bristow sliced it and passed around plates.

I poured the tea and handed a cup and saucer to Brockwell. It was a relief to see him distracted from his interrogation by refreshments.

"I've looked into Walker's case on the stolen coronet," Brockwell said without lifting his gaze from the cake resting on his knee. "He has no evidence against the maid. He'll not arrest her."

"That is good to hear, Inspector," I said.

"Not for Walker. His superiors aren't happy with his lack of a conviction. Walker will be feeling the pressure. If he can't find evidence soon, I wouldn't put it past him to make it up. His colleagues suspect he has done so in the past. He has a suspiciously successful arrest record."

"That would account for his rapid rise through the ranks," Matt said.

Brockwell ate his cake in silence except for the sigh accompanying each bite. When he finally finished, he brushed the crumbs off his fingers and picked up his teacup. "Now, where were we? Ah yes, the reason for my visit."

"You mean you're not here to see us?" Matt asked with a pout in his voice. "I am disappointed."

"As it happens, I'm here about the assaults on Mr. Longmire. I visited the suspects Mrs. Glass suggested." He nodded thanks in my direction. "They match the descriptions you gave and have no alibis for the time of both assaults."

"Have you told Longmire about the arrests?" Matt asked.

"Not yet. I wanted to speak with you about something the assailants alluded to."

"Go on."

"Both men were interviewed separately. Both had the same story. They claimed to have received their instructions by letters signed by your uncle, Lord Rycroft."

"That's absurd," Matt said. "He doesn't know those men. They're magicians who assaulted Longmire because he wrote letters calling them cheats. My uncle dislikes Longmire for other reasons, but he has no connection to those thugs. He has been set up."

"That's what I suspected. A guilty man doesn't sign his name on a letter that would implicate him. Thank you for confirming my suspicions. But the question remains, who set him up?"

I had my suspicions, but I kept quiet. Matt did too and Brockwell left a short while later, without a name.

After he'd gone, we both looked at one another. "Coyle," Matt said.

"Shall we confront him now?" I asked.

"Not yet. I want to find out if my uncle had any involvement at all. I suspect he's not entirely innocent."

* * *

A NOTE ARRIVED from Lord Coyle just as we were about to leave. Matt read it then screwed it up and tucked it into his pocket. I dug into his pocket and retrieved it.

'Twenty-four hours,' the note read.

I screwed it up again and handed it to Bristow. "Dispose of this."

Matt and I left. Neither of us mentioned the note or Hope and Lord Coyle's proposal. It played on my mind all the way to the Rycroft's townhouse, however. I couldn't stop thinking about it.

By the time we reached our destination, I'd decided I

wouldn't interfere in her life. I couldn't convince her to marry him. The decision was hers to make and hers alone.

I told Matt so. He grasped my hand before I stepped out of the carriage. "You must do as your conscience demands."

"Thank you, Matt. I'm glad you understand."

As it turned out, Hope wasn't at home. It was a relief not to have to endure polite conversation with her. Both of her parents were there and greeted us civilly, if somewhat briskly. We had debated on the way whether Matt should speak to Lord Rycroft alone, but I suggested Lady Rycroft ought to hear what we had to say. We might gauge as much from her reaction as his.

We sat with them in the drawing room but declined refreshments. "We won't be staying long," Matt said. "We have just spoken to a detective inspector acquaintance from Scotland Yard. He informed us that he arrested two men who assaulted Mr. Longmire."

Lady Rycroft made a miffed sound through her nose. "And you expect us to be sympathetic towards him? The man deserves what he got. Pity they didn't finish him off."

"They didn't, did they?" Lord Rycroft asked.

"No," Matt said.

They didn't seem too concerned about Mr. Longmire's well-being. I could hardly blame them. Mr. Longmire was changing the course of their daughter's life.

"Is there a point to telling us this?" Lord Rycroft asked.

"The two assailants accused you of paying them to do it," Matt said.

"What!" Lord Rycroft shot to his feet, his face red with fury. "How dare they! This is absurd! I'll march down to Scotland Yard myself and tell them so."

He didn't leave, however, and simply sat again.

It was his wife's reaction that interested me more. Lady Rycroft sat quite still, except for her eyes. She watched her husband intently from beneath her lashes.

"I told him it wasn't you," Matt said. "The police agreed that you've been framed."

Lord Rycroft settled back in the chair. His jowls settled too, folding into the fat around his neck. "Quite right. Good to see there's a sensible head down at the Yard."

"Someone wanted to implicate you," Matt went on. "Any idea who?"

Lord Rycroft shook his head, but did not meet Matt's gaze.

"Richard," Lady Rycroft snapped. "He doesn't deserve your protection. Whoever it is has thrown you right in it and doesn't care a whit. If Matthew hadn't been friends with this detective, you could have been in enormous trouble."

"I'm a peer of—"

"Don't be naive. Not everything can be swept under the carpet. If the newspapers sense blood, they'll send out the dogs." She blinked at him, then at us, and touched her turban self-consciously.

Lord Rycroft cleared his throat. "Very well, I'll tell you. It must be Coyle."

"Lord Coyle?" Lady Rycroft stared hard at her husband. "But…why?"

"I don't know why he used my name. You'd have to ask him that."

"Did you approach him about Longmire?" Matt asked.

Lord Rycroft hesitated.

"There's no point defending him now," Matt said. "If this is his doing, you need to tell me."

"That's the thing. It's not entirely his doing." Lord Rycroft cleared his throat and studiously avoided his wife's fierce glare. This seemed to be news to her. "The morning after our dinner with Patience and Cox, I approached Coyle. Patience told us the night before about Longmire's claim. I asked Coyle if there was something he could do to…make the problem go away."

"Those were your precise words?" Matt asked.

"More or less."

Then it was fortunate Lord Coyle had stopped at assault. On the other hand, he was a manipulator, not a murderer.

"I told him I would give my permission for him to marry Hope if he would get Longmire out of our lives. For Patience, you understand."

"You sold one daughter to save another," I said.

Lady Rycroft turned hard, glittering eyes on me. "That's a simplistic view. *You* wouldn't understand, India."

I kept my mouth shut. I wouldn't be drawn into a verbal sparring match with these two. I hoped Matt wouldn't either. Not before we had all the answers we'd come for.

"Hope still has to agree to the match," Lord Rycroft told me. "I won't force her."

Lady Rycroft gave the slightest shake of her head at her husband's concession.

"I told Coyle about Longmire's threatening letters to magicians," Lord Rycroft went on.

His wife made a scoffing sound in the back of her throat at the mention of magic.

"Patience told us about the letters. I thought then and there that if the recipients knew Longmire sent them, they might retaliate."

"You told Coyle it was Longmire," Matt said. "You thought if he wanted to marry Hope so much, he'd get rid of Longmire for you, and the recipients of those letters would be the perfect scapegoats."

I gasped. Now I understood. Lord Rycroft didn't have the stomach to assault Longmire himself, but he knew Lord Coyle would. Or, at least, had contacts among the sort of men who would take justice into their own hands after learning who sent them threatening letters. Coyle gave Longmire's name to the two thug magicians knowing they would mete out justice.

"But what would that achieve?" I asked, as much to myself as anyone else. "Longmire wouldn't give up the claim for the Cox title just because some magicians assaulted him. He wouldn't connect the two. Did you plan on telling him that you could stop the assaults if he gave up his claim on the Cox title?"

Lord Rycroft looked away. "You have it."

But I didn't think I did. There was only one explanation that made sense of it all—the men were not supposed to stop at assault. When Lord Rycroft asked Lord Coyle to get rid of Mr. Longmire, he didn't mean from the city, or to get him to give up his claim on the title. He meant for Coyle to end Longmire's life.

Oh God.

Matt had gone very still, as had Lady Rycroft. She stared and stared at her husband, her lips parted, her face pale. They had come to the same conclusion as me.

"But it was all for nothing," Matt said quietly. "Cox will lose everything to Longmire anyway. He hasn't given up, nor will he."

Lord Rycroft expelled a heavy breath. I couldn't fathom what was going through his mind. Relief that the thugs hadn't killed Mr. Longmire after all? Or disappointment?

"I don't understand why Lord Coyle would sign your name on his orders?" Lady Rycroft said to her husband. "Why would he try to damage your reputation? Doesn't he want to marry Hope?"

"Perhaps we should reconsider his offer," he said.

"Absolutely not! He's an excellent choice. We can overlook this. We must overlook it. We need him and the qualities he brings to the family, now more than ever. We can't save Patience, but Hope will rise from the ashes of her sister's disgrace."

Her husband nodded thoughtfully. "And there's Charity to consider too. You're right, I will overlook Coyle's indiscretion. Nothing more will be said about it." He stamped both hands down on the chair arms and regarded Matt. "Thank you for bringing this to my attention. Please reassure your detective friend that I didn't employ those thugs."

Matt approached his uncle. He stood over him, calmly doing up his jacket button. But his jaw was hard and his glare equally so. "Do not get involved in anything like this again. Next time, I won't defend you."

We exited the drawing room, but Matt paused then retraced his steps. "When will Hope return?"

"This afternoon," Lady Rycroft said. "She should be home by three."

I had the devil of a time keeping up with Matt's strides as we left the house. His temper was still steaming when we took off after giving Woodall directions to drive to Belgrave Square.

But my temper was equally fierce. Not just over what I'd heard in the Rycrofts' drawing room, but because I knew why Matt wanted to speak to Hope.

"We agreed we wouldn't try to convince her," I said. "Don't deny that's why you want to speak to her this afternoon."

"*You* agreed not to speak to her. I didn't."

"Matt!"

He arched a brow, challenging me.

I wasn't going to let a brow defeat me, no matter how severe the arch. "It must be her decision," I said. "Do you understand? I can't live with myself if we force her down that path."

He turned away to stare out the window, presenting me with his uncompromising jaw. "The Glasses make the Johnsons look like children. At least my American family face their enemies. They don't try to kill them by proxy."

We remained cool toward one another for the entirety of the short journey, but Matt suggested we go for a stroll in the leafy square to calm down before confronting Lord Coyle.

"I need my wits about me and I can't do that if you're mad at me, India."

I sighed and agreed. A brief walk would do us both good.

Matt sent Woodall home to Park Street with the carriage. It wasn't far and we could walk there when we'd finished with Coyle. He opened the gate to the garden square and we immediately spotted Lord Coyle not far away, leaning heavily on his walking stick. He'd stopped to talk to someone on the path and they appeared to be having a rather intense conversation.

"It's Whittaker," Matt said.

I squinted at the figures. He was right. I recognized Sir Charles's slim, dapper figure. "Should we hail them?"

"I want to hear what they're saying."

"Why?"

"It could be important."

"But—"

"Come on, India."

He grabbed my hand and together we ducked behind a tree then approached swiftly, using the thick trunks and foliage as cover. We stopped behind a plane tree near Lord Coyle and Sir Charles, and Matt took me in his arms. He kissed me. It was a distracted kiss, designed to obscure our faces if they happened to glance our way. I could just make out what the two men were saying.

"She asked after his cousins," Sir Charles said.

"Interesting," mused Lord Coyle.

"There are none, but the fact she asked is telling. They must be working on a spell that requires wool magic."

Fortunately Matt swallowed my gasp or I would have given us away. I knew precisely who they were talking about—me. I had asked Mrs. Delancey about her husband's magical family, and then we'd seen her meeting with Sir Charles. She had passed on that information to him.

But the question was, why did it interest these two?

CHAPTER 17

"We're not going to confront them," Matt said after they'd gone. His tightened grip hadn't let me go until the two men walked away. They had not seen us. Or if they did, they had thought us just two lovers in the park.

"Why not?" I asked hotly. "Sir Charles is feeding him information about me, and Mrs. Delancey is passing it on to Sir Charles! How could she do that to me? She says she considers me a friend, but to turn around and do this!"

He rubbed my arms up to my shoulders and dipped his head to meet my gaze. "She has betrayed you, it's true. But I don't think confronting her, Whittaker or Coyle will get us answers."

I stretched out my fingers, releasing some of my anger. He was right. We wouldn't get the truth by questioning them.

"Besides," he went on, "if they don't know that we know, we can give them false information to throw them off the scent of your real research."

I smiled as the last residue of tension left my body. "Good thinking."

He kissed my forehead and took my hand. "Let's visit Coyle as we originally planned. We might not get the truth about why he sent the magicians after Longmire and blamed my uncle, but the truth isn't too important in this instance. I simply want him to be aware that we know."

Sir Charles was nowhere in sight as Lord Coyle's butler greeted us at the door. We waited in the drawing room for his lordship, whose arrival was announced in advance by the *thunk* of his walking stick on the floor.

"This is a surprise," he said, easing himself into an armchair by the fire. "Does this mean you have good news for me, Mrs. Glass?"

"Hope's decision—"

"This isn't about Hope," Matt said, cutting me off. "It's about James Teller and Donald Grellow."

"Who?" Lord Coyle asked mildly.

"One is a brick magician, the other a carpenter magician, as you well know. They assaulted Mr. Longmire, on your orders."

Lord Coyle rubbed the head of his walking stick with a hand marked by age spots. To think that a young, beautiful woman like Hope was considering marrying this old, corpulent schemer beggared belief. But as her mother pointed out, I wouldn't understand. I had not been brought up knowing that I would be sold into matrimony to the bidder with the best pedigree.

"And you want to know why I ordered the assault?" Lord Coyle asked.

"We know why," Matt went on. "My uncle asked you to."

Lord Coyle acknowledged the point with a single nod.

"You paid Teller and Grellow to beat up Longmire and you signed the instructions with my uncle's name. Why?"

Lord Coyle showed no sign of surprise that we knew that much. Indeed, he must have suspected we'd eventually find out, considering our contacts within the police force. "Insurance."

"Pardon?" I asked.

"Insurance, Mrs. Glass. If the police arrested the thugs—which I assume they have or you wouldn't be here—they would learn of the payment and the letter signed with Rycroft's name. Very few of our city's detectives would look beyond the signature. They would take it at face value. The upshot is, I didn't want them digging further and linking my name to it. Rycroft asked me to orchestrate it. He should get the blame, not me."

"But you must have known that the detective in charge would notify the commissioner when he saw a peer's name on the letter, and that the commissioner would notify me before sweeping it under the carpet."

"That's why I knew it would come to nothing."

"But the commissioner would have done the same thing for you, my lord," I pointed out. "You're ranked higher than Lord Rycroft, after all."

"I am not related to one of the commissioner's favorite private inquiry agents, or whatever you want to call yourselves these days." He pointed his walking stick at Matt. "I also didn't want my good name tarnished by this, even if it is just in the commissioner's eyes and that of a few policemen."

While his words held a ring of truth, I didn't quite believe them. It seemed unnecessary to sign a name at all.

"No harm done," Lord Coyle said. "Nothing will come of it. The two magicians will go to trial without the letter being mentioned at all."

"I don't know," Matt said.

"It wasn't a question, Glass. I can assure you, the letter and the orders contained within will not be presented."

It was chilling that he could be so assured, but he spoke with utmost confidence. This man was powerful indeed if he could suppress that detail in court.

Matt didn't seem nearly as surprised as me. "No doubt it will come out that they were angry about the letters Longmire sent. I'm sure there are witnesses who will testify as to how angry."

"And not a single one will have to be paid to be there," Lord Coyle said. "They will simply speak the truth. I believe Teller and Grellow became quite loud about their hatred of the author of those letters in their local pub, and even louder once they learned his name from an anonymous source. They mentioned in great detail how they would 'show him,' as they put it."

Matt and I stood to go, but Lord Coyle pointed his walking stick at the sofa. "Sit, sit. Tell me how your investigation is going. Found the coronet yet?"

"Yes," Matt admitted. He did not sit, and I took my cue from him and remained standing too. "I'm on my way to notify the police now."

"Who was it?"

"None of your business."

Coyle chuckled. "Fine, fine. Have it your way. I assume the coronet is back in Cox's hands?"

"Almost."

"I look forward to seeing it. I hear the gold is very beautiful."

"It is," I said.

"You ought to give it directly to Longmire. Cox tells me he's giving up and won't contest the claim."

"His lawyer advised him he couldn't win," Matt said.

"He decided not to try anyway, for the sake of his children," I added. "A lengthy public trial will hurt his family more. Anyway, he seems to have made his peace with his change in circumstances, and I know his wife doesn't care about losing the title of Lady Cox. She loves her husband and just wants him to be happy."

"What a pretty domestic picture you paint of them, Mrs. Glass." He rocked himself to his feet, using his walking stick to push up. "Speaking of domestic bliss, will I be able to join the ranks of happily wedded couples?"

"That is Hope's decision to make," I said defiantly. "We will not influence her."

"You have less than twenty-four hours."

"We won't influence her," I said again, louder.

He simply smiled.

Matt took my arm and steered me out of the drawing room.

"I don't know why Hope hasn't refused him yet," I said as we drove home. "She can't possibly be seriously considering marrying him."

Matt put his arm around my shoulders and nuzzled my hair near my ear. "Not everyone thinks like you, India. People get married for all sorts of reasons other than love. Hope is merely following in the footsteps of centuries of ancestors who married for position or wealth."

I sighed into him, relaxing for the first time since entering Coyle's house. "Thank goodness you broke with tradition."

"My father did it first. Blame him for setting a precedent."

I smiled against his mouth. "He started a new tradition. One that I hope will continue for generations of Glasses."

* * *

MATT WAS GONE A LONG TIME. Too long for a visit to the police station to simply hand over the coronet to Detective Inspector Walker. He must have called on Hope. It was most infuriating. He knew my thoughts on the matter.

I was very aware, however, that he had never agreed with me.

"How is Hope?" I asked when he strolled into the sitting room late in the afternoon.

"I didn't visit Hope," he said, matching my casual tone. "I went to see Cox after speaking to Walker."

I lowered my book to my lap. "Oh. Sorry."

He bent down and gave me a delicate kiss.

Willie made a sound of disgust in her throat. "Do you have to do that in here?"

"Ain't you got something better to do than complain all the time?" Duke said to her.

Willie shot to her feet. "You're right. I'm going out. Don't wait up."

"But it's almost dinner time," Cyclops said with a frown. "Don't you want to eat first?"

"I'll eat later. Tell Mrs. Potter to leave something out for me."

"Don't go to the docks," Matt said. "You can't risk the constables catching you again."

"I'm going to find me a poker game," she said.

"You ain't got no money," Duke reminded her.

She glared at him. "Wish I'd never told you that."

"Why not visit Brockwell instead," I said. "He'll be at a loose end now that his investigation into Longmire's assault has concluded."

She didn't dismiss the idea outright but pursed her lips, considering.

I took that as a good sign. "This morning when he visited, he couldn't stop looking at you as you walked away," I said. "He was admiring your, er, buckskins."

Her gaze snapped to mine.

"And he spoke about you after you left," I added.

She walked off, only to stop at the door. "What'd he say?"

"He said he admires you."

She looked pleased for a fleeting moment before regaining her stoic composure.

"And he thinks your uniqueness is an integral part of what makes you beautiful," I went on.

Her lips flattened. "You took it too far, India. He don't care for beauty." She walked out of the room.

"I meant beautiful in character!" I called after her. "Not that he doesn't think you also have a beautiful face, but it's just that your character is more important to him!"

She didn't respond.

Cyclops, seated nearest the door, peered through it. "She's gone."

I sighed and slumped into the sofa. Aunt Letitia patted my knee. "Never mind, India. You tried and that's the main thing. If Willemina and the inspector are meant to be together, fate will see to it."

"Perhaps," I said. "But sometimes fate needs a helping hand."

"Especially in Willie's case," Duke said. "She's too stubborn to take notice if fate bit her on the nose, pointed at Brockwell, and pushed her in his direction."

***

MATT WAS out of sorts the following morning. He ate very little at breakfast and hardly spoke a word, even when Willie announced with a yawn that she would never entertain another lover ever again. I was too worried about Matt to ask her why, and Duke and Cyclops gave her no more acknowledgement than a nod. She pouted and returned to staring at the fireplace.

"I'm going for a walk," I said. "Matt, will you accompany me?"

He looked up from the newspaper he was reading. "Hmm?"

"Would you like to accompany me on a walk?"

"Yes, of course."

We did not get the opportunity to leave the house, however. Lord Coyle arrived with Hope on his arm.

"We are engaged," she said simply upon taking a seat in the drawing room. She smiled. It didn't convince me of her happiness.

"Congratulations," Matt said, not bothering to hide the relief in his voice. "When did this happen?"

"Last night," Lord Coyle said. "She graced me with her presence at dinner and gave me the good news." He lifted her gloved hand to his mouth and kissed the knuckles. "She's everything I could wish for in a bride."

Hope's smile turned serene. "Thank you, my lord." To us, she said, "I'm honored that he was still willing to marry me after my sister's husband's situation came to light. It's a testament to the depth of his feelings for me. No woman could ask for more in a marriage."

"As the heir to the Rycroft barony, I wanted to assure you of my good intentions toward your cousin, Glass. I will take care of her. She'll want for nothing and my name will shield her from any repercussions to come of Cox's predicament."

"I'm glad to hear it," Matt said blandly. "Are your parents happy with the union, Hope?"

"Immeasurably," she said. "My mother is urging us to wed as soon as possible, but I insist on waiting a month."

"So soon?" I asked.

"I don't want a winter wedding. We plan to marry here in London rather than the country."

I saw no chink in her armor. No slip of her smile or recoiling from her fiancé's touch. She seemed content.

"Hope, would you mind giving me your opinion of our library furniture?" I asked. "It's rather old and I'm considering changing it."

Matt looked as though he'd protest but swallowed it when he realized my true motive. He fell into conversation with Coyle as we exited.

"This isn't about furniture, is it?" Hope asked as we entered the library.

I rounded on her. "Did Matt visit you yesterday?"

"No."

"Did he talk you into marrying Lord Coyle?"

She laughed a sweet, musical laugh. "No. It was my own decision. Although…"

Did I want to hear this? Did I want to know that Matt had somehow conveyed the importance of her accepting Coyle's proposal?

"Go on," I prompted.

"I was influenced by recent events," she went on. "My parents advised that Lord Coyle can protect me from Patience's scandal and any future scandal Charity may cause. They told me how he made the recent attacks on Mr. Longmire appear to be my father's fault."

She watched me carefully, perhaps looking for a sign as to the truth of that suggestion. I hoped my face gave nothing away.

"I've always known he was powerful, but now I understand what power truly means," she said. "He has contacts in the palace and Whitehall. People respect him. They listen to him and do as he bids. As his wife, I will share that."

"You want his power?" I asked.

"Of course. What woman doesn't?"

I stared at her, long and hard, trying to understand. She merely smiled back, as if she knew what I was thinking and knew it was impossible for me to understand her. We were so different.

"As your cousin's wife, I feel obligated to tell you what I know," I said. "Lord Coyle might be powerful, but he wields that power to get what he wants. It was he who informed Mr. Longmire that he had a strong claim to the Cox title."

"Thank you for confirming it. I was told as much, but I wasn't sure."

"Told by whom?"

"Aunt Letitia."

My mouth opened and closed but nothing came out. I couldn't find the words to voice my opinion. I wasn't even sure of my opinion. Should I be pleased or concerned? Did Aunt Letitia know that Hope's acceptance would eradicate the favor I owed Lord Coyle? I couldn't quite recall if she knew about it or not.

Or had she acted purely out of self-interest for the Glass name? It wouldn't surprise me if she had. She was a terrible snob.

Hope laughed again. "You are sweet to worry about me, India, but I assure you, marriage to Lord Coyle will suit me well."

"Wait," I said as she walked off. "Are you not concerned that Coyle told Longmire about his claim to the barony?"

"Not at all. I'm flattered. It just goes to show how much he wanted me as his wife."

I frowned. I felt stupid for missing the point that she seemed to think was obvious.

She gave a little roll of her eyes, as if she couldn't quite believe my stupidity either. "Can you not see, India? He wanted to bring my family down and make my parents desperate to accept him into the family. And believe me, they were fiercely in Coyle's favor ever since Cox informed us. By causing this scandal, Coyle knew it would be almost impossible for me to refuse him. My parents said they would never force me to marry him, but they didn't mean it. While I saw their point, it wasn't until I learned how Coyle set the ball in motion that I realized the power he wields. Not only did he have knowledge of Cox's illegitimacy, but he saved that information for a time when he needed it. Powerful, wealthy and clever. It's an intoxicating combination in a man."

She smiled and headed out of the library, her steps light, her hips swaying. I stood a moment, watching her retreat, wondering if she was as mad as Charity or cleverer than everyone. One thing was certain, however; she was greedy. Greedy for power. She'd found a way to get that power through Coyle.

Lord Coyle rose as we entered the drawing room. They said their goodbyes and asked us to inform Aunt Letitia of their good news. I sat again after they left and asked Peter to fetch tea.

"Are you sure you don't want smelling salts?" Matt asked, sitting beside me on the sofa. "Or strong liquor? You look as though you're going to faint."

I blinked slowly at him. "I just had the strangest conversation with Hope in the library."

"As did I, with Coyle. But you first."

I told him about Hope's greed for power and the reason behind her decision to accept Coyle. "I'm sorry I ever doubted you, Matt. You told me you didn't try to convince her, and I didn't quite believe you. A letter from Aunt Letitia explaining all about Coyle being behind Longmire's claim is what finally convinced her."

"Aunt Letitia!" He shook his head, disbelieving.

"Tell me about your conversation with Coyle."

"First of all, I wanted his assurance that you are now off the hook. He gave it. You no longer owe him a favor."

"Even though we didn't influence Hope?"

He chewed his lip.

"*Go on,*" I said darkly.

"I told him I pointed out to Hope how he can help her achieve whatever she wants," he said.

"What if she tells him you said nothing of the sort to her?"

"He thinks I told Aunt Letitia what to write in a letter to Hope. I suspected she'd write to her and you just confirmed it. I'll have a word with Aunt Letitia later to make sure she knows what to say if Coyle interrogates her. But I doubt he will." He grinned. "I feel like a weight has been lifted from my shoulders."

"I suppose, but I am worried about Hope. I'm afraid I can't feel as glad as you do."

He shrugged. "Is it so bad that I'm glad my wife no longer owes Coyle a favor? That's not all we talked about, anyway. He told me he bought the coronet off Longmire. In advance, of course. Longmire hasn't got it in his possession yet."

"So Coyle will add a magical gold object to his collection. He'll be the envy of the others."

"They'll offer him an enormous sum to buy it from him, but I doubt he'll sell."

He certainly wouldn't. Not after going through so much to get it. That coronet not only symbolized the power he had over the lives of several people, but also of Hope's acceptance of his marriage proposal. He wouldn't sell it for even more magical gold.

* * *

Mr. Longmire was in the middle of packing his own bag when we arrived at his lodgings in the early afternoon. His valet was nowhere in sight.

"He left yesterday," Mr. Longmire said. "Good riddance. He was a mere servant yet *he* looked down on *me*!" He shoved a creased shirt into the bag. "All he did was complain and tell me I did everything wrong. A gentleman should do this or that in a particular way, according to him. Bloody snob."

"You're leaving London," Matt said.

"I hate this city, and I'm not needed here. My lawyer has his instructions. I'm going home to pack my things and move into the big house." He looked up from his bag and smirked, only to wince when it hurt his cut lip. "I suppose you heard? Cox gave in."

"We heard," Matt said. "We also heard you sold the family coronet to Lord Coyle. Is that wise, considering it's the symbol of your family's power?"

"Symbol of the devil's work, you mean. I don't want that thing anywhere near me. Coyle's welcome to it."

"I hope you charged him a fortune for it," Matt said idly.

Mr. Longmire straightened. "How much should I have asked?"

"Double of what he offered."

"Triple," I said. "It's incredibly rare."

Mr. Longmire's eyes gleamed. Well, one did. I couldn't see the other through the swelling.

"All in all it's been a profitable visit." He managed to shut the carpet bag, but the seams stretched almost to breaking point.

"Speaking of money," Matt said, "we came here in a last ditch effort to have you reconsider the effect your actions are having on Lord Cox's family."

"He's Lord Cox no more," Mr. Longmire said cheerfully. "What *is* his name?" He shrugged, not caring.

"He's your family," I pointed out.

"My mother was my family. When she died…" He shook his

head as if to shake off the memory of her. But I heard the vulnerability in his voice, the sadness. This man had grown up with one family member and she was gone. Still, it was hard to have any sympathy for him. He was pushing away the only family he had left with both hands.

"I'm sorry for your loss," I said, somewhat automatically.

"Being alone doesn't bother me," he said. "I prefer it. I don't need anyone."

"Be prepared for the gold diggers," Matt said with a wry twist in his tone. "The matchmaking mothers will come out of the woodwork now that there's a new eligible bachelor available among the peerage."

Mr. Longmire's face was one of horror, made even more gruesome by the bruises and cuts. "I don't want a wife."

"What about children?" I asked.

"Can't think of anything worse."

"But you're a baron now," I said. "You have to think of the future."

"I don't care what happens to the estate and title after I die. Let Cox and his people fight it out in court. It's not my problem. Now, if you don't mind, I have a train to catch."

An idea formed, one that seemed a little mad at first, but quickly took root. It was a neat solution to a sticky problem, and might just work.

I followed Mr. Longmire down the stairs. "May I suggest something?"

"Only if you're quick," he said.

It was irritating talking to his back, but he was giving me no choice. "If you remain childless for the rest of your life, will you make Lord Cox's eldest son your heir in your will?"

"Only a *legitimate* male can inherit," he said over his shoulder. "Aside from me, there are none. Not even going back generations. My lawyer checked. When I die, the title will become extinct."

I stopped and stared after him. All this upheaval, all this

distress, and for what? He wasn't even doing it for his future children, to make a better life for the generations to come after him. He was doing it for himself. The man was despicable.

Matt rushed down the steps to where Mr. Longmire stood alongside a small trunk at the base of the staircase. The landlady watched on in silence from the sitting room beyond.

"In the case of an extinct title, the estate is severed from the title and the lands and other assets go to whomever is named in your will," Matt said.

"I told you, I don't care what happens after I die."

"But—"

"I'm not paying a lawyer to draw up the paperwork. It's a wasted expense. Good day."

"I'll have my lawyer draw it up," Matt said. "It will cost you nothing."

Mr. Longmire paused at the front door. "Why should I do anything for that man? He knew about me and did nothing."

"That's why I'm suggesting you leave it to your nephew," I said. "Not your brother."

"I don't have a—" He swallowed his protest and averted his gaze.

"You have a family," Matt said quietly. "You are not alone now. Consider my wife's suggestion."

"There is no one else to leave the estate to, so why not Cox's eldest son?" I said brightly.

Mr. Longmire blew out a long breath as if releasing a lifetime of frustration with it, but he did not agree to my plan.

"If you do this," Matt said with dark intensity, "I will make sure the two men who assaulted you do not get off lightly."

Mr. Longmire's gaze snapped to Matt's. "How?"

"That's the thing about belonging to the British peerage. You can do whatever you want. You'll find that out soon."

I eyed him sideways. He didn't believe what he was saying, but it only mattered that Mr. Longmire did.

The Yorkshireman picked up one end of the trunk and waited

for Matt to pick up the other. "If your lawyer draws something up, I'll sign it. I have nothing against the boy, only his father."

They carried the trunk to the waiting hack and lifted it onto the roof. I watched as Matt strapped it down while Mr. Longmire fetched his bag. He spoke to the landlady then closed the door and rejoined us.

"Now that you have been exposed as the author of those letters, you won't write any more, will you?" I asked.

He threw his bag into the cabin and climbed in after it.

"Will you, Mr. Longmire?" I prompted.

He went to close the door but Matt caught it. Mr. Longmire pulled hard, but Matt didn't let go.

"My wife asked you a question," Matt growled.

"Very well," Mr. Longmire growled back. "I won't send any more letters to magicians. But I won't stop my crusade against them. Driver! Move on!" The coach lurched forward and Matt had to let go or be dragged with it. Mr. Longmire closed the door, pulled down the window, and said, "Magicians are cheats!"

Matt's jaw hardened. He looked to our coach, parked at the curb.

I slipped my hand into his. "Let him go," I said. "He's not worth another moment's thought."

"Agreed."

We headed home. Neither of us mentioned Mr. Longmire, the assaults or his letters again. We had truly let him go, in every sense. In fact, the journey was quite pleasant as we talked of happier things.

To our utmost surprise, we arrived home to find Aunt Letitia in the drawing room playing poker with Willie and Lord Farnsworth. It was such an odd thing to see that both Matt and I paused in the doorway.

"There you are, Glass," Lord Farnsworth said with a toothy smile. "The ladies are teaching me poker."

"I keep telling you," Willie said. "I ain't a lady."

"You are to me." He patted her hand then laid down his

cards. "Two pair, ace high. That's good, isn't it?"

Aunt Letitia set her cards on the table too. "Not as good as mine. Three of a kind. Can you match that, Willemina?"

"Nope. All yours, Letty."

"I say, you do have the most interesting way of speaking," Lord Farnsworth said. "Indeed, everything about you is interesting, Willie. It's not just the accent—which is a breath of fresh air—but your choice of phrases, your clothing, even your attitude. I've never met anyone like you."

"Why thank you, Farnsworth."

I cringed at the familiar use of his name, that only his male friends would call him by. She should be addressing him as "my lord" or "sir." If I found it slightly awkward, Aunt Letitia seemed positively horrified.

"Willemina," she scolded. "Lord Farnsworth is your cousin's distinguished guest! Don't embarrass Matthew."

Willie looked to Matt then me. "What'd I do wrong?"

Lord Farnsworth threw his head back and laughed. "Nothing, nothing at all. It's quite all right, Miss Glass. If Willie wishes to take her obsession with all things American beyond the accent, then I'm willing to go along with it. It's quite harmless, after all."

"Obsession?" Willie's brow creased. "What're you talking about? I ain't obsessed with being American; I *am* American."

Lord Farnsworth laughed as he gathered up the cards. "Of course, of course." He winked at Matt and me.

Willie's frown deepened. "Are you all sharing a joke at my expense?"

"I have no idea," Aunt Letitia said. "Will someone please deal? I'm having a winning streak and don't want to lose momentum."

"Of course, dear Miss Glass." Lord Farnsworth shuffled the deck with quick, agile fingers.

Willie crossed her arms. "You do know I am American, right?" she asked. "I ain't a fake."

He cast her a benign smile without pausing his shuffle.

Willie turned fully to face Matt. "Tell him I really am American."

"She is," Matt said simply.

Lord Farnsworth winked at us again. "I believe you."

"I don't think you do," Willie said. "I was born and raised there. I've only lived in London a few months. Why do you think *I'm* a fraud and not Matt?"

"His accent isn't very strong. It sounds worldly, and more authentic to my cultured English ear."

Willie rolled her eyes. "My accent is *authentic* American. His was corrupted by a childhood spent all over Europe. Anyway, just because you ain't heard an accent like mine before don't mean it ain't real."

"Besides," Lord Farnsworth went on as if she hadn't spoken, "you introduced yourself as Glass's cousin, and I happen to know his three cousins are British born and bred."

I pressed my lips together, suppressing my smile as I realized his mistake.

"That's his father's side," Willie said. "I'm his cousin on his mother's side. The Johnsons are Americans."

Lord Farnsworth stopped dealing the cards. "Johnson?" he asked weakly. "Glass, what's going on?"

Matt fought back his smile. "She's a Johnson from California."

"So…she's not the daughter of Lord Rycroft?"

"Didn't she introduce herself as Miss Johnson?"

"Simply as Willie."

Aunt Letitia sighed as she picked up her cards. "If only I'd been here when you arrived. I am very sorry, my lord. You must forgive her. She's quite mad."

"I am not!" Willie cried.

Lord Farnsworth gave Matt an apologetic shrug. "You can see how I made the error. You did say your cousin's top drawer was unhinged." He tapped his forehead.

Willie scowled at Matt. "You called me mad?"

"I was referring to Charity," Matt assured her.

She grunted. "Just so you know, Farnsworth, Charity makes me seem normal."

Aunt Letitia suddenly lowered her cards. "*Now* I understand why you've been flirting with Willemina. You thought she was my niece."

"An honest mistake," Lord Farnsworth muttered.

Aunt Letitia settled a hand on his arm. "Charity is very much available. Shall I set up a meeting between you?"

Lord Farnsworth frowned at Willie. "She's madder than Willie, eh? Best not. Not unless the other fillies suddenly all get married."

Aunt Letitia sat back and regarded her cards again. "At least I tried. That's my duty done."

Willie threw her cards down and shot to her feet. "I ain't sitting here listening to my character being shredded. I may be a bit eccentric, but you're a caboose short of a full train, Farnsworth."

"Willemina!" Aunt Letitia scolded. "Apologize this instant."

Willie spun on her heel and marched out.

Lord Farnsworth's gaze followed her exit. Or, rather, followed her backside. He almost fell off his chair trying to see her until she was out of sight. "What an interesting outfit. I hope it catches on."

"We are very sorry about her behavior," Aunt Letitia gushed. "She was brought up by the most despicable people."

He patted her hand. "It's all right, Miss Glass. I understand eccentricity better than most. My mother was away with the fairies." He stopped suddenly as Duke and Cyclops entered.

My stomach dropped to my toes. Oh no. He couldn't fail to recognize Cyclops. He'll know we've been spying on him.

He regarded Cyclops with a finger tapping against his lips. He looked as though he was trying to place him.

Cyclops turned and walked quickly out without a word.

The rest of us remained silent. I tried to think of something to explain why Lord Farnsworth's previous coachman was strolling around our house, but couldn't. Even Matt, who always knew just the right thing to say, was at a loss for words.

Lord Farnsworth regarded his cards again. "That fellow reminds me of the coachman who left my employ the other day. Hated losing him. He was a good man, knew his way around the city and always got me to where I wanted to be on time. I wondered why he left suddenly. Perhaps, like your friend there, he had a better place to be."

He couldn't possibly be so stupid as to think his coachman had an identical twin who also wore a patch over his eye. I refused to believe he could be that thick-headed and still function in society.

I looked to Matt. Matt looked to me. We both shrugged at the same time and sat at the card table.

"Deal us in," Matt said. "Duke, do you mind pouring drinks?"

"It's far too early for liquor," Aunt Letitia protested.

"Thank you," Lord Farnsworth said. "Don't mind if I do."

Aunt Letitia gave a thin smile. "Perhaps just this once."

"Duke, eh?" Lord Farnsworth said as he watched Duke splash whiskey into the tumblers at the sideboard. "Which one?"

"What?" Duke asked.

"I know you're not Cornwall." He snickered. "You're too young to be Norfolk or Somerset..." He clicked his fingers. "I've got it! You're the Duke of Wellington!"

Look For:

THE KIDNAPPER'S ACCOMPLICE

The 10th book in the *Glass And Steele* series

by C.J. Archer

Sign up to C.J.'s newsletter at www.cjarcher.com to be notified when she releases new books. Subscribers also get access to a FREE Glass and Steele short story. More details on the next page.

GET A FREE SHORT STORY

I wrote a short story for the Glass and Steele series that is set before THE WATCHMAKER'S DAUGHTER. Titled THE TRAITOR'S GAMBLE it features Matt and his friends in the Wild West town of Broken Creek. It contains spoilers from THE WATCHMAKER'S DAUGHTER, so you must read that first. The best part is, the short story is FREE, but only to my newsletter subscribers. Subscribe now at www.cjarcher.com

ALSO BY C.J. ARCHER

SERIES WITH 2 OR MORE BOOKS

The Glass Library

Cleopatra Fox Mysteries

After The Rift

Glass and Steele

The Ministry of Curiosities Series

The Emily Chambers Spirit Medium Trilogy

The 1st Freak House Trilogy

The 2nd Freak House Trilogy

The 3rd Freak House Trilogy

The Assassins Guild Series

Lord Hawkesbury's Players Series

Witch Born

SINGLE TITLES NOT IN A SERIES

Courting His Countess

Surrender

Redemption

The Mercenary's Price

ABOUT THE AUTHOR

C.J. Archer has loved history and books for as long as she can remember and feels fortunate that she found a way to combine the two. She spent her early childhood in the dramatic beauty of outback Queensland, Australia, but now lives in suburban Melbourne with her husband, two children and a mischievous black & white cat named Coco.

Subscribe to C.J.'s newsletter through her website to be notified when she releases a new book, as well as get access to exclusive content. Her website also contains up to date details on all her books: http://cjarcher.com

Follow her on social media to get the latest updates on her books:

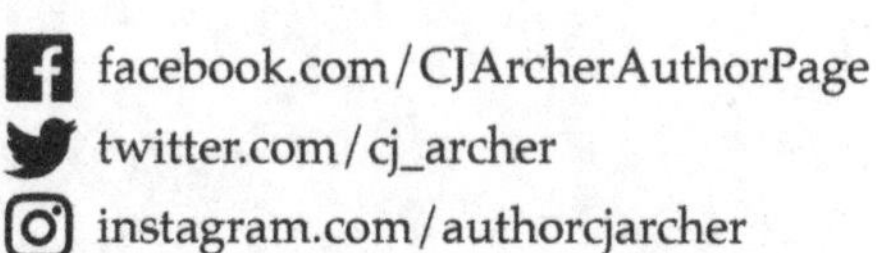

www.ingramcontent.com/pod-product-compliance
Lightning Source LLC
Chambersburg PA
CBHW010447310726
48979CB00018B/2845/J

* 9 7 8 1 9 2 2 5 5 4 6 5 9 *